Hawkshaw went over the Kanaday woman's file again.

Now that he'd met her and the kid, the case no longer seemed an abstraction, nor did they. They were flesh and blood.

And the reality of her was distracting, too distracting. Because she wasn't the woman he wanted. He forced himself to look at the fuzzy reproductions of the snapshots that Corbett had sent of Kate. There were only three.

The first showed her and the kid sitting before a towering Christmas tree. The kid, Charlie, was mugging for the camera, and she was smiling with what seemed like real joy. Her smile was nice, full of life. He wondered if she would ever smile that way again. He set the photos aside and took a sip of beer.

A lone light shone from the farthest window of the house. Kate had left the bathroom light on for the kid, a gesture that touched him in spite of himself.

Don't be touched, he warned himself. *Don't feel anything.*

The woman and kid had come into his life suddenly, and with luck they'd disappear just as suddenly. Until then, he'd watch out for them because they were a legacy from Corbett, a favor to be returned and a debt to be paid.

But nothing personal. He would stay uninvolved. He had made it his specialty.

Dear Reader,

My husband and I visit Florida's Lower Keys as often as possible and have explored the backcountry by kayak. I love the loneliness and wildness of the place—although I could have done without getting to know a certain sea slug quite so well.

Before writing this story, I read a lot about the backcountry, stalkers and attention deficiency in children. There's a lot of my son in Charlie—a bright, imaginative kid intensely frustrated by reading problems and handicapped by an overabundance of energy and a tendency to march to a different drummer. He overcame his difficulties much as Charlie does. Today he teaches composition and Shakespeare at the University of New Orleans. Writing this book made me aware again of the challenges such children—and their parents—face. The best part was the reaffirmation that such challenges can be met.

Sadly, writing *The Guardian* also made me painfully conscious of the inadequacy of stalking laws in the United States. I hope we can work to better them.

Sincerely,

Bethany Campbell

Bethany
Campbell
THE GUARDIAN

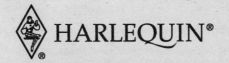

HARLEQUIN®

TORONTO • NEW YORK • LONDON
AMSTERDAM • PARIS • SYDNEY • HAMBURG
STOCKHOLM • ATHENS • TOKYO • MILAN • MADRID
PRAGUE • WARSAW • BUDAPEST • AUCKLAND

ISBN 0-373-70837-8

THE GUARDIAN

Copyright © 1999 by Bethany Campbell.

This edition published by arrangement with Harlequin Books S.A.

Look us up on-line at: http://www.romance.net

Printed in U.S.A.

To Margot Dalton—

Who, like E. B. White's Charlotte, is not only a
good friend, but a good writer.

CHAPTER ONE

THE SHARK WAS DUSTY.

Nearly six feet long, it was stuffed, mounted and hung on the wall above the sagging couch. Its downturned mouth grinned with cruel teeth.

On the shark's head was a black baseball cap. In white letters, it said UNITED STATES SECRET SERVICE.

A tall man, naked except for a towel knotted around his middle, stood before the shark. He held the phone and listened to a voice half a continent away. His face was grim.

I don't want to get involved, he thought with deep distaste. *Those days are over. I'm out of the game. For good.*

But because it was Corbett talking on the other end of the line, Hawkshaw listened.

"There's no choice," Corbett said. "She's got to get out of town. She knows it. I can't keep her safe."

Hawkshaw adjusted the towel around his waist. He was dripping salt water onto the old braided rug.

He said, "I was about to get into the shower."

Corbett said, "This guy who's after her—this stalker— he's getting dangerous. Not just to her, to her kid. He's started to look on the kid as some sort of rival."

A kid, Hawkshaw thought with weariness and guilt. He tried to keep himself indifferent, unassailable. "Why can't the police handle it?" he asked.

Corbett said, "The guy's smart, Hawkshaw. He doesn't

threaten her outright. But he never stops watching her. And he lets her know he's watching—and that he wants her."

Hawkshaw sighed in disgust. He didn't like the sound of this. An anonymous stalker was the worst and most slippery kind. "You've got no idea who this psycho is?"

"None. He's a voice on a phone. He's a note in the mail. He's the ice pick in your tire. The dead bird on your doorstep."

"How long has he been after her?"

"Eighteen months," Corbett said. "It started with a couple of notes. Anonymous calls. It built. She changed her number, kept it unlisted. I encrypted her computer so nobody could get into her e-mail. But nothing works. She needs to get the hell out of here."

Hawkshaw stared at the shark. It returned his gaze with a glassy, emotionless eye.

"What's the matter?" he asked. "Hasn't she got people of her own to go to?"

"No. Her parents are dead. She's a widow. She's got a friend in another city who'll help. But I don't want her going straight there. I want to throw this bastard a curve. Have her take such a crooked path, he can't follow."

"And I'm the crooked path she takes."

"Don't get me wrong, Hawkshaw. This woman doesn't *want* charity. She doesn't want to run—she's a fighter. If the guy was a threat only to her, I don't think she'd budge. But there's the kid."

I don't want to help widows and children, Hawkshaw thought with resentment. *Throw them to the sharks.* He ran a forefinger along the edges of the shark's teeth. They felt pleasantly sharp.

"She's no shrinking violet," Corbett insisted. "She's an extremely independent, self-reliant woman—"

Then let her be independent and reliant by herself, Hawkshaw thought.

"—listen, Hawkshaw," Corbett continued, "this guy who's after her, he's getting ready to explode. All the signs are there. Something very bad is about to happen unless she and the kid get out of here. It's instinct. I can't shake it. You understand?"

Corbett's instinct. Hawkshaw understood all too well. He stared at the scar that snaked up the tanned flesh of his right forearm. Oh, yes, he would always remember Corbett's instinct; he was beholden to it for the rest of his life.

But he said, "My Galahad days are over, Corbett. I'm a hermit now. I like it."

"But you're staying there?" Corbett asked, slyness in his voice. "In Florida?"

"No. Yes. I don't know," Hawkshaw said. "I'll probably sell the place. I've got to fix it up. One of these days."

"That's what you said six months ago."

"Time flies."

"Look, she could help you. She's got energy, she's enterprising," Corbett said. "Up here she can't even work anymore. The stalker—he disrupts her workday, calls her co-workers. He's starting to harass everybody she comes into contact with."

Bingo, thought Hawkshaw with a sure, sickening realization. Suddenly he knew he wasn't going to get out of this. "Everybody?"

"It's a figure of speech," Corbett said.

Hawkshaw closed his eyes. As in a vision, he saw Corbett's round, good-natured face, the receding hair, the mustache that never seemed even on both sides.

He saw Cherry, Corbett's wife, pretty and ever-generous. He thought of Corbett's adolescent twin girls in last year's Christmas snapshot, their smiles silvery with braces. He was godfather to both.

Hawkshaw opened his eyes. He wiped a cobweb from the shark's fin. "Everybody includes you, doesn't it, Corbett? It includes Cherry and the girls, too. Don't bloody lie to me. I know you too well."

There was a moment of silence. Finally Corbett said, "That's not a factor. It goes with the territory. My major concern is for the woman and her son. That's the truth."

Oh, hell. Depression stole over Hawkshaw like a long, cold shadow.

He sat down on the old couch. He thought of Corbett and all he owed to Corbett.

A hopeless sensation yawned within him. He knew what he was going to say and wished with all his heart that he could say something else.

"All right," Hawkshaw said. "Fax the details to me, in care of the Flamingo Motel." He gave Corbett the number. "Tell the woman and kid I'll take them on. For a while. A couple weeks maybe."

"Good. If we cover her tracks well enough, maybe she can break free of him. Go her own way."

"Amen," said Hawkshaw. *The sooner the better.*

There was another awkward silence. Then, with feeling, Corbett said, "You won't be sorry about this."

Yes, I will, thought Hawkshaw.

He was already sorry.

THE DETECTIVE, CORBETT, came back from the downstairs pay phone and into his private office. He was a stockily built man with thinning hair and a mustache that always seemed slightly off-center.

He gave Kate a smile that had no happiness in it. "You're going away," he said. "It's set."

Kate's arm tightened around Charlie, her six-year-old son. "Can't you at least tell me where?" she asked.

Charlie wriggled. He hated sitting still and was fidgety.

Corbett shook his head. "It's best you don't know yet. Out of the Midwest. That's all I can say. I'm sorry."

I have no secrets, Kate thought numbly. *Wherever I am, whatever I do, the stalker knows. He always finds out. Always.*

She let Charlie slip away from her. He ran to the window, stood on tiptoe and looked out at the summer afternoon.

Her hand fell uselessly to her lap. She could only stare at Corbett's kind, jowly face.

"I'm sorry," he repeated.

She swallowed. "How—how long do you think we'll have to stay there?"

"I don't know," Corbett said. "Till we're sure he hasn't tracked you. Once we know that, you're free to move on."

To move on.

The words tolled ominously in Kate's mind. She had known it might come to this, of course. She and Corbett had talked about it, insane as it was.

Wordlessly, both she and Corbett turned their gazes to Charlie. The boy shifted his weight from foot to foot and hummed as he stared outside. He tugged restlessly at his brown forelock.

She had tried to prepare Charlie for the possibility that they would have to leave. But how, really, did one prepare for such an extreme and desperate action?

"I—I—" Kate stammered "—well, it's necessary. It has to be done. That's all there is to it."

"Yes," Corbett said. He came to her, put his hand on her shoulder. "If we can't keep him away from you, then you've got to get away from him. Both of you. Where he can't find you."

We have to run. Like hunted animals. Because there's a madman out there. This can't be happening. Not really.

Kate shook her head to clear it. "I didn't want anybody else involved. Why can't Charlie and I just leave on our own? I could go straight to my friend. Eliminate this middle person, this stranger—"

"We were in the Secret Service together," Corbett said. "He retired two years ago. He's the best, Kate. And he's worked with kids. Consider it a security move for a while, that's all. I couldn't trust you to anyone better."

But his words didn't reassure her. She felt stunned, shocked, empty, unreal. "Won't you at least tell me his name?"

"Kate," Corbett said wearily, "the less you know the better. I want you to go home, pack the bare necessities. I'm taking you someplace else tonight. In my car, not yours. I'll get your plane tickets. You'll have to travel under another name."

She straightened her back and tried to square her jaw, which felt twitchy, undependable. "How soon? When do you want us to go?"

"As soon as possible."

"How long are we supposed to stay with this—person?"

"Until we think you're safe."

Safe. A bitter giddiness filled her. She smiled at the irony of the word. *Safe.*

"Until we make sure he hasn't traced you," Corbett said.

"He," Kate echoed. Her stalker was nameless, faceless, shapeless. He was nowhere and everywhere. He seemed like some monster out of mythology, with a thousand eyes to watch her, a thousand ears to listen to her, a thousand invisible tentacles to reach out at her.

"Our things—" she said, thinking of their small condominium, stuffed with its trove of mementoes. There were the photos, the antiques, Charlie's toys, her precious books.

Corbett kept his expression matter-of-fact. He folded his arms. "I'll see you get them when you're settled. I'll arrange it so it can't be traced."

"My bank account," she said. "I'll have to transfer the funds. But if I don't even know where we're going—"

"I'll take care of it."

She thought fretfully of the man to whom Corbett was sending them. "This person—this friend of yours—I'll need to reimburse him. I don't want to owe anybody."

Corbett's only answer was an ironic smile. "I know you, Kate. You'll pull your own weight."

"But how?"

"There'll be something. He's thinking of selling his place. He needs to put it in shape. Maybe you could help him."

"Yes," she murmured. "I can do that, all right." She'd worked her way through high school and most of college as part of a cleaning crew for a real estate company. She didn't like the work. But she knew how to do it.

Charlie, bored with looking out the window, ran to her, tugged her hand. "Come on," he said. "Let's go home."

Kate bit her lip. How did you tell a child that this might be the last time he'd see home? That you were fugitives now, and that perhaps you could never come back?

But she stood, forcing herself to smile. She gave Charlie's hand a confident squeeze.

"Charlie," she said, injecting all the cheer she could into her voice, "remember that trip I told you we might take?"

THE WOMAN AND KID were arriving that night. Hawkshaw was no happier than before about the prospect; he felt as evil-tempered as a snake shedding its skin.

Still, he was nagged by the alien thought that he should clean house. This was such a distasteful impulse that he promptly quelled it.

He did, however, force himself to put sheets on the twin beds in the guest room. At least, he supposed it was a guest room. Up until now he'd been lucky enough to avoid having guests.

Outside, rain poured down, hammering on the roof and streaming down the windows. The weather was too vile to fish or kayak, so restless, he stayed inside and did push-ups.

He told himself he would do a hundred, then make himself examine the file of material Corbett had faxed him about Katherine Kanaday.

But after a hundred push-ups, he still felt too restless, so he started a second hundred. After three hundred, he gave up. He lay on the floor for a moment. He swore, muffled, into the braided rug.

Then he rose, snagged a beer from the refrigerator and picked up the Kanaday file. He wore only a pair of denim cutoffs; he didn't bother much about dressing these days, and he didn't intend to.

He swung his long body down on the couch, kicked a couple of boating magazines out of his way. He plumped up the ancient sofa pillow, settled back and opened the file Corbett had faxed.

There were a couple of fuzzy pictures of the woman and kid. The kid was cute. In his heart of hearts, Hawkshaw liked kids; he considered them a sort of separate species and thought it a damn shame they grew up to be human beings.

The woman he dismissed as nothing special. Too thin, her hair too long and curly. Corbett said her hair was reddish. Hawkshaw had never been attracted to redheads. Carrot-tops, he thought dismissively.

He began to read about her. She was thirty-two years old, had a college degree, and had worked as assistant manager in a new-and-used bookshop. Had been married to a professor of computer science at the local college.

Ho-hum, thought Hawkshaw, looking over her background: a quiet life, boring and bookish. Nothing out of the ordinary.

Until a year and a half ago. Then her husband had suddenly and unexpectedly died of a brain tumor. Ten days later, the stalking began. An odd sequence—was it a coincidence?

Hawkshaw stretched. He scratched his bare chest and took a sip of beer. He read on.

Corbett had written,

On the morning of February 11, Kanaday opened front door of her apartment to get paper. On doorstep found single white rose wrapped in cellophane. Beneath it, note, unsigned. Note laser-printed on white paper. See attached.

Hawkshaw picked up a separate stack of papers clipped together. He read the top one, which was labeled, in Corbett's firm handwriting, "First Note."

I THINK OF NOTHING BUT YOU. I WANT YOU WITH ALL MY BEING. IF I CAN'T HAVE YOU, I DON'T KNOW WHAT I WILL DO. GIVE ME A SIGN THAT I CAN COME TO YOU. WEAR THIS ROSE ON YOUR COAT TODAY.

Hmm, Hawkshaw thought, cocking an eyebrow. Mildly interesting. Not overtly threatening, just psycho enough to make a person nervous.

He went back to Corbett's account. The Kanaday woman said she at first thought the incident was only a "sick joke." She'd thrown away the rose and thought no more of it. Until the second rose appeared.

Again the nameless admirer asked her to wear the flower. Again she threw it away. Then the phone calls started. A man's voice, low, unrecognizable, breathless, hungry.

Wherever she went, he seemed to know. He told her what she had done, whom she had seen, to whom she had talked, what she wore. Somehow he seemed to watch her all the time.

The stalker's threats were always veiled, never explicit. Small things appeared—like the roses, the notes. Others disappeared—like the dog's leash or a pair of muddy tennis shoes left outside beside the door mat.

And the calls, wrote Corbett, never stopped. It didn't matter how often the Kanaday woman changed her number; the stalker always found out the new one. Then, angry that she'd tried to elude him, he would plague her even more unmercifully. At last, when she no longer answered the phone at home, he began to harass her at the bookstore, and he did so until she had to quit her job.

Hawkshaw frowned at the closing paragraphs.

Kanaday had just started a new job at the Columbia Mall bookstore. Near closing time, she received a call from the stalker.

He claimed at that moment he could see her son. He described the boy's clothing and play activity. He said, "I know why you don't come to me. It's because of the boy. You feel guilty because you have to pretend to want him more than you want me. I'll take care of that, and then I'll come for you. And then you'll be mine forever."

Hawkshaw swore under his breath. He closed the folder and tossed it on the floor. He stood, restless again. He walked to the window. The view was still obscured by rain.

Stalkers, he thought with loathing. He stroked the scar along his forearm, then turned and glowered at the file.

"Find the bastard, Corbett," he said between his teeth. "I'm not up to these games anymore."

He drained the beer and glanced at the clock, calculating the hours of freedom he had left. It was a silly clock, shaped like a cat, whose tail was the wagging pendulum. The phone rang. The back of Hawkshaw's neck prickled in apprehension.

His phone seldom rang these days. Somehow he knew this call meant more bad luck.

THE MIDNIGHT SKY WAS BLACK and starless. The plane taxied down the wet tarmac, came to a stop before the small air terminal.

Key West, said illuminated letters that rose from the terminal's roof. Their pastel color was haloed by mist.

Key West, thought Kate. *Florida. We're really here.* Corbett had told her their destination only when he had taken her inside the terminal back home.

Now she and Charlie were exiles, strangers in a strange land. Everything felt unreal—how could it seem otherwise? They had come to the Florida Keys to live with a man she had never met, had never even spoken to.

A wave of anxiety surged through her, but she ignored it. Keeping her head high, she carried her sleeping son down the stairs of the plane.

Charlie was exhausted. They had been traveling since dawn, and their flight had been delayed in Miami for five hours because of the torrential rains.

Here in Key West the drizzle was light. The moon was masked by clouds. Beyond the airport's chain-link fence, Kate saw palm trees mistily gilded by the parking lot lights. The air was sultry and pungent.

Charlie stirred against her shoulder. "What's that smell?" he asked crankily.

"It's the ocean," she told him, although the scent was as new to her as it was to him.

He yawned and relaxed, snuggling his face into her neck. She held him more tightly and made her way inside the terminal's glass doors. The boy was growing heavy, and their carry-on bag was sliding awkwardly from her shoulder. She paused, trying to hoist it more firmly into place. She glanced about.

Even at this hour the terminal was lively. She heard Jamaican accents mingling with those of Brooklyn; she saw a Muslim woman in a black veil and a Sikh man in an azure turban.

College students crowded elbow to elbow with retirees,

and a young Asian couple, looking tired, carried sleeping twin infants. There seemed to be almost every sort of person—but nowhere did Kate see anyone who might be looking for her and Charlie.

Her clothing was purposefully nondescript: faded jeans and a heather-gray T-shirt. Sunglasses hid her brown eyes, and a scarf covered her red-gold hair.

She had done everything in her power not to be attractive or have an ounce of sex appeal. She did not want to be noticed or remembered.

She shifted Charlie in her arms and took off the scarf. She took off the sunglasses, too, which seemed silly so late at night, and stuffed both into her carry-on.

She shook her head to clear it and gazed at the crowd around her. No one seemed to take the slightest notice of her or her child.

She eyed the crowd again, unsure for whom she searched. Charlie sighed again and buried his face against her neck, as if wearily begging her to make everything normal again.

Normal. The word mocked her. *Normal.*

Her arms tightened around her son with fierce protectiveness. A now-familiar anger swept through her, and she welcomed it; it was her friend and it kept her going.

But Lord, she was tired. She squeezed her eyes shut, willing the fatigue away, marshaling her strength. She took a deep breath, then another. Suddenly, a voice spoke her name. It was a male voice, gravelly, yet oddly soft.

"Katherine Kanaday?"

Her eyes flew open. As if by magic, a tall man had materialized in front of her. His lean face filled her vision, and she blinked, disconcerted.

Her gaze met his, which was an intense blue-green, and

unreadable. Her chin jerked up, and she eyed him with the suspicion that had become second nature to her.

She had pictured a bland-faced older man much like Corbett. But this man must be only in his early forties, and he looked anything but bland.

Corbett's words came flashing back to her. *You can depend on him.*

But Kate's breath stuck in her chest because this stranger didn't seem like someone to depend on. He looked more like a man who created danger than safety.

He towered over her, all height and hard muscle. A wide-brimmed Aussie hat hid his hair and shadowed his eyes. He had an angular jaw and a cleft chin. His cheekbones were high and prominent, and he was deeply bronzed by the sun. He had not shaved for several days.

His khaki shirt looked weathered, and Kate could see a triangle of brown chest. Around his neck was a leather thong from which dangled some sort of small stone fetish.

He said, "If the phone doesn't ring, it's me."

If the phone doesn't ring, it's me. It was the strange sentence Corbett had picked to serve as a password, and only he and she and this man knew it. The knots in her nerves untied themselves, and she almost smiled.

He didn't. His face remained impassive. But he took off the hat. His brown hair was thick and streaked by the sun. The sideburns showed the faintest glint of silver.

"W.W. Hawkshaw. I'm a friend of Corbett's."

He offered her his hand, and she took it. A small, unwanted tingle of sexual awareness swarmed through her nerves.

Guiltily, she drew her hand away. Sex wasn't to be trusted. It was what had gotten her and Charlie into this insanity in the first place.

Charlie clutched her more tightly and burrowed his face

against her. He muttered something nearly incoherent about going home.

"Shhh," she whispered. She no longer knew where home was.

Once again resentment warred with her fatigue. But before she could sort out her feelings, before she could even try, Hawkshaw had jammed on the hat again, pulling the brim back to its stern angle. He was ready to get moving.

"Allow me, ma'am," he ordered, reaching for Charlie.

"I can handle—" she began, but he ignored her. Somehow, he had the boy out of her grasp and expertly cradled in his right arm. Charlie stirred, but didn't waken.

Kate stared at the hard-looking man, but he only nodded toward her carry-on bag. "That, too, ma'am," he demanded.

"It's not that heavy."

But he stripped it from her, slung it over his own free shoulder.

She stood, feeling half-naked without her burdens, and oddly nettled to be so efficiently relieved of them. He was a high-handed man, and she didn't like it.

"You have other luggage?" he asked.

"Yes," she admitted reluctantly. "The most important's the dog—I hope they haven't lost her."

"Dog," he repeated, completely without enthusiasm.

He made Kate feel awkward, and she resented it. "Corbett said it was all right to bring the dog. He said he asked you about it, and—"

"It's fine," Hawkshaw said, holding up his hand as if to silence her. "Don't mention it."

He started toward the baggage pickup area. "This way."

Kate had no choice but to follow him. Why was he so

damned *preemptory?* Because they were late? Maybe he'd been waiting for hours, and it had soured his mood. Well, it was good of him to have waited at all, and she supposed she should apologize, just to be polite.

"I'm sorry we're late," she offered, hurrying to keep up with him. "Our plane was delayed in Miami a long time—"

"Yes, ma'am. I'm aware of that," Hawkshaw said.

"I know it was an inconvenience. Thank you for—"

"Don't bother," he said curtly.

"I just want to apologize for any—"

"Don't bother," he repeated and looked away pointedly, as if he found her irksome.

Oh, to hell with him, she thought tiredly. *If he's a boor, he's a boor. I didn't come down here for a friendly guy. I came for a tough one.*

He stopped before the luggage carousel. He didn't say, "How was your trip?" He didn't say, "How's my old friend Corbett?" He didn't say anything.

She didn't, either. Suddenly all she wanted was a bed and eight hours of sleep. She'd deal with Mr. Charm, here, in the morning, when she'd got her strength back.

She studied him furtively, taking his measure. His eyes had permanent creases at the outer edges. They gave him the look of a man who had spent his life watching the world around him and watching it carefully.

He didn't look at her. She had the impression he was purposefully ignoring her. But then, almost against his will, it seemed, he gazed down at Charlie. His craggy face didn't mellow.

"So this is Charlie?" he said.

Kate looked at her son, so young, so innocent of what was happening to him, lying so trustingly against this stranger's chest. A rush of tenderness swept away her other emotions, and she felt a lump like a fist in her throat.

"Yeah," she said. "That's Charlie."

HAWKSHAW HAD WAITED for the plane with deep misgivings. He was a private man about to surrender his privacy, and he had already damned himself for it a thousand times.

And his mood was frankly rotten. Right before he'd left for Key West airport, his ex-wife had called from Hawaii. She had an engagement singing in the lounge of a very upscale hotel on Waikiki Beach. "I'm in love," she'd announced. "I'm finally over you. I think I'm going to get married."

Suddenly Hawkshaw had remembered everything he'd worked to forget: the loss, the guilt, the failure, the incredible emptiness.

He'd forced cheer into his voice and congratulated her with all the heartiness he could muster. He didn't ask her the details. He didn't want to hear them.

She deserved to be happy, God knew. But basically what Hawkshaw had wanted to do was get drunk and stay that way for about a week. Maybe put his fist through a wall or two, that sort of thing.

But instead of mourning for the woman he wanted, he was stuck baby-sitting for one he didn't want in the least. The Kanaday woman was prettier than he'd expected, and for some obscure reason, this annoyed him.

Certainly Corbett's fuzzy photos had given no hint of her attractiveness. She'd looked thin and uninteresting in the pictures.

In the flesh, she was slender, not skinny, and her fea-

tures, although not perfect, were good enough, and the
red-gold of her hair was stunning.

Hell, he'd thought, *no wonder somebody's after her.*
And then he'd thought, *Dammit, Corbett. What have you
done to me now?*

CHAPTER TWO

HAWKSHAW RECOVERED HIMSELF, more or less.

This woman was one last assignment—and there was a rigid rule about assignments: Do Not Get Emotionally Involved. In his present mood, it seemed a laughably easy rule to keep.

He loaded the woman's luggage in the back of his van and swung the heavy dog cage inside. The dog snuffled and whined.

It was a basset hound, for God's sake. One of those low-slung, bowlegged lugubrious-looking dogs with ears that nearly dragged the ground.

Except for the dog, the woman and kid were traveling remarkably light. That was good. That was probably Corbett's doing. (Couldn't Corbett have talked her into leaving the fool dog behind?)

The kid was strapped into the back seat. He'd wakened briefly when his mother put him in the van, but now he was dead to the world again.

Hawkshaw got into the driver's seat. The woman sat in the passenger seat, staring up at the ink-dark sky. The lights of the airport parking lot fell through the windshield, illuminating her profile. It was a nice profile, he noted, but she wasn't Helen of Troy.

He started the van. From the back, the dog gave a pathetic yodel of canine heartbreak.

Hawkshaw headed out on South Roosevelt Street, toward the highway. The street ran beside the shore of the Atlantic side of the island, and the sea was rough tonight.

"We've never been in Florida before," said Kate Kanaday, staring out at the ocean. Its darkness was dimly streaked with lines of white foam breaking.

She had a low voice, the kind that would sound sexy over a telephone. He hadn't noticed her voice before. Funny. Maybe it was the darkness that made him notice now. He thought of a man listening in the dark to that voice, becoming excited by it.

She said, "Where are we going? Will you tell me that much? Corbett wouldn't say. Only that we'd meet you here, in Key West."

He narrowed his eyes against the glare of oncoming headlights. Traffic was heavy, even at this time of night. Key West was a party town, and the party never stopped.

He said, "It's in the lower keys. A place called Cobia Key. Not many people know where it's at."

Which is to your advantage, he thought. *Which is to your very great advantage.*

"I do," she said without hesitation. "It's the island sixteen miles north of Key West. There's a heron preserve there."

He allowed himself to lift an eyebrow in surprise, but kept his gaze fastened on the road. "You've heard of it?"

"I read about it," she said in her low voice. "When we were delayed so long in Miami, I bought a book."

Of course, he thought. She'd read about it. She would. "Yeah," he said. "You worked in a bookstore."

"Yes," she said. "I used to."

There was no self-pity in her voice, only resignation.

Hawkshaw stole a sideways look at her. The van's windows were down, and although her hair was pinned back in some sort of braid, strands had escaped and fluttered around her face.

The van was on the highway now, crossing one of the dozens of bridges that linked the islands that formed the Keys.

The Kanaday woman said, "You live on Cobia Key?"

"For now," he said. "It's nothing fancy. It's in the backcountry. Off to itself."

"I don't mind," she said, still gazing moodily at the Atlantic. "As long as it's safe."

In the back of the van, the basset hound gave a throaty complaint followed by a series of mournful snorts.

She said, "You were in the Secret Service with Corbett?"

"Yeah," he said.

"Until he retired, went into business on his own?"

"Yes."

"And you've retired, too?"

"Yes."

Two years ago he'd taken an early retirement, at age forty-two, exactly twenty years after signing up with the Treasury Department. He'd loved the job, but he'd left it in self-disgust after he'd lost Sandra.

He didn't want to talk about himself or the Service or his relationship to Corbett or to think about Sandra. So he said, "Tell me about this problem you've got. Do you think Corbett's got some lead on the stalker? Something he's not ready to tell you or me?"

She stiffened as if the word *stalker* sent a bolt of electricity ripping through her system. She drew her breath between her teeth. "No," she said. "I don't think he does. He's afraid my only option is to go away." She turned to him. "I have a friend, Carol, in Denver who'll help. I worked it out with her over a pay phone, so nobody could tap into the conversations. But Corbett still didn't want us to go straight there. He's very cautious. I hate imposing on you.''

"Don't mention it," muttered Hawkshaw.

"I mean it," she said. "I *hate* it. My money situation's complicated right now, but somehow I'll reimburse you. I pay my own way. We're not a charity case, Charlie and I." She turned away again. "So tell me about yourself," she said. "What do you do, now that you're retired?"

"As little as possible."

"Do you have a first name?" she asked.

"None that I answer to."

"How long did you and Corbett work together?"

"Fourteen years, off and on."

"All of it in Washington?"

"A lot of it," he said.

"Like where else?"

"Here," he said. "There."

She shifted in her seat and he could feel her looking at him. "Would you rather we not talk? Is that it? All you have to do is say so."

The words surprised him. There was a certain sassiness in them he hadn't expected. But, what, God help him, if she was a talker, one of those women who never shut up?

"I'm out of practice," he said dryly.

"If you're worried that we're going to intrude on your life, don't be," she said. "We'll keep to ourselves as much as possible."

"Umph," he said.

"The last thing I want to do is be a bother."

"Um."

"I mean, I, of all people, know what it's like to have your privacy invaded."

Touché, he thought. *A good point, that.*

"I have plenty to do," she said, as if to herself. "I've got a lot of decisions to make, things to plan. I mean, if I look at the bright side, I've got a whole new life ahead, a completely fresh start."

He almost said something sarcastic. Already she was trying to look on the bright side? To be optimistic? *Lady, don't you understand what's happening to your life?*

He stole another glance at her. She had one elbow on the window's edge, her knuckles pressed hard against her jaw.

The moon, nearly full, had broken through the clouds, silvering her profile. She looked like a face delicately carved on a coin.

With a start, he realized she was biting her lip. He thought he saw the glitter of tears in her eyes, but she blinked hard twice, then three times. The glitter disappeared.

He said nothing.

In the back, the dog whined as if its heart were irreparably broken. But Katherine Kanaday kept her back straight, her eyes looking straight ahead, and her chin up.

HAWKSHAW'S PLACE WAS in "the backcountry," he'd said, but his words had given Kate no hint of how desolate the backcountry could seem.

The van left the main highway, meandered through a small development of homes that stood dark and lifeless as tombstones. Then the houses grew fewer and farther apart, and when, at last they came to an end, civilization seemed to end with them.

The dark land stretched out blackly on either side, thatched with scrub wood. The air was heavy with a rich, swampy scent. The winding road narrowed and seemed to roll on forever, but at last Hawkshaw turned in at a graveled drive. He got out of the van and opened a pad-locked gate.

Kate could make out a tall chain-link fence glinting faintly against the trees. After Hawkshaw moved the van through the gate and refastened the lock, he drove on into a darkness so thick it gave her a twinge of claustrophobia.

A small deer leaped across the road and was caught briefly in the van's headlights. It was such a tiny, elfin creature, Kate thought she was hallucinating.

She gasped in surprise.

"Key deer," Hawkshaw said, sounding bored. "That's all."

She blinked and the animal was gone, as if it had vanished back into the magical world where it belonged. Of course, she thought, it had been one of the miniature deer peculiar to these islands. "Oh," she said softly. "I read about them."

He gave no response. He pulled up next to a house that even in the darkness seemed neglected, almost deserted. She heard the lapping of water when she got out of the car and thought she could smell the ocean nearby, but she could not see it.

Hawkshaw carried Charlie up a narrow flight of stairs to what seemed to be a long deck. He unlocked the front door, switched on the inside lights, and took the boy inside. Kate followed, blinking at the disarray.

Hawkshaw was lean of body and spare of speech, and she had expected the house to be lean and spare, as well. But the living room was crammed with run-down furniture and cluttered with fishing and boating paraphernalia. Some sort of huge stuffed fish hung on the wall; it gave her an unwelcoming stare.

"It's kind of a mess," Hawkshaw said, in a master-piece of understatement.

Kate smiled weakly. The decor, she decided, could be described only as Late Bachelor Hellhole.

"Your room's this way," he said, moving down a narrow hallway. "Watch out for the oar."

He hit another light switch with his elbow, and stepping over an abandoned oar, he carried Charlie down the hall to a back room. He turned on yet another light.

Kate followed warily. The bedroom gave off the air of being unused for years, perhaps decades. Boxes were piled haphazardly against the walls, as if Hawkshaw had been moving out, then suddenly changed his mind.

There was little furniture: an old wicker dresser, a metal desk and folding chair, a pair of twin beds with mismatched spreads.

The Ritz it isn't, thought Kate, with sinking heart.

But Hawkshaw turned down the cover and sheet of one bed with the air of a man who knew what he was doing. She was surprised to see that the sheets and pillowcase seemed crisp and clean, freshly laundered.

He laid Charlie down and started to untie one of the child's scuffed running shoes, then abruptly straightened. His eyes met hers. "You'll want to do that," he said gruffly.

The room was small, its ceiling low, and suddenly Hawkshaw seemed even taller and wider-shouldered than he had at the airport. He hooked his thumbs on either side of his belt buckle and cocked one hip. He looked her up and down, his eyes narrowed. The slant of his mouth was resigned.

"There's a bathroom in there," he said, nodding toward a badly chipped door. "I'll get the rest of your things. And your dog."

Kate winced. The dog, still caged in the van, had started to bay piteously.

Hawkshaw shook his head, then pulled the brim of his hat down even more. He made his way past her, but the room was so small that he accidentally brushed his arm against hers as he headed toward the door.

The fleeting touch of his body was unexpectedly electric. Once again his gaze locked with hers, and the complexity she saw in those green depths shook her.

Quickly he glanced away, and then he was gone, striding down the little hall. She felt a strange, inner shudder. She'd read a profound resentment burning in his eyes, and she was sure it was resentment of *her.*

He did not want her and Charlie here. She had almost been scalded by the rancor she had felt flaring in him. Yet she sensed more than rancor in that swift, telling look. There had been something like desire, all the sharper for not being welcomed.

She knew because she had felt the same sensation; a sudden hot spark of sexual attraction that she disliked, and wanted to disclaim.

The slightly musty air of the room seemed to throb with his presence, even though he was gone. *Don't be asinine,* she scolded herself. She was so tired that she was drugged by fatigue; it was making her imagine foolish things.

She sighed and bent over Charlie and finished untying his shoes. She slipped them off, loosened the button at the throat of his polo shirt. Then she shook him gently.

"Charlie," she whispered. "Everything's fine. We're in Florida. Get up and go to the bathroom. Then you can go back to sleep."

Charlie stirred grumpily. His long lashes fluttered open, and he squinted, frowning at her. He tried to roll over and ignore her.

But she persisted. She wanted him to know he was in a new place, but that he was safe and that she was there with him. Finally she roused him enough to lead him into the bathroom.

"We're in Florida," she told him, "with a man named Mr. Hawkshaw."

"I don't care," Charlie grumbled.

"I want you to understand. We're in Florida. With Mr. Hawkshaw. What did I just say?"

"Florida," Charlie muttered. "Mr. Shocklaw."

"Hawkshaw," she repeated, taking him back to the bedroom. "There's your bed. The bathroom's right over there. I'll leave the light on in case you have to get up."

The boy climbed back into bed and struggled, frowning, to get between the sheets.

"Do you want your pajamas?"

"No," he yawned. "Let me *sleep*."

He fell back against the pillow, his eyes already closed.

Hawkshaw came in the door, carrying their few pieces of luggage. He set them down near the doorway. The fat basset hound, Maybelline, waddled behind him, her eyes wells of sorrow over what she had suffered.

Maybelline gave sadly accusing looks to both Kate and Hawkshaw. Then huffing and straining, she managed to clamber onto Charlie's bed. She shot the two adults another aggrieved glance, then turned around several times and, with a grunt, plopped down beside Charlie.

"I hope you don't mind," Kate said. "The dog always sleeps with him. He'll feel more at home if she—"

"No problem," Hawkshaw said, cutting her off. He turned and left, closing the door behind him as if he was glad to have a barrier between them.

Kate sighed and sat on her own bed. She stared at the shut door and suddenly felt as if she were in prison.

If Hawkshaw found it so damned disagreeable to have them here, why on earth had he said they could come?

He might be a fine bodyguard, a protector par excellence, but did he have to be so silent and surly and turbulent?

On top of it all, he had some weird sexiness, and he knew it. As if *she*, of all people, was going to go for the dangerous, mysterious type. No, thank you. If she ever got mixed up with another man, she hoped it was a mild-mannered teddy bear of a fellow who gave off an aura of danger no greater than a marshmallow.

Oh, hell, she thought wearily. Why was she criticizing Hawkshaw? He might be edgy and rude, but he'd been good enough to take them in, hadn't he? Perhaps she should no more blame him for his prickly coldness than she should blame an attack dog for being vicious.

She sighed, rose, and got ready for bed. She wouldn't let this man get her spirits down. She simply would not allow it.

She left the bathroom light on and the door partly open, in case Charlie awoke. She turned out the overhead light and settled into the bed, which was surprisingly cool and soft.

From beneath the closed bedroom door came a wedge of yellow light, and there was the sound of music somewhere, muted and rather haunting. Hawkshaw must still be up.

She was stricken with a sudden, piercing memory of his sea-green eyes. *No, my girl, none of that,* she told herself firmly. She would not think that way.

The stalker had stolen a few small items from her—possessions that she had left near the doorstep or on her patio—nothing that seemed of great consequence.

But, in truth, he had stolen far larger things: her job, her home, her peace of mind. He had stripped trust from her life, especially trust of men. And along with it, he had thieved away desire.

HAWKSHAW SAT AT HIS father's battered desk in the living room, going over the Kanaday woman's file again. Now that he had met her and the kid, the case no longer seemed an abstraction, nor did they. They were flesh and blood.

Yes, he thought, and the reality of her was distracting, because all he wanted to think of was Sandra, who was marrying someone else and would never be his again.

Sandra, he thought hopelessly. The memory of her was always like a knife in the heart. He forced himself not to think of her sensual blondness. He made himself look instead at the fuzzy reproductions of the snapshots that Corbett had sent of Kate Kanaday. There were only three.

The first showed her and the kid sitting before a towering Christmas tree. The picture was dated two years ago. The kid, Charlie, was on Kate's lap, mugging for the camera, and she was smiling with what seemed like real joy.

The camera didn't love her, he told himself. Not the way it had loved and flattered Sandra.

But the smile—Kate Kanaday's smile was nice, and it was full of the love of life. He wondered if she would ever smile that way again. He set the photos aside, face down.

He scanned the file again, looked at one of the notes from the stalker. The man had written:

I WANT TO TOUCH YOU EVERYWHERE. TO KISS YOU EVERYWHERE. TO EXPLORE EVERY INCH OF YOUR BODY. YOU WILL OPEN YOURSELF TO ME, AND CRY OUT WITH UNBEARABLE PLEASURE AT THE JOY MY BURNING THRUSTS WILL BRING YOU...

Hawkshaw shook his head in disgust. He knew what the police had probably told her, that guys who wrote such muck seldom acted on it. They got their jollies through the words and didn't have to do the deeds.

But Hawkshaw knew this was not always true. He closed the file, pushed away from the old desk. He got to his feet and took another beer from the fridge. He went outside, to the deck.

The boards creaked beneath his feet. The deck was sagging and in disrepair like the rest of the property. He would have to make up his mind sooner or later: either fix up the house or tear it down for good.

He sipped the beer and stared off into the velvety darkness. This point of land was surrounded by tidal streams and mangrove islands. He heard the splash of a fish, perhaps even a dolphin, for dolphins sometimes came into the waters.

He inhaled deeply of the salt, humid air. He had spent much of his youth here, in this very house.

Now the house was decaying around him. He stared up at the featureless sky. Man-made dwellings were fragile in this climate; they took constant maintenance. Hawkshaw decided he was not good at maintaining things, at least the things that were supposed to belong to him.

He turned and looked at the lone light that shone from the farthest window. The woman had left the bathroom light on for the kid, a gesture that touched him in spite of himself.

Don't be touched, he warned himself. *Don't feel anything. Don't get involved.*

The woman and kid had come into his life suddenly, and with luck they'd disappear just as suddenly. Until then, he'd watch out for them because they were a legacy from Corbett, a favor to be returned and a debt to be paid.

But nothing personal. Hawkshaw would stay uninvolved.

He had made it his specialty.

A RAGGED SCREAM WOKE KATE. In panic she raised herself on her elbow, staring about the strange room.

The morning's first light poured between the curtains. Charlie slept in the bed next to hers, his brown hair dark against the white pillowcase. His breathing was even and deep.

Maybelline slept beside him, her squat body curled up against his legs. She opened one bloodshot eye, limply raised one ear. She sighed a doggy sigh.

The scream rent the air again, and Kate's heart pounded in confused dismay. But Maybelline closed her eye, lowered her ear. Her body relaxed, and in the fraction of a moment, she snored.

The scream sounded again, this time farther away, and Kate thought, *A seagull. That's all. Seagulls make an awful sound like that.*

It came back to her in a surreal rush that she and Charlie were somewhere in the Florida Keys. The realization jarred her, and she sank back against the pillow. She caught her lower lip between her teeth.

She and Charlie had arrived in Florida last night, and now were hidden away with a friend of Corbett's. And that friend was a tall, lean unfriendly man named Hawkshaw....

Her muscles stiffened at the recollection of Hawkshaw. Like Corbett, he had been in the Secret Service, and that, in truth, was almost all she knew about him.

She raised herself again on her elbow. She barely even knew where she and Charlie *were,* for God's sake. She had better find out, because she was going to have to explain it all to Charlie. And prepare him for Hawkshaw.

The room was musty, and she thought she could smell the ocean—or was it the Gulf? Or both? She also imagined the aroma of coffee in the sultry air. Squinting at her watch, she saw that it was just after six; with luck Charlie should sleep for another hour.

She slid from bed, opened her suitcase and snatched up her toiletry case and a change of clothes. The face that stared back at her from the mirror startled her. She looked pale and uncertain of herself. She hated that uncertainty; it had once been so foreign to her.

She clambered into jeans and a pale-green T-shirt, put on her old running shoes, then slipped out of the bedroom, leaving the door open in case Charlie awoke. She cast a last, worried glance back at him, the dog still snoring by his side.

She padded down the hall. The living room looked as cluttered and disheveled as it had last night. Almost everything in it seemed dated, as if the contents had come from an era older than Hawkshaw's own.

The kitchen was overcrowded, but she found a freshly brewed pot of coffee warming on the counter and a clean mug. She filled it and stepped to the front door.

She eased open the screen door and looked up and down the deck for Hawkshaw. Her heartbeat quickened as she saw him, sitting on a bench, hunched over a weathered picnic table. He had a manila folder open in front of him and seemed to be deep in study.

He sat in profile to her, a forelock of hair falling over his eyes. He wore olive drab shorts and that was all. The rest of him was as naked as the day God made him.

The morning sun was still mellow, and it spilled over on his shoulders, gleamed on the muscles of his back. His arms and legs were sinewed and bronzed, and she could see the tracery of veins that etched his biceps.

The azure-blue of the sky framed the sharp angles of his profile. He looked at ease with himself, as much a part of nature as an eagle or a stag might.

He did not look up at her, and not even his slightest motion betrayed that he knew she was there. But he said, "Hello, Katherine. Bring out your coffee and sit down. We have things to talk about. By the way, your socks don't match."

She blinked in surprise and her gaze fell involuntarily to her feet. On one foot was a navy-blue sock, on the other a black one.

Almost reluctantly she came to his side. She sat down on the bench as far from him as she could. He sipped at his coffee, but he didn't look at her.

"How did you know I was there?" she demanded. "How did you know I had coffee? How did you know my socks don't match? You never even saw me."

"I saw you," he said in his soft growl. "It's my business to notice things. Or it was."

He had shaved. The lean planes of his face were clean, and the scent of something piney hovered about him.

"How long did you say you and Corbett worked together?" she asked uneasily.

"Fourteen years," he said.

He raised his eyes to hers. They were keen eyes, and for the first time she realized they also seemed intensely intelligent.

"But you don't want to talk about me," he said. "You want to talk about where you are. Right?"

"Exactly," she said. "Charlie's already confused about everything. Somehow I have to explain this to him."

"Right," he said, turning his gaze from her. He set

down his coffee mug. From a stack of papers on the table's corner he drew out a map.

He unfolded it and set it between them. "This chain of islands is the Lower Keys."

He picked up a red pen. She noticed the long, jagged scar on his right arm. With the precision of an artist or an engineer, he circled the last island in the chain. "That's Key West, where you landed."

She nodded mechanically. A breeze sprang up. From the corner of her eye, she saw how it fluttered the lock of hair that fell over his forehead.

"We came up the one main road," he said, tracing a line. "We're here, Cobia Key. We're at the edge of the heron sanctuary. More or less surrounded by mangrove islands. Like I say, we're isolated."

His gaze met hers again, and it seemed to her that it held a strange mixture of coolness, distance, and unwilling hunger. Uneasy, she turned her face from his and stared out at the dark tangle of the mangroves. "You're alone here?" she asked.

"Yes," he said in a tone that implied, *And that's how I like it.*

She heard gulls crying in the distance, but she realized that this place was oddly still, almost hushed. The landscape did not seem tropical or exotic. Instead it seemed brooding, the mangrove forests full of mystery.

She had imagined Florida abloom with flowers and bright with colorfully plumaged birds. She had not envisioned these thick, low woods, deep with secrets. It was an alien atmosphere, and she took a drink of coffee to steel herself against it.

"What is this place?" she asked, giving the worn deck a critical glance.

"It used to be a guide service. Mostly kayak tours. Not anymore."

She looked at him questioningly. "You bought this when—when you retired from the service?"

"I inherited it," he said. "When my father died."

"I'm sorry," she said, although she could detect no sorrow, no grieving in him.

"It's getting ready to fall down," he said from between his teeth. He tapped the map with the pen again. "But that's where you are. What's left of Hawkshaw's Island Adventures. In Nowhere, Florida."

"Over there," she said, nodding toward the patch of green-gray water glinting between the trees. "Is that the ocean?"

"No. Just a channel."

Unexpectedly he stood. The tattered shorts rode low on his hips. He handed her the map, his hand brushing hers. She found that the touch made her draw in her breath.

"Look," he said. "I'm not much of a host. I'm out of practice. But can I get you something to eat?" he asked. "More coffee?"

"No," she said hastily. "I'm fine. But Charlie will probably be hungry. I wish I'd thought last night to ask you to stop, to let me buy a few things."

"It's okay," he said. "I put in plenty of supplies."

Seeming restless, he moved to the edge of the deck and put his bare foot on the lower railing. He stared out over the trees.

"It's going to get hot," he said quietly. "Really hot. Can you feel it?"

CHAPTER THREE

THE BREEZE CHANGED DIRECTION, making the mangroves drone and sigh as if whispering ancient riddles.

Hawkshaw leaned his elbows on the top railing, not looking at her. The sun made his bare back and shoulders gleam like copper.

"So," he said, "let's talk about this mystery man, this stalker."

Her stomach tightened. "I should go see if Charlie's ready to wake up."

"In a minute," Hawkshaw said. "This guy—he's been harassing you for a year and a half, right?"

"Yes." *And he's brought me to this,* she thought fatalistically. *To depending on the kindness of strangers.*

"You have no idea who he is?"

"None." The word was a knot of gall in her throat. Suddenly, her future loomed before her with all its unspeakable uncertainty.

She was not even sure about her past. Was the stalker someone she knew? She had come to suspect, at one time or another, almost every man she knew.

Hawkshaw turned, almost lazily. He leaned back, his elbows resting on the railing. "So you went to Corbett."

"I had to do something," she said with a surge of spirit. "The police couldn't help. I had to fight back someway."

"You knew Corbett from before," he said.

"Only in passing. His office—his and his partner's—is in the same building as the bookstore. I checked him out. I heard his qualifications were excellent."

"They are. Frankly, I'm amazed he hasn't been able to ID this guy."

She shook her head in frustration. "Every time he thinks he has a lead, it melts, turns into air. It's like chasing a ghost."

She knew that Corbett was good. But the stalker was better. Corbett had followed half a hundred clues and hunches, but they'd led only to half a hundred nowheres.

On Corbett's advice, Kate had changed her phone number six times. She would have changed where she lived, but she could not find a buyer for the condo. She'd come to fear it would not matter if she did. The stalker would always find her, it seemed. She was stymied. So was Corbett.

Now, she who had prided herself on being so independent was on the run. By the harsh light of morning, it seemed an extraordinary and frantic move.

"You told nobody you were leaving Columbia?" he asked.

"Nobody," she said. "Except my friend in Denver. I said we'd be coming soon. But I didn't tell her where we'd be until then. I didn't know myself."

"And Corbett told nobody," he said. "Not even his partner?"

"Not even him," Kate said. She liked Corbett, but not his partner, Bedlingham. Bedlingham was married but flirtatious; to her it seemed he always exuded an air of sly, forbidden sexuality.

"And Corbett's checked out the men closest to you?"

"Yes," she said, although there weren't that many.

George Chandler, her husband's stepfather. George

lived in the city, but he and Chuck had fallen out years ago. They had not socialized, had hardly spoken to each other.

There was Chuck's brother, Trevor. Trevor lived in Minneapolis, where he was confined to his house because of multiple allergies and never went out. She communicated with him mostly by e-mail because it was cheaper than phoning. She felt guilty, for she had lied to him about what she was doing. She had told him she was taking the computer in for repair and would be out of touch.

And there was her former boss, the bookstore owner, Winston McPhee. McPhee was a kind, fatherly man who'd promised he'd take her back when it could be done. But the stalker had made McPhee's life hellish with jealous calls day and night, and he'd disrupted the business until Kate knew she had to leave.

"Your father-in-law," Hawkshaw said. "Your brother-in-law. Your former employer. Corbett's checked them out. And they seem clean?"

"Yes," she said, ashamed because at one time she'd suspected each of them. But she had come to look on every man she met with suspicion these days. It was a tense, terrible way to live.

"Corbett says it could be somebody I don't know at all," she said. "Or somebody I've known for years."

Her gaze drifted to the picnic table. The breeze rustled the papers in a file folder that lay open next to a black ball cap.

With an unpleasant shock, she recognized the top page—a copy of one of the stalker's notes. She knew those hideous notes by heart.

This one said,

I SAW YOU TODAY. YOU WERE WEARING
YOUR GREEN PANTSUIT AND BLACK
JACKET. IN MY MIND I TOOK OFF YOUR
CLOTHES. I WANTED YOU SO MUCH IT WAS
LIKE POISON IN MY VEINS. I IMAGINED YOU
NAKED AND KNEELING BEFORE ME. THIS IS
WHAT YOU DID—

She realized that Hawkshaw had read these filthy notes,
and her face blazed with shame. Hastily she rose from
the bench.

"I'd better go see about Charlie," she said. "If he
wakes up in a strange room…"

"If he wakes up in a strange room, what?"

"He'll be upset. Charlie has—a few problems. He has
an attention deficiency."

She nodded, rather bitterly, toward the papers on the
table. "Corbett seems to have told you everything else.
Didn't he tell you that?"

"It's no big deal."

"Maybe not to you," she said defensively. "But it
makes it harder for him to adjust to change than it is for
most children. He doesn't understand any of this—"

Hawkshaw shrugged one shoulder, as if what she said
didn't matter. "He'll have breathing space here."

He obviously didn't understand, didn't want to. "Listen," she said, her voice brittle, "I'm not asking any fa-
vors for myself. But you might show a little sympathy for
Charlie. He's only a child, he has special needs, this is a
horrible situation."

"I happen," he said coolly, "to be rather good with
kids."

I'll bet, she thought. *I'll just bet.*

The breeze tossed Hawkshaw's hair, flapped the worn

cloth of his shorts. He crossed his arms across his chest. He tilted his head in the direction of the stalker's notes.

"Katherine," he said, "you think I haven't seen letters like that before? I have. Plenty of them. You can stop blushing."

She didn't want to hear more. She turned and took refuge in the quiet of his strange, disordered house.

CHARLIE'S EYES FLUTTERED open, struggled to focus. Mama leaned over him, smiling. An instant uneasiness swept over him.

These days Mama's smile was different than it used to be, it no longer seemed real or alive. The smile was like a mask. Charlie could not explain this, he only knew it was true.

"We're here, Charlie," Mama said. Her voice was cheerful, but her eyes weren't. "We're in Florida. We got here last night. You were asleep—"

Charlie sat up, frowning and rubbing his eyes. She had told him yesterday they had to go to Florida, she had showed him meaningless shapes on a map, she had said a lot of words. Now she was saying them again.

You're in Florida.

Florida seemed to be a room that was little and not very nice and smelled funny. He didn't like it. He wanted to go home.

He rubbed his eyes harder, till he saw colored sparks whirl and swoop across his vision. Then he stopped. Warily he opened his eyes again.

Florida was still there, the whole room of it. And the scary thing about Florida was that it was *different* from all he knew. His bed was not really his bed. The walls were not his walls, the window not his window.

"This house belongs to a man named Mr. Hawkshaw,"

Mama said. ''Mr. Hawkshaw's a friend of Mr. Corbett. You remember Mr. Corbett? He drove us to the airport—''

The mask of Mama's bright smile made Charlie feel something was badly wrong. Her words beat against his ears the way moths beat against a screen at night. Like moths, the words wanted in, but they couldn't get in.

Charlie stared at the curtains as if hypnotized. They were not his real curtains with the pictures of the *Star Wars* people on them. These curtains were ugly-brown with blue-and-white fishes on them. The fishes had little blue dots for eyes.

Mama was still talking, her words softly going *bat, bat, bat.* She had him up, leading him to a bathroom that was not his real bathroom. Her words couldn't get inside his head. He was too busy looking at all the different things, all the wrong things, all the *Florida* things, in this bathroom.

The wallpaper was enough to make him dizzy. There were more fishes on it, silly pink-and-yellow fish on a watery green background. He felt as if he were underwater, that Florida had turned him into a fish-boy.

''Hello,'' he called in his mind to the other fish. *''Hello, I'm a boy who's trapped here. How do I get back home?''*

''Swim, you must swim very hard,'' said a pale-yellow fish. *''You must swim with all your might.''*

''Charlie, stand still!'' Mama ordered. ''Just brush your teeth.''

''I'm swimming home,'' Charlie said around his toothbrush. His arms made wild windmill motions, as if he were swimming at a heroic pace.

He imagined he was friends with all the fish. He began to sing ''Under the Sea.'' He imagined himself singing and dancing with all the fish and a big red lobster and pretty little mermaids.

His mother told him to quiet down, but her words were only more moths flying airily around his head. "Under the sea," he sang and did a fancy fish-dance step. "Under the se-e-a—"

Mama said something about breakfast. She pulled a clean shirt down over his head.

Help! thought Charlie. *I can't see! I can't breathe! Mama's a sea witch! She's put me in a bag!*

But he sputtered out of the neck hole of his shirt, safe again. "To the kitchen—" said Mama, opening the door into a hallway. From the first look, he didn't like this hallway. It was long and narrow and different—it was more of nasty Florida.

But fat old Maybelline was up now, and she wanted out. She waddled down the hallway, her short legs chugging, her ears nearly trailing on the ground.

Charlie the fish-boy swam behind her, his arms churning again. "Glub," he said. "Glub-glub." He pretended Maybelline was a squid and that he was following her.

Then he was out of the sea and into a living room, and wow, it wasn't his living room, it was *really* different— not all neat like Mama kept their place, and there was *stuff* everywhere!

He stopped to gape. His mind spun, trying to take it all in as his eyes danced from one object to another. Such a wealth of things! A cascade of things—fishing poles, a net with a handle, a tackle box, an oar, hooks, bobbers, flies, weights, a hundred things that he had no names for.

"Cool!" Charlie breathed. He felt dizzy with wonder. He looked up at a big fish stuffed and mounted on a wall. Was it a *shark?* It was, it was a shark, he was sure of it—what a paradise of stuff.

"Way cool!"

He reached toward a fishing pole, the biggest fishing pole he'd ever seen. Surely such a pole was used to catch whales!

"Charlie, don't," his mother warned, pulling his hand back. "That's Mr. Hawkshaw's. Come on. Let's take Maybelline outside. Then we'll find some breakfast."

But Charlie couldn't help himself. He picked up a colorful fishing lure with all sorts of bright mirror-things glittering on it. It had red plastic tentacles like an octopus—it even had little eyes!

"Charlie!" his mother said sternly.

But the lure was too wonderful, and he was turning it over and over until it *bit* him—

"Yow!" Charlie sprang back, dropping the lure. A bright drop of blood welled at the tip of his thumb. "I'm stabbed!" he cried. "I been stabbed by an octopus!"

"You should mind your mother, kid," said a man's voice.

Something in that voice paralyzed Charlie. *A lion-voice,* he thought wildly. *I hear a lion-voice.*

He turned and saw a big, tall man standing in the doorway. This man looked like a superhero to Charlie, except he was dressed strangely. All he wore were shorts and a black baseball cap. His skin was tawny-brown all over, like a lion's. Charlie stared up at this wondrous being.

"Charlie, now you've hurt yourself," his mother said, but he barely heard her. He was too busy looking at the superhero.

"Let me see your hand," Mama fussed, but the words fluttered in confusion at his ears. They didn't really register. He shook off Mama's questing hand.

"Let's see, Charlie," the tall man said, kneeling beside

him. He took Charlie by the hand and squinted at the bleeding thumb.

"I was bit by an octopus," Charlie said, hoping to impress him. "Maybe I'll die of octopus poison."

"I doubt it," said the man. "Come over to the sink. We'll wash it and put on some antiseptic."

"It hurts," Charlie said, "but I'm not crying. See?" He pointed at his tearless eyes.

"I see," said the tall man, rising to his feet. He was so tall his head seemed to almost touch the ceiling. He kept hold of Charlie's hand and led him to the cluttered sink.

"Wow," Charlie breathed, looking up at him. "Maybe I'll have a big, massive scar."

"Maybe," said the man, running cold water on the stinging thumb. "You should have minded your mother."

Charlie ignored the advice. He also ignored his mother, who stood by with an oddly disapproving look on her face. He would *fix* her for bringing him to this old Florida. He'd fix her by liking the tall man better than he liked her—so there.

"Who are you?" Charlie asked. "How come you don't got no shirt?"

"Don't have any shirt," his mother corrected, but he hardly noticed.

"My name's Hawkshaw," said the man. "I don't have a shirt because I don't need one. This is the Florida Keys. It's warm all year."

"Then why do you have a hat?" Charlie asked.

"To keep the sun out of my eyes," said the man, picking up the antiseptic. "Hold still. This is going to hurt."

"I won't cry," Charlie vowed, but the smarting of the medicine made him dance in place.

"Charlie," his mother asked, "do you need a bandage on your thumb?"

Charlie didn't answer. He just gazed up, up, up at Hawkshaw. *Hawkshaw,* it was a good name, he thought. Like Batman. Or Rambo. Or Han Solo.

Hawkshaw's cap was black with white letters. "What's your hat say?" he demanded.

"I don't think he needs a Band-Aid," Hawkshaw told Mama. To Charlie he said, "It says United States Secret Service."

Charlie's eyes widened. "Secret Service? Like the guys who guard the president?"

"Yeah," Hawkshaw said in the purr-growl of his lion's voice. "Like that."

Charlie was swept up by excitement. "Are *you* in the Secret Service?"

"I was," Hawkshaw said easily. "What say we take this dog out? She's standing cross-legged, she has to pee so bad."

Charlie saw his mother leading the dog outside, but the fact hardly registered. He was too rapt with admiration. "Did you have a *gun* and everything?"

"A gun and everything," Hawkshaw said. "Come on. Your mother's doing all the work." He headed for the door and Charlie followed as if fastened to him by a string.

"Did you ever guard the president?" Charlie asked in awe.

"Sometimes," Hawkshaw said. "Mostly I guarded other people."

"Did you ever shoot anybody?" Charlie asked hopefully. "Did anybody ever shoot you?"

Hawkshaw's lean face seemed to grow leaner, starker and sterner. "Outside, kid," he ordered, holding the door.

And Charlie, dutiful as a page in training to a great knight, obeyed.

IN THE YARD, next to a cluster of flowering shrubs, Maybelline squatted modestly. Kate stared off in the opposite direction, trying to seem too dignified to notice.

She saw Hawkshaw come out on the deck. He tilted back the bill of his cap and stared down at her.

Self-conscious, Kate tried to ignore him. She was a mess, of course. She was pale with a Northerner's pallor, and she hadn't fastened her hair back, done anything to it except brush it.

Her jeans were baggy, her shirt mannish, and Hawkshaw probably wondered why anyone, least of all a stalker, would want her.

His gaze seemed to settle on the slight thrust of her breasts under the shirt, and, in embarrassment, she looked away. She was imagining things, she told herself. And if she wasn't, the last thing she needed was anybody's sexual interest. She'd had enough for a lifetime.

Her son was chattering a mile a minute to the man, and Hawkshaw answered with grunts and nods. But when she stole a glimpse at him, she saw his eyes were still on her.

Maybelline plodded a few steps into the shade and sat down among the deep-red phlox. Delicately, she began to gnaw at her haunch, as if besieging a flea.

Kate knelt beside her, slipping her arm around the dog affectionately. She nuzzled one of the velvety ears. Maybelline kept pursuing the flea.

Kate raised her eyes and stared toward the patch of sea that showed between the trees. The sun beat on her face, and she thought of Charlie, who was as fair-skinned as she. The both of them would need hats and sunscreen, or they'd be burned and blistered.

She turned to look at Charlie again and saw Hawkshaw take off his own cap and adjust it to make it tighter. "Here, kid," he said, setting it on Charlie's head. "You want to wear this?"

"Wow," Charlie breathed, reverently fingering the bill. "You'll let me?"

"Sure," said Hawkshaw.

The boy smiled more widely than Kate had seen him smile in weeks. She swallowed.

He was a nice-looking boy, she thought, handsome, even. He had his father's straight brown hair and angular, masculine features. But his eyes were the same color brown as hers, and in them shone a lively intelligence, a bright imagination.

But sometimes, because of his attention deficit, Charlie's liveliness was too unfettered; it needed taming.

It seemed profoundly unfair to her that the boy had faced so many problems. The loss of his father, the insanity of her being stalked, his own disability—sometimes her feelings of protectiveness for him almost overwhelmed her.

Hawkshaw turned his attention back to Kate. She dropped her gaze to the dog and started to unfasten the leash.

"Wait," Hawkshaw ordered. "I wouldn't do that if I were you."

She looked up, surprise mingled with resentment. His tone had been abrupt, even imperious.

"What's wrong?" she demanded.

He made his way down the narrow stairs, Charlie tagging behind him like a puppy.

"I just wouldn't let her off yet," Hawkshaw said. "The Keys aren't like the city. Nature gets a little snarky down here."

"Snarky?" she asked dubiously. It seemed an unlikely word for him to use.

"Dangerous," he amended. "Come on. Let's walk her around the yard. I'll explain what I mean."

"Look at me, Mama," Charlie said, fairly dancing before her, adjusting the oversize cap on his head. "I'm a Secret Service man—I guard people."

He dived on the unsuspecting Maybelline and caught her in a possessive embrace. "You're a spy!" he informed the startled dog. "I got you!"

Maybelline sighed, martyrlike, and let him wrestle her to the ground. Kate stared down at the boy in shock. "Charlie! Where's your shirt?"

He had been wearing a shirt only a moment before, she was certain of it. Now his thin, white back was as bare as Hawkshaw's tanned one.

"Charlie, Charlie," Kate said, pulling him off the dog. "I asked you—where's your shirt?"

"I don't remember," he said carelessly. He picked up a stick and aimed it into the trees like a gun. "Bang!" he yelled. "Stick 'em up—you're under arrest!"

Kate knelt before him and pushed the stick down firmly. "Why?" she said, very clearly, very carefully. "Why did you take off your shirt?"

"I don't have a shirt because I don't need one," Charlie said, echoing Hawkshaw exactly. "This is the Florida Keys. It's warm all year."

She looked back toward the deck and saw the boy's polo shirt lying inside out on the bottom stair. He had stripped it off and tossed it aside.

"Charlie," Kate said firmly, "you have to wear a shirt. You'll get a sunburn—a bad one."

"I don't need one," the boy repeated stubbornly. "This is *Florida*." He adjusted the cap again and looked up at Hawkshaw with shining eyes. "I like Florida better than I did," he said.

Hawkshaw put his hands on his hips. "Charlie, your mother's right. Put your shirt back on. Go on. Do it."

Charlie stood, his face indecisive for a moment. Then he brightened and said, "Okay." He dashed away and ran back to the stairs. He struggled with his shirt and at last got it on, but inside out.

Kate dropped the dog's leash, rose to her feet and gave Hawkshaw a sarcastic look. She strode to where Charlie twisted and wriggled. She pulled the shirt off and then expertly put it on him again, right side out.

He jammed the hat back on his head and ran over to Hawkshaw. "I got my shirt on, see?" he said eagerly.

Hawkshaw nodded, keeping his face impassive. "That's good," he said. "A boy should mind his mother."

Kate picked up Maybelline's leash. She made her voice controlled, almost frosty. "You were going to give us the safety tour, Mr. Hawkshaw?"

"Yes," Hawkshaw said. "Now the Keys are a special environment. This island we're on—"

"We're on an *island?*" Charlie interrupted, tugging at Hawkshaw's bare knee. "An *island?* Where's the ocean?"

Hawkshaw pointed between the trees. "Over there," he said.

"I can't see it," Charlie almost wailed in disappointment. "Where?"

Hawkshaw hoisted him up easily, so the boy's head was as high as his own. "Over there. See it?"

"Oh," Charlie said with disappointment. "I thought it'd be bigger."

Hawkshaw laughed. "It is bigger. You can't see much of it from here, that's all."

"Can we go closer?" Charlie begged.

"Sure," Hawkshaw said. "Why not? You better ride on my shoulders. There's poisonwood between here and there. You'll have to learn how to identify it, stay away from it."

"Poisonwood?" Charlie asked, charmed at the exotic and dangerous sound of it.

"Yeah. I'll show you." Hawkshaw let the boy settle on his shoulders. He turned to Kate, who stood, holding the dog's leash and eyeing him warily. "You should come, too," he said. "You need to learn these things."

"Then by all means," she said with a shrug, "let the lesson begin."

For the first time, he smiled at her, the barest curve at one corner of his lip. He seemed to be saying, *You have a problem with this, lady?* He moved off through the trees, Charlie on his shoulders.

She felt a strange, primal emotion surge deep within her, a feeling so foreign that at first she didn't recognize it. And when she recognized it, she was ashamed.

Even when her husband had been alive, Charlie was very much her child. Since Chuck's death, it had seemed like her and Charlie, the two of them, together against the world. She was used to being the most important person in the boy's life.

Now, in a matter of moments, he had fallen under the spell of Hawkshaw—Hawkshaw, of all people. And Kate, suddenly relegated to second place in the boy's regard, was shocked to feel the sting of jealousy.

CHAPTER FOUR

IN HAWKSHAW'S BOYHOOD, Cobia Key had been wild and solitary, and it had suited him; he had been wild and solitary himself.

Now he felt the slight weight of the boy on his shoulders and remembered being carried by his own father the same way in this same place. He remembered how his father had introduced him to this mysterious land that could be at once both beautiful and fearful.

The famous Keys highway had run through Cobia to end in Key West, its tipsy and not quite respectable final destination. But in those days hardly anyone stopped in Cobia, for it seemed there was nothing to stop for.

But the island had its inhabitants. They were few but hardy, independent souls who relished Cobia's privacy and its isolation for their own reasons, sometimes legal, sometimes not.

Over the years, while Hawkshaw had been gone, the edges of Cobia's splendid loneliness had been eaten away. The highway through it now sported an ugly restaurant, an uglier motel, and a small but hideous strip mall.

A new housing subdivision had grown up along the open water, concrete dwellings colored in pastels like different flavors of ice cream. They looked as if they were made for mannequins, not people, and Hawkshaw didn't like them.

He was glad that here, in the backcountry, the wilderness remained, and so did the loneliness.

He walked across the weedy yard, conscious that the loneliness was violated now by the boy and his mother. He was an unwilling host, and they were his unwilling guests.

He might begrudge their presence, but he would have to make the best of it. He would begin by pointing out the boundaries and setting the rules. The woman beside him walked gingerly and so did the basset hound, like the city creatures they were.

"There," Hawkshaw said to Charlie. He pointed at a tall, spindly tree on the opposite side of the tidal stream. "That's a poisonwood tree. You don't want to touch any part of it or put it in your mouth. You have to memorize how it looks, the big shiny leaves, the black splotches on the bark."

"Wow," Charlie breathed, clearly awed. "Will it kill you?"

"No, it's more like poison ivy. But it makes some people pretty sick," said Hawkshaw. "So steer clear of anything that looks like it. That's an order."

Kate Kanaday shifted uneasily and gripped the dog's leash more tightly. "Snakes," she said. "There are snakes here, aren't there?"

"Yes, ma'am," Hawkshaw said. "Coral snakes. And cottonmouths. And rattlesnakes."

"Rattlesnakes—that's awesome," Charlie said. "Can we catch one?"

"No, you certainly can't," Kate said. "If you see a snake, don't even think of touching it—run."

Hawkshaw glanced down at her. Her pallor clearly marked her as an outsider to this world of perpetual summer. But the sunshine did dazzling things to her hair, making it glint with live sparks of red and gold.

"There are plenty of harmless snakes," Hawkshaw said, looking away. "You just have to learn to tell which is which."

"Yeah, Mama," Charlie said enthusiastically. "You just have to learn to tell which is which."

"I don't care what it is," she said, putting her fist on her hip. "If you see one, run."

Charlie bent down to Hawkshaw's ear and said in a conspiratorial voice, "Girls are sissies."

Kate looked both crestfallen and insulted. "Charlie!" she said, "That's *not* true."

"Your mother's not a sissy," Hawkshaw said. "But she's right. Don't mess with a snake if you don't know what it is."

"Can *you* tell a poison one from a good one?" Charlie asked.

"Yes," said Hawkshaw.

"Who taught you?" Charlie demanded.

"My—" Hawkshaw hesitated. He'd almost slipped into his old Southern speech habits and said, *My daddy.* He corrected himself and said, "My father. I grew up here. This was his house."

"And your mother's?" Charlie said brightly.

"No. She never lived here."

"Where is she, then?" Charlie asked with a child's bluntness. "Did she die?"

"No," said Hawkshaw. "She lives someplace else, that's all."

"Well, where?" Charlie insisted.

"Montreal." A cold place for a cold woman, his father had always said. Hawkshaw's father hadn't been able to hang on to the woman he'd loved, and Hawkshaw had rather despised him for it. Now history had repeated itself, like a bad joke. *Like father, like son.*

"Montreal," Charlie mused. "Did your father go there, too?"

"Charlie—" Kate began, her tone warning.

"No. My father's dead," Hawkshaw said. He had no taste for sugarcoating the expression nor did the kid seem to want it.

"Did he die of a brain attack?" Charlie asked. "Mine did."

"Charlie—" Kate warned again.

"No," Hawkshaw said. "Not that."

"Then what?" Charlie asked, all amiable curiosity.

"Something else," Hawkshaw said vaguely. *Drinking,* he thought. *He died from the drinking.*

Hawkshaw had never been sure if his mother had left because his father drank, or if his father drank because his mother had left. It was odd. After all these years, he still didn't know.

"Well, what?" Charlie persisted. "Did a snake bite him? Did a shark eat him?"

"No," said Hawkshaw. "He just died, that's all."

Kate looked humiliated by this exchange. "That's *enough,* Charlie." To Hawkshaw she said, "I'm sorry. He doesn't mean to pry."

Hawkshaw changed the subject. He turned so that he and the boy could see where the tidal stream ended and the ocean began. "That's the Gulf of Mexico," he said, pointing out toward the open water. "Can you swim, kid?"

"No, he can hardly swim at—" Kate began.

"Some," Charlie contradicted. "I can swim a little."

"Well, don't go near the water without a life jacket until you can swim a lot," said Hawkshaw.

"Can you swim a lot?" Charlie asked.

"Yeah," Hawkshaw said. "I can."

"You could teach *me,*" Charlie said.

"Charlie," Kate almost wailed, "stop *bothering* Mr. Hawkshaw."

"Somebody needs to teach me," Charlie told her righteously. "And you can hardly swim at all."

Hawkshaw studied Kate, raising a critical eyebrow. She'd probably never swum in anything other than a chlorinated pool in her life or seen any water creature more fearsome than a duck in a park pond.

He saw the worry in her eyes, and he saw the questions.

"These are dangerous waters," he said.

"How dangerous?" Charlie asked, delighted.

Hawkshaw realized his gaze had been locked too long with the woman's, reading too many things in it. She didn't want to depend on him, but she had no choice. He hoped she understood that he intended to take care of her and the boy.

But she could probably also read a reluctant hunger in his eyes. He wondered if she knew how primitive and selfish that hunger was. *The only reason I would want you is because I can't have Sandra.*

"How dangerous?" Charlie repeated, insistent.

"Very dangerous," Hawkshaw said, "if you don't understand them."

He shifted the boy to a more secure position. "Come on. I'll show you the boundaries of the land. We'll worry about the water later."

CORBETT HAD PROMISED to call at twelve noon, Florida time. The crawling hours seemed like eons to Kate. This morning, she'd been able to make Charlie settle down only long enough to eat a few spoonfuls of cereal and sip distractedly at a glass of orange juice.

The orange juice was fresh, squeezed that morning by Hawkshaw himself on an old machine that looked like a medieval torture device. He said the oranges were picked only yesterday.

Kate found this a small comfort. She felt anchorless, cast adrift. She had left behind everything and everyone except Charlie, and at the moment even Charlie seemed to have deserted her.

The boy was besotted with hero worship; he couldn't get enough of Hawkshaw. He followed him like a dog and echoed him like a parrot.

Kate had fought down her first, unexpected wave of jealousy and was now working on her second. She had figured Hawkshaw would tire quickly of having Charlie underfoot; after all, with her he was such a prickly, private man.

But with Charlie, he seemed to have almost infinite patience. He was out on the ramshackle dock now, teaching the boy to use some fishing contraption he called a Cuban reel. He seemed prepared to answer any question Charlie had, so long as it wasn't too personal, and had promised him a kayak ride tomorrow, if Kate would go along.

The kayak looked like a long, glorified floating banana to Kate. It was made of polystyrene and seemed no more substantial than a child's toy. She had no desire to get into such a flimsy craft nor to float over the mysterious, brackish water.

Hawkshaw's catalogue of hideous things that dwelled in the water was as intimidating as it was lengthy: water snakes, eels, sea slugs, rays, barracudas, alligators, sharks and poison jellyfish. Each item on the list enchanted Charlie as much as it repelled her.

Kate sat moodily on the deck, watching the man teach the boy to tie a hook onto his line. Charlie still wore the black Secret Service cap and had colored sunscreen on his nose.

Maybelline had deserted the scene of all this male bonding and lay beside Kate's chair. Kate stared out at the brooding water and the dark mangroves and was haunted by two sinister lines of poetry:

Yea, slimy things did crawl with legs
Upon the slimy sea.

Yet, she had to admit the place had a strange beauty, somehow both dangerous and serene.

When the phone rang at precisely noon, she tensed and automatically rose from her chair. But she was supposed to wait for Hawkshaw. She was not, under any circumstances, to answer the phone herself.

At the first ring, he came bolting up the stairs at remarkable speed. The man's reflexes, she marveled, were hair-trigger. He slammed into the kitchen with her and a panting Charlie at his heels. He himself was not an iota out of breath.

He snatched up the receiver and leaned almost languidly against the counter. "Hawkshaw here," he said, his voice so level it seemed emotionless.

He listened for a moment, keeping his face impassive. Then his mouth crooked down at the corner. "Ask her yourself," he said.

His expression blank again, he handed the receiver to Kate. "It's Corbett," he said. He touched Charlie's shoulder. "Come on, kid. Let's fish."

Charlie beamed as Kate took the phone, but his grin wasn't for her. He had eyes only for Hawkshaw. The two of them went out, and the screen door banged behind them.

Kate, an orderly person, winced at the sound. "Hello," she said into the phone. "We made it. We're here."

"I know," said Corbett. "He phoned me last night as soon as he saw the two of you get off the plane. Didn't he say?"

Kate blinked in surprise. "No. He hasn't told me much at all. Including that."

Corbett chuckled. "That's Hawkshaw. He plays it close to the vest."

He doesn't wear a vest, Kate wanted to retort. *He wears hardly anything.*

Instead, she said, "You didn't tell me you were sending us to the Great Dismal Swamp. This place is precisely in the middle of nowhere."

"The middle of nowhere is where you need to be," Corbett said. "How are the accommodations?"

Kate glanced ruefully around the cluttered kitchen. "'Primitive' might be the word."

"And your host?"

"'Primitive' might still be the word. I think I can teach him to say, 'Me Tarzan.' I'll pass on telling him 'Me Jane.'"

Corbett laughed again. "He said after twenty years of suits, ties, and protocol, he was going back to nature again. Sounds like he did."

"More than I can tell you," said Kate, not in admiration.

"He deserves it," Corbett said.

"I offered to clean up his house and he nearly bit my

head off,'' Kate said. This was an exaggeration, but when she'd raised the subject, Hawkshaw had been curt.

''You'll get used to him. How's Charlie like him? Just fine, I bet.''

''Just fine would be putting it too mildly,'' Kate said from between her teeth. ''Charlie's—quite taken.''

''Oh, yeah,'' Corbett said, ''he's great with kids, always was. A legend in his time.''

''Doesn't he—'' she hesitated, curious but not wanting to appear so ''—he doesn't have any of his own?''

Hawkshaw was in his early forties by her reckoning; he might well have children who were grown up by now. *Even grandchildren,* she thought, rather shocked at the idea.

''No, he never did,'' said Corbett. ''Damned shame.''

She chose her words with care, said them as casually as she could. ''But he's been married?''

''Hawkshaw? Lord, yes. Most married man I ever knew.''

What's that mean? she wondered in bewilderment. ''But he's alone now? What happened?''

''Divorce,'' Corbett said. ''It goes along with the territory too often, with the Secret Service. But it's not my place to talk about his private life.''

But you told him all about mine, Kate thought rebelliously, then was ashamed of herself. Corbett was an honorable man who had done everything in his power to help her.

She said, ''Where are you calling from? A pay phone?''

''Yes.''

She suppressed a sigh. The stalker knew so much about her that Corbett believed it was possible the man could be tapping into phone lines, even Corbett's own. To be safe, Corbett had been keeping in touch with Hawkshaw through pay phones chosen at random.

Squaring her shoulders, she said, "Any leads, Corbett? I'd love to call this trip off and come home."

"Sorry, Kate. If the stalker knows you're gone, he's given no sign. You need to stay put for the time being. You're in good hands."

I don't want to be in anybody's hands. Except my own.

But she forced herself to be calm, businesslike. "You've checked my apartment? Nothing on my answering machine?"

"Nothing out of the ordinary. An insurance salesman. A call from some woman named Mitzi, says she's in your reading group."

Kate winced. Her reading group, which met once a month to discuss a current book, had been the only adult social life she'd had left. But she'd skipped it for so long that it already seemed part of a distant past.

"Any significant mail?"

"Mostly junk," said Corbett. "A notice from your vet. Maybelline's due for some kind of shot and checkup."

"Drat," she said. "I forgot. She's got a bad hip and a weird allergy. She has to have her shots or she gets all achy and itchy. I'll have to find a vet here. If I can find one that doesn't specialize in alligators."

"Let me know if you need her records sent. I'll get it done."

"Thanks," she said, her throat suddenly tight. "I appreciate it. I appreciate you."

"Kate—I'm sorry it's come to this. That you and Charlie have to suffer this dislocation. I wish it were different. This guy's long overdue to make a slip. If he does, I'll do everything in my power to get him."

"I know you will."

"Take care, Kate."

"Corbett?"

"Yes?"

"Be careful yourself. He may get angry at you when he finds out I'm gone."

"Hey, let me do the worrying for a while. You've held the monopoly on it too long."

After Kate hung up, she missed the sound of Corbett's familiar voice, felt a rush of loneliness for home. But, she told herself sternly, homesickness was futile. It was good for nothing.

"This guy's long overdue to make a slip," Corbett had said. *"If he does, I'll do everything in my power to get him."*

"If," Kate murmured. That was the word that cast such a long, cold shadow over her life and Charlie's, even in the bright sunshine of Florida.

HAWKSHAW LIKED THE KID. He had a quick, lively mind, although sometimes it was too lively for the boy's own good; Hawkshaw had seen that immediately.

He decided the best strategy for the day would be to keep the kid too busy to notice how troubled his mother was. Kate Kanaday might toss her fiery hair and speak with a tart confidence, but she was worried, deeply so.

She'd sat on the deck much of the morning with a book she didn't read, mostly looking off into the distance like a sad princess held prisoner in a tower.

Hawkshaw knew the dark mangrove islands and the twisting tidal streams could make some people feel closed in, even trapped. The backcountry seemed both marsh and jungle to them, its heart full of shadows.

When Kate came out of the kitchen after Corbett's phone call, she went to the far corner of the deck. She stood, staring out longingly toward the one small, distant glimpse of open ocean.

Beside him, Charlie was solemnly reeling in his line to check his bait.

"Let's go out for lunch today," Hawkshaw told the boy gruffly. "To celebrate your first day here. And see a little more of the Keys. What say?"

"Will we see the ocean?" Charlie asked, looking up at him eagerly. The boy had his mother's eyes, so deeply brown they seemed almost black. They gave Hawkshaw a strange twinge.

"We might see some of it," Hawkshaw said, and gave the bill of the boy's cap a teasing tug. "Go wash your hands."

Hawkshaw decided to take them in his father's disreputable convertible, an ancient Thunderbird that was partly robin's-egg-blue, but mostly red with rust. The kid immediately fell in love and clambered into the back seat and buckled his seat belt. The woman eyed the car as if it were the wreck of a particularly sinister flying saucer, but she got in.

Hawkshaw gunned the big motor and took the winding road back to Highway 1. He headed for his favorite fish and chips shack, with outside tables overlooking the Gulf of Mexico.

They had conch fritters and French fries, and for dessert slices of tart Key lime pie topped with clouds of meringue. Charlie was enchanted by a brassy old seagull who would skydive for French fries tossed into the air. Kate smiled to see the kid laugh, but her smile was sad, and she said little.

After lunch, Hawkshaw drove farther north to the beach at Bahia Hondo. He disliked the beach because it always teemed with people, but it was a good beach for a kid to learn to play in the sea, to literally get his feet wet. The water was shallow for a long way out, and the bottom mostly sandy and smooth.

Charlie ran ahead of them, darting right and left, dashing into thigh-deep water, then wading, laughing back.

The tide was going out, the water was calm, and a soft breeze stirred the afternoon heat. Kate and Hawkshaw strolled barefoot at the edge of the surf, ankle deep in the cool, foaming water.

They walked against the breeze, and Hawkshaw tried not to notice the way the soft wind sculpted Kate's pale-green shirt to her breasts. She'd plaited her hair into one gleaming braid, but strands had come loose and fluttered about her face like delicate streamers of fire.

Overhead the gulls shrieked and squabbled in flocks, but the more majestic birds wheeled alone, aloof from them and from each other.

"Hawkshaw! Hawkshaw! What's that?" Charlie cried. He nearly danced in the surf as he pointed upward at an elegant black shape sailing high in the blue.

"A frigate bird," Hawkshaw told him. "They call it the 'magnificent' frigate bird."

Charlie stood, staring up for a moment, then ran on, playing tag with the waves.

Kate put her hands in the pockets of her shorts and cast him a sideways look. "How many times today have you heard that?"

"Heard what?" he said.

He'd put on a shirt for her benefit, but now he unbuttoned it and let it blow back in the wind. He liked the feel of the salt wind on his bare flesh.

She looked up at the sky, the hovering frigate bird. "That question: 'Hawkshaw, what's that?'"

"About four thousand," he said.

"You don't get tired of answering?"

He shrugged. "Not really."

"It's very good of you to be so patient with him."

He was not good at taking compliments or thank-yous. He shrugged again and looked out to sea. "It's okay."

"He gets very—hyper—about things sometimes," she said. "When he's interested in something, the questions never stop."

"Kids are curious," he said.

"If he gets too curious, if he becomes a pest, you have to be firm with him, that's all. I don't want him to be a bother to you."

"He's no bother," Hawkshaw said. That was God's truth. Hawkshaw had nothing else he needed to do, not one damn thing.

"His attention usually flits around a lot," she said. "It's been a problem. But when he's really interested in something, he can become almost obsessive. So I'll understand—" Her voice trailed off, pensive, resigned.

Hawkshaw leaned down, scooped up a fragment of broken conch shell from the surf and hurled it into the sea. "He's a smart kid," he said.

"He *is* smart," she agreed. "And he's very imaginative—the doctors say that's really in his favor. That's a plus."

He stole a glance at her. Her face, framed by the rippling strands of loose hair, was sober. She kept her gaze on the boy running and wading ahead of them.

"He's also an only child," she said. "That's actually a plus, too, in a case like this. He *needs* extra time. Extra attention. And all these things have been hard on him, his father's death, and then—"

She went silent.

"The stalker?" Hawkshaw added.

"Yes. *Him.* God, I don't even have a name for him. He's trying to destroy our lives, and I don't even know his name. I hate it. I hate *him.*"

She shot him a look so volatile that it startled Hawkshaw. Beneath her sadness was passion, a firestorm of it. Then she looked down, as if ashamed of letting her emotions fly free for even an instant.

"It's not about me so much," she said, kicking at the surf. "It's Charlie, what it's done to him. That's what I can't forgive."

Hawkshaw frowned. To him, it was the mother, not the boy, who seemed hurt and disturbed.

"Charlie seems fine," he said. "Maybe you worry too much."

She gave him another sharp look, just as turbulent as the first. "I *can't* worry too much. Charlie's got a special problem. It's affected his learning. He—he can't read. He has to repeat first grade."

She acted as if her words were some sort of horrible confession. Hawkshaw said, "That's no sin."

Her chin jerked up, and her eyes went straight back to the boy. "It's hardly a blessing. He hates school—with a passion. He misbehaves. He doesn't make friends. He has problems with self-esteem."

"Self-esteem," Hawkshaw repeated, sarcasm in his voice. To him, it sounded as if she'd read too many psychology books.

She said, "Self-esteem is a big issue for children with attention deficiencies."

"Issue," he echoed in the same tone.

"Never mind," she said curtly.

"He's a good kid. What more do you want?"

"He's good *here,*" she answered. "He's good now.

But you make it seem like a big vacation. I mean, it's kind of you, and he loves it, but it's not the real world."

"It's my real world," said Hawkshaw. "And you didn't answer. What more do you want from him?"

She shook her head. "I'm not asking that he turn into a genius. I just want him to be able to read, for God's sake. That's all."

"I see," said Hawkshaw.

She sighed and passed a hand over her hair to tame it, but it refused to be tamed. "I know," she said. "I sound like a neurotic mother. Maybe I am. I don't even know. Being stalked is hard work, you know? It wears you down. You lose perspective. Oh, hellfire."

Against his will he gave her a one-cornered smile. "I hear the pay's lousy, too."

"It is lousy." She didn't smile in return, but a dimple appeared in her cheek. It played intriguingly and for all too short a time. He wanted it to come back.

"But," she said, trying to smooth her hair again, "I'm not a freeloader. I pull my own weight. I see a lot of things around your house that need to be done. I want you to let me do them."

A primal suspicion flared in Hawkshaw. *Danger,* it cried like a siren, *Danger, danger!*

He stopped and stared down at her, the surf lapping around his ankles. "Do things? What?"

She stopped, too. "Your house is a mess, to put it politely. I could clean it up. KP, janitor duty, that's all."

"I like my house the way it is," he said and started walking again. For some reason the cold of the surf coursed up from his feet into the marrow of his leg bones and straight to his spine and brainstem.

"Corbett said you're thinking of selling it. If you do, you'll have to clean it up," she argued, splashing along beside him. "It'll bring a better price—that's the truth. I know. I used to work for a real estate company. On a housecleaning team, in fact."

"I haven't decided to sell," he said. "Maybe I'll keep it."

"If you keep it, you should keep it up," she said. "Have you done anything to it since your father died?"

Hawkshaw would not stoop to lie. "No."

"How long ago did he die?"

He grimaced in displeasure. "Sixteen months ago."

"And how often did *he* clean? Hardly ever, I'll bet."

"Look," he said, "it's not your concern. You may think it's full of common, ordinary dirt and clutter, but it's not. It's *family* dirt and clutter. It's a heritage."

"But I owe you, Hawkshaw. I don't like being beholden. I wouldn't mind—I'd welcome it. I could burn off nervous energy."

"You want to reimburse somebody, reimburse Corbett. This isn't between you and me. You don't owe me. I owe him." He walked faster.

"Owe him what?" she said, keeping up.

"A favor."

"Must be a big one."

"Big enough."

"What sort of favor makes you take in two strangers, for—for weeks, maybe?"

"That's between Corbett and me."

"Look," she said, "just let me try, all right? Starting with the kitchen. I mean, my God, it's practically self-defense. My child could die of botulism. If you don't like what I do there, tell me to stop and I'll stop."

"No," he said from between his teeth. "I told you. You owe me nothing—zip—zero—*nada*."

"Good grief, what did Corbett do for you? Donate both his kidneys?"

He stopped again, wheeled to face her. "You want to clean the kitchen?"

She put her hands on her hips, locked gazes with him. "Yes."

"It'll make you happy to clean the kitchen?"

"Yes."

"All right, dammit, clean. But on one condition."

She put up her chin again, in that way she had. "What?"

"Don't ask any more personal questions. None. Not about Corbett or anything else. You and I do not have a personal relationship—get it?"

She looked him up. She looked him down. "I get it. And you're on."

"Deal?" he said.

"Deal." She offered him her hand.

He looked at it a moment, then took it in his own, shook it brusquely. It was a strong little hand with a surprisingly firm grip. He couldn't let go of it fast enough.

They walked on in silence, following Charlie's erratic, weaving lead. Hawkshaw didn't look at Kate. She didn't look at him. He thought of Sandra.

Come back, Sandra. I love you. I don't want this woman in my house. I want only you.

CHAPTER FIVE

CHARLIE LOVED THE CONVERTIBLE and everything about it—the flow of the wind whisking his face and tangling his hair. Looking straight up and seeing sky until he was dizzy with it.

He loved the impossible highway; it was like a great silver chain linking island to island. The highway leapfrogged the very ocean itself, not once, but again and again. Hawkshaw said there were forty-two bridges hooking the islands together—and one was *seven miles* long!

The bridges filled him with marvel. What sort of supermen had built them? How had they erected such great pillars on the floor of the sea? By what magic had they arched steel and concrete over the foaming waves?

Charlie was bewitched by the sea itself, how it moved and sparkled and changed colors. He loved the mysterious way it stretched, hazy, to the very horizon. He loved the briny tang of its scent, the lively edge of its breeze.

What could be better than wading in the cool water, feeling the rush and tug of the surf against his legs? The sea was not like the pond in the park back home; the pond just *sat* there, growing yucky green junk on its top. The sea was alive and powerful. His feet still tingled from it and felt deliciously crusty with salt.

He was delighted by the idea that the water's changing blue-and-green surface hid a multitude of secrets. Hawkshaw said sharks of all kinds lived in the water, and dolphins and squids and octopuses. Gigantic turtles, big enough for a boy to ride, swam in the sea, and in the deeps there were shipwrecks, and yes, even treasure.

Charlie was enchanted with everything about Florida, even the telephone poles. At home a telephone pole was only a pole, but on top of many of these were huge, prickly looking nests made out of sticks. The big birds that lived in them were ospreys, large hawks that dove in the water for fish.

He could lean back, the wind on his face, just watching the birds. Back in the city, he had seen only ordinary birds, like pigeons and sparrows and robins and starlings. Here, the birds seemed enchanted, as if a wizard had created them with a magic wand.

There were different kinds of gulls, those rude, graceful clowns who tumbled and soared through the air. There were pelicans, both brown and white, with their enormous beaks. There were magnificent crested white birds called egrets. When Charlie saw them on the wing, they gave him an incredibly sweet feeling of peace and satisfaction.

Tomorrow Hawkshaw said he would take them in the kayak to the mangrove islands, and they would see even more sorts of birds. Charlie sighed with happiness. Hawkshaw knew everything about the Keys. Hawkshaw knew everything about *everything*.

When the big convertible pulled into the unkept yard at Cobia Key, Charlie looked fondly at the ramshackle house on its skinny stilts. It was a sort of funny house, he supposed, but to him it seemed the stuff of Paradise.

He unbuckled his seat belt and clambered out of the Thunderbird's backseat. His mother was slightly sunburned and her hair was tossed and tangled by the wind. Charlie thought she looked beautiful, but strangely unhappy.

Hawkshaw got out of the car and had to wrench open his mother's door because it wouldn't open from the inside. It occurred to Charlie that Hawkshaw ought to notice how pretty Mama was, that he might like her; he might even like her enough to *marry* her, and then they could stay here, in Paradise, forever.

But Hawkshaw hardly looked at Mama, and Mama hardly looked at Hawkshaw. There seemed to be a secret sort of tension between them that Charlie couldn't understand and didn't like.

Mama got out of the car and thanked Hawkshaw with her Very Polite Voice. It was usually a bad sign when Mama used her Very Polite Voice, and it made Charlie uneasy.

Still using that voice, Mama turned to him and said, "Charlie, thank Mr. Hawkshaw for lunch and the trip."

Charlie mumbled, "Thank you, Mr. Hawkshaw, for lunch and the trip. Do you want to fish again?"

"Sure, kid," said Hawkshaw. "Why not?"

"You shouldn't take up all Mr. Hawkshaw's time," Mama said with her frosty politeness.

"Mr. Hawkshaw has no other plans," Hawkshaw said. "Otherwise, Mr. Hawkshaw would just lie in his hammock."

"Well, in the meantime, I'll just clean up Mr. Hawkshaw's kitchen," Mama said, trying to smooth her tousled hair. "As agreed."

"Clean away," Hawkshaw said, but he didn't look pleased at the prospect. "We men," he added, giving Charlie a comradely glance, "will fish."

"Charlie, come inside first," Mama ordered. "I want you to comb your hair and brush your teeth and put on some more lotion and take your pill."

"Ah, Mom," Charlie complained. "That's sissy stuff. We men want to fish."

Mama gave Hawkshaw a narrow-eyed look. Hawkshaw shrugged. "Mind your mother, kid. I need to comb my hair and brush my teeth and maybe put on some lotion myself."

"Do you have to take a pill, too?" Charlie asked hopefully.

"Charlie, come on," Mama said, taking him firmly by the hand and walking him up the stairs. Hawkshaw followed, his unbuttoned shirt flapping in the breeze.

"Well, do you take a pill?" Charlie insisted, twisting around to see the man.

"Sometimes," Hawkshaw said without emotion. He unlocked the door.

"I have to take pills all the time," Charlie grumbled, but he let Mama lead him off into the bathroom. He grimaced and twisted as she scrubbed his face, neck and ears with a cool washrag.

Maybelline had followed them and stood in the doorway, gazing up with sad eyes, her tail wagging dubiously.

Mama shook a pill out of the bottle, and he grimaced again as he washed it down with a sip of water. Grudgingly, he brushed his teeth. Grumbling, he combed his hair. Resentfully, he slathered sunscreen on his face and arms and knees.

Mama forced him to calm down and spread it more evenly, then wash his hands again. "I'm going to fish," Charlie said. "I'm gonna put *bait* on a *hook*. Why do I have to wash my hands again?"

"So you don't poison the bait with sunscreen," said Mama. "Don't splash."

He half dried his hands on the towel and started to run out the bathroom door. Mama caught him by the back of his shirt. She knelt and put her hands on his shoulders. "Charlie, I know you're having a good time here—"

"I love this place," he said. "I don't want to go home. I want to stay here."

She sighed and squeezed his shoulders more tightly. Again she had the unhappy look in her eyes, the look that always made Charlie unhappy, too. "We can't stay here. We'll be here a few weeks at most. Mr. Hawkshaw's being especially nice because it's your first day here. But every day won't be like this. So don't get too—attached. We'll have to move on."

Charlie's emotions took a wild, dizzying dip. She was telling him something bad, but he didn't completely understand. "What do you mean?" he demanded. "Get too attached? What's that mean?"

She smiled, smoothed his hair. "Don't get to like it too much. Don't get to like *him* too much. It's a—vacation, that's all. We'll be leaving."

Charlie felt disappointment, and he felt anger. Why would Mama bring him to this wonderful place, then tell him not to like it? It wasn't fair, it wasn't right.

He glared at her.

"Charlie," Mama warned, "keep your temper. Enjoy yourself while you're here. But remember we'll be moving on."

"Where?" he said petulantly. "Back home? I don't want to go home. Denver? I don't want to go to Denver. I don't know anybody."

She got a funny look on her face, almost scared, almost as if *she* was going to cry. Charlie felt tears of his own coming on.

"Honey," she said, "don't worry about it. Enjoy it while you can. You men go fishing."

She kissed his cheek, but he was already struggling to

get out of her grasp. He grabbed the Secret Service cap and jammed it on his head, and ran out of the bathroom, dodging Maybelline.

He thundered down the hall, jumping over the boat oar, nearly tripping over a deep-sea fishing pole, and maneuvered his way through the crowded kitchen. He swung open the back door and half ran, half danced to the deck.

"Hawkshaw," he called in joy edged with desperation, "I'm here, Hawkshaw!"

KATE ROSE from her kneeling position and looked after her son until the back door slammed.

"Well," she muttered to Maybelline in self-disgust, "I certainly blew *that*."

She had meant only to warn Charlie, not to alarm and upset him. But Charlie, always volatile, was too excited to understand.

Hawkshaw had cast a spell over the child, but the man couldn't understand Charlie, didn't realize he was doing the boy as much harm as good.

She was going to have to talk to Hawkshaw, frankly and sternly. It wouldn't, she knew, be pleasant.

She wished Corbett would call up and say, "Guess what? We caught your stalker. But he tried to escape and fell into the sewage processing plant and was turned into compost. Come home and relax."

"Fat chance," Kate said to Maybelline, who looked appropriately doleful.

In the meantime, her fate was in Corbett's hands, and there was nothing for her to do but wait. If she waited idly, she'd go mad.

Well, her work seemed cut out for her. Revolting as she found the idea, she would become Hawkshaw's cleaning woman. It was easiest for Charlie to navigate a world when it was tidy and ordered. She put her hands on her hips and looked down the hall. This rat's nest of Hawkshaw's was the essence of clutter.

"Come on, Maybelline," she told the dog. "You can be charwoman number two. You're in charge of any mice or badgers we find burrowing in this dump."

She strode purposely to Hawkshaw's wildly disordered kitchen. A kite, of all things, hung from the knob of one of the scarred kitchen cabinets. The kite looked ancient, its silk faded and dusty.

There was enough junk to fill several trash bags and enough old knickknacks and trinkets to stock a good-sized flea market. A dead cactus in a chipped pot sat on the windowsill above the sink. Beside it lay a large dead insect, its legs stretched heavenward as if praying for deliverance.

In the corner was an oversize cracked plastic wastebasket, nearly full of empty beer cans. Kate frowned. Did Hawkshaw have a problem?

She'd keep a sharp eye for any indication. He certainly wasn't going to watch out for *her* son while he was drinking.

Under the sink, she found a few cleaning implements that had possibly been new when dinosaurs roamed the earth. There was also a moldy can of cleanser, and a jug of household cleaner that had never been opened and was covered with dust and cobwebs.

Kate wrinkled her nose in distaste and gathered up these few pathetic weapons in the War Against Dirt. She had no illusions that she was a flawless housekeeper; she was not. But she'd never been afraid of work, and she would show Hawkshaw she could earn her own way. She would show him with a vengeance.

AN HOUR LATER, Kate wiped her forehead with the back of her hand. She had filled two trash bags, scrubbed the counters and started in on the old stove.

She'd wiped years of grime off the window over the sink so that now the sunshine gleamed through. If she glanced outside, she could see Hawkshaw and Charlie sitting in the shade of a palm tree, fishing. From time to time the man pointed into the sky and Charlie squinted up at a bird soaring across the blue.

Kate frowned, shook her head, and went back to scouring the stove. Part of her disliked the scenario of men lazing while the woman worked. Yet another part of her was grateful that Charlie was amused and quiet.

She finished the stove and decided to pace herself and take on an easy task. She would work her way up to tackling the sink, which was so dirty she thought of it as the Great Pit of Crudmore.

There were only four drawers in the tiny kitchen, and three were so crammed with oddments that they wouldn't close completely. With a sigh, she opened another trash bag and started clearing the drawers.

She jettisoned things mercilessly, including old flashlight batteries, bits of string, empty rolls of tape. She paused when she came to a yellowed envelope stuffed with photographs.

She set the envelope aside, thinking Hawkshaw might want to go through the pictures. But the envelope was unsealed and a spill of snapshots cascaded to the floor, several skittering to rest under the bottom edge of the counter.

She knelt to pick them up and was startled to see Hawkshaw's image. At first she hardly recognized him; he was dressed in a suit and the expression on his face was—happy. He was younger, and he had his arm around a beautiful young woman.

She had upswept blond hair, ornamented by a veil held in place by a crown of pearls. She wore an elaborate long white dress with a train and carried a large bouquet of pink and white roses.

She was obviously a bride. Just as obviously, Hawkshaw was her groom. He smiled down at her as if he took notice of nothing else in the world. The woman's smile, aimed directly at the camera, was small and triumphant.

Kate looked at the next photo, which showed the bridal party. She blinked in surprise when she realized the best man was a younger, thinner Corbett, looking rather wan.

Beside Corbett was a teenage girl wearing a short veil and carrying a pink-and-white nosegay. She bore such a startling resemblance to the bride that Kate was sure she must be a younger sister.

The kitchen door suddenly burst open, and Charlie ran, lickety-split, for the bathroom. Hawkshaw, who was right behind him, ignored Kate. He opened the refrigerator, pulled out a can of beer, and popped open the top.

Then he noticed the photos in her hand. "What are those?" he demanded, his tone close to hostile.

Kate looked him in the eye. "Pictures. I was going to put them aside for you. Some of them fell out of the envelope. I was picking them up."

"Where'd you find them?"

"There," she said, with a nod at the open drawer. She thrust the snapshots back into the envelope and held it toward him. "I thought you might want to save them."

For an instant, he looked as if she were offering him a tarantula. Then he made his face blank. "No," he said. "But I'll get rid of them." He took the envelope and stuffed it into the back pocket of his shorts.

"I'm sorry," she said mechanically. "If I find any more—"

"Forget about it."

His curtness piqued her. She hadn't meant to go through his damned photos, and she wasn't going to apologize again.

She stared pointedly at the beer can in his hand. "You've got about a thousand of those," she said, nodding toward the trash. "Do you recycle them around here, or what?"

"Yeah," he said and took a drink. "Just set them aside."

"Excuse me," she said, "but it looks like they've been set aside for a couple of years."

"Whatever," he said.

She poked the sack with her foot so the cans clinked together accusingly. "I hope all these aren't yours," she said.

He sighed and turned from her. He went to the back door and gazed off into the distance.

"Because I don't want my child around the water with you if you're drinking. It's too dangerous."

He shot her a killing look. "One beer on a summer afternoon isn't 'drinking,'" he said and went back outside.

Through the window she could see him pacing the dock's edge, staring across the tidal river. Either the photos or her remarks about the beer had offended him. He slapped his bare chest and stalked the water's edge like a sun-god in a bad mood.

"Jerk," she muttered under her breath.

But to her surprise, he emptied the beer into the river. Then he crushed the can between his hands. For a moment she thought he would pitch it over the water into the mangroves, but he didn't. He just stood there, holding it, almost as if it were a relic only he understood.

THAT AFTERNOON Charlie caught a small hammerhead shark, about four pounds. The kid danced around so excitedly Hawkshaw was afraid he was going to wet his pants.

Kate had to come out of the kitchen and admire the fish as if it was the size of the one in *Jaws*. Charlie was beside himself with pride.

Then Hawkshaw expertly unhooked the shark, avoiding its razorlike teeth, and put it back in the water. He explained to the kid the sharks were important to the balance of nature, and the kid seemed to understand.

Hawkshaw himself caught a couple of ronco, good-tasting panfish, and he grilled them on the deck. Once again Kate only picked at her food, but she smiled at Charlie as he talked shark, shark, shark.

After supper, Charlie wanted to do everything again—go fishing, run all over the yard and name the plants, take the convertible back to the sea and play in the waves by moonlight.

Hawkshaw sensed Kate would have an easier time with Charlie if she was alone with the boy, so he made himself scarce. He sat by himself in the yard, gazing at the moon.

He thought of a small, trim yacht. He thought of sailing to Cozumel and beyond, alone and unencumbered.

Solitude. It was all he wanted if he could not have Sandra. But he could not rid himself of the unpleasant awareness of the strangers in his house. He liked the kid, liked him more than was probably wise.

As for the woman—he found her disturbing. So she was pretty. So what? He didn't want her, he wanted his wife back. It was as if the gods had sent Kate to mock him.

With a grinding stab, he thought of the wedding pictures in his pocket. Soon Sandra would be having another wedding, and the thought of her in another man's arms made him half-sick with jealousy.

Jealousy was stupid, he told himself. He'd had other women in Washington after she'd left him. For a time, he'd used other women as his drug of choice, until he'd overdosed on them and realized Sandra was the only one he wanted.

He'd been celibate now for almost a year. He'd gone at celibacy as if it were magic, a sacrifice he could make to bring back Sandra. Now, he thought disgustedly, the magic had failed and he was horny, plagued by animal urges.

He watched the first stars glowing in the darkening sky. He thought again of the wedding pictures and of Sandra.

She's found somebody else. Be happy for her. Let her go, he told himself.

He slapped at a mosquito and turned back to face the house. He saw the main light in the back bedroom wink out. Charlie must be asleep at last, he thought.

He rose from the old lawn chair and headed rather grimly back to the house. He intended to sit alone on the deck, listen to the night sounds, stare at the constellations, and have a few beers. If Kate objected, to hell with her.

The kitchen seemed so clean it was unnatural, almost frightening. He opened the refrigerator and took out a can of beer. Kate came quietly down the hall, stood at the kitchen's edge.

She was barefoot, and she'd unplaited her hair so that it hung down her back. She wore cutoffs and a dark-brown T-shirt that was the same color as her eyes.

Her skin was faintly touched with tan, and it struck him that she didn't look as out of place as she had this morning. She crossed her arms and stared up at him, her gaze steady.

"Thanks for going outside," she said. "He needs routine at bedtime—it reassures him, calms him. He especially needed it tonight. It was a bad day."

Hawkshaw felt his back stiffen with rancor. He'd done everything in his power to keep Charlie amused, and the kid *had* been happy; he'd acted as if he'd been in seventh heaven. He'd remember catching that shark as long as he lived.

"Excuse me," Hawkshaw said. "A bad day?"

An odd look came into her eyes. "I'm sorry," she said softly. "I said it wrong. It was a different day."

"'Different' is 'bad' in your book?"

"Not my book, Hawkshaw. His. This move, everything about it, is a crisis for him."

He shrugged and opened the beer. "You want one of these?"

She shook her head. "His sleeping schedule was thrown off yesterday. And today was a big day for him—a lot of excitement. The newness of everything. The trip to the beach."

She paused and her expression went rueful. "And, of course, that—shark."

"He's a good little fisherman. A natural."

"Is he?" she asked, her face brightening. "That's good, because he's not well-coordinated in things like sports. They're usually not fun for him. Other kids laugh at him."

"That's the nice thing about fishing. All you need is patience."

Her mouth took on a sad smile. "Patience is generally in short supply for Charlie."

Hawkshaw shrugged again. "He's got it when he fishes."

She nodded, crossed her arms more tightly. "Yes. Well. That's one of the ironies. When something does catch his interest, his concentration's so absolute, it's almost scary."

He took a long pull of the beer. "Maybe he's got a gift."

"Maybe he does," she said pensively. "Some children with attention deficiencies *are* gifted. They can be imaginative—spontaneous—and really curious."

Hawkshaw felt a sudden and unwanted rush of curiosity of his own. He wondered if her long hair felt as silken as it looked. He imagined touching it, winding it around his hand as he drew closer to her.

It was time, he realized, to end the conversation.

"At any rate," she said, "I wanted to thank you for *your* patience. You've been very kind to him."

"Don't mention it," he said brusquely. "Make yourself at home in here. I'll be out on the deck. Alone."

He said *alone* so pointedly that he thought when he moved toward the door, she'd step out of his way quickly. She did not.

She set her jaw and looked up at him. "I understand your need for privacy," she said evenly.

"Good," he said, just as evenly.

She shot a cool glance at the beer can in his hand. "And I'm grateful—I mean this sincerely—that when you want that stuff, you hold off until Charlie's not around."

"Hey," Hawkshaw said, his lip curling, "discipline is my middle name."

"I'm glad," she said, meeting his eyes again. "And there's one more thing I want to say to you."

His nerve ends rippled with the sense of trouble coming. "So say it."

"Corbett said you were good with children. You are. Charlie obviously likes you a good deal. I think he finds you—glamorous."

He blinked in displeased surprise at her choice of words. "Glamorous," he echoed sarcastically. "That's me, all right." He tipped the beer back and took another long drink.

"All right," she said, fisting her hands and putting them on her hips. "This is what I'm asking. Don't show my son too good a time here. Don't make him enjoy it too much. Don't play the big hero, okay?"

He drew his head back slightly, narrowed his eyes. Was she crazy?

"I'm not playing hero," he said. "No way. You said yourself this whole thing's a crisis for the kid. If he can forget the crisis for a while, have a little fun, it gives you a problem? Excuse me?"

Her mouth took on a stubborn tilt. "First, all this is too—too stimulating for him. It's not good. He needs quiet, routine, continuity."

Hawkshaw leaned toward her and spoke through gritted teeth. "You want him to learn. He learned to fish. He learned the names of five different trees, ten different birds. He learned what the ocean looks and sounds and feels like. This isn't good for him?"

She made an impatient gesture. "His brain chemistry is different from most people's. He's not equipped to handle so much—"

"He's got a sharp little mind, and it seems to be hitting

on all cylinders. He seems to handle it all better than you. What's wrong? Want him to sit by his mama and worry?''

"Of course not,'' she retorted. ''But there's a lot at stake here. It won't be long until I take him off to Denver. Denver has to be home. I don't want him falling in love with this place, Hawkshaw. And pining for it. Or for you.''

Hawkshaw swore under his breath and turned from her in disgust. ''You're really something else.''

"I want us to move forward, Hawkshaw. Not to be looking back. We don't have much left behind us, back in Columbia. The stalker saw to that. So maybe—if we're lucky—very lucky—Charlie won't miss it much. But I don't want him thinking that you're God and this is Paradise. And that I've snatched him away from it.''

Slowly, he turned to face her again. ''Cripes, I'll be like somebody he met on vacation once. Who gets dimmer and dimmer in his memory all the time. You don't understand that? You don't know anything, do you?''

She took an aggressive step forward. ''What I understand—''

The phone rang, as if the tension between them had made it call out. It clearly startled her, for she stepped back, clutching at the counter behind her.

Hawkshaw reached for the receiver and snatched it up. ''Hawkshaw here,'' he said, hoping his tone sounded more neutral than he felt.

"It's me,'' said Corbett's voice. ''It's about Kate. I've got good news and bad news. Which do you want to hear first?''

CHAPTER SIX

KATE SAW HAWKSHAW'S body tense. "What is it?" he asked sharply.

His face was unreadable, yet his stance, his expression, his eyes, all told her something was happening. *Trouble,* she thought sickly. *It's more trouble.* She gripped the counter more tightly.

Hawkshaw didn't look at her. He listened to his caller, his attention as concentrated as a laser.

"Who?" he demanded. "Where? When?"

Kate moved closer to him, so he would have to acknowledge her. She mouthed a silent question: "Corbett?" He did not seem to see her, but gave her a curt nod. "How much damage?" he asked.

Damage? Alarm frayed her nerves, her stomach clenched. She turned away. Behind her, Hawkshaw's unemotional voice said, "Anybody hurt?"

Half-sick, Kate put her hand to her midsection.

"How badly?" Hawkshaw asked, as calmly as if he were discussing the extent of a car repair.

Oh, Lord, Kate thought, squeezing her eyes shut, *now somebody's hurt. Who? Why? Is it my fault? Why is this happening?*

"She's okay?" Hawkshaw said. "Good. Good."

She wanted to turn and demand who had been hurt, but she no longer felt in control of her emotions. She stood, both arms wrapped around her waist now.

Hawkshaw said, "So much for the good news. What's the bad?"

Kate's eyes sprang open, her head snapped up. There was worse news? Hawkshaw spoke so calmly she wanted to scream. She could stand to listen to no more.

She spun around and fled out the kitchen door, letting it slam behind her. She ran down the rickety steps to the farthest edge of the dock.

For a few seconds she stared out across the water and the dark islands that surrounded her. High in the sky hung the full moon. The restless water shattered its image into a thousand ghostly shards.

Somewhere a night bird shrilled its cry. Somewhere an animal answered with the low growl of a predator. Kate felt as if she stood, poised on the edge of the world. She was pursued, but there was nowhere left to run.

Charlie, she told herself fiercely. *I've got to stay strong for Charlie. I'm all he's got. I can't feel sorry for myself. I cannot. I will not.*

But the old weariness came over her, pressing like a relentless weight. She sank to the boards of the dock and sat cross-legged. Her heart beat against her ribs like a bird struggling to flee a trap.

She did not want to look into the darkness around her, so she put her face in her hands, trying to calm herself. She breathed deeply. She kept saying Charlie's name over in her mind, like a mantra that would keep them both safe from harm.

She did not hear Hawkshaw come down the stairs. She was not aware of him until his hand closed on her shoulder. He startled her, and she gave a nervous little jump that made her feel foolish.

She raised her head and made sure her chin was high.

She gazed at the broken light dancing on the tide. She drew up her knees and put her arms around them.

Hawkshaw knelt beside her, his hand still on her shoulder. "Are you okay?" he asked in his low voice.

"You shouldn't creep up on people like that," she said. She was afraid to ask what she really wanted to know. She kept staring ahead, waiting for him to tell her.

"Are you crying?" he asked. "You're crying, aren't you?"

She thought she heard concern in his voice, which would be a sure sign she was going insane. "No," she almost snapped, but she could say nothing more.

He bent nearer, and she could sense him examining her face in the moonlight. She kept her expression impassive. He would see no tear tracks streaking her face. Not a one. Not now or ever.

He didn't speak, but he kept his hand on her shoulder, kneading it softly. It felt comforting, almost sensual, and she resented it. She shook herself free from his touch.

"Just tell me what Corbett said," she ordered, preparing herself for the worst. "Just spit it out, will you?"

He settled himself beside her. "He said he had good news and bad news. The good news is they've got somebody in custody that may be your stalker."

Stunned, Kate whipped her head around to stare at him. "The stalker? The police have him?"

He raised a cynical eyebrow. "Maybe. Maybe not."

"Well, what *happened?*" she demanded.

"Somebody robbed your place. Vandalized it and set it on fire."

She recoiled in disbelief. "My place? I have an alarm system. Corbett insisted on it. How could anybody get in?"

Hawkshaw kept his gaze on her face, as if intently

studying her reaction. "He cut the phone line in the middle of the night. Jimmied open a window. No signal could get through to the security company."

"Y-you said someone was hurt," she stammered. "Who?"

"Your neighbor. A Mrs. Mona Snelling. The fire spread—not badly, but enough that she had to go to the hospital for smoke inhalation. She's fine."

Kate's shoulders sank, as if the news were too heavy to bear. "Mrs. Snelling," she murmured. "I hardly knew her. She moved in last year. She tried to be kind to Charlie and me. But I wasn't friendly to her—by that time I was afraid to be friendly to anyone."

"She's fine," Hawkshaw repeated. "She's got some kind of little dog. It woke her in time."

Kate was ready to take back her vow not to cry in front of Hawkshaw. Her mouth quivered. "A little old poodle. I thought it was just a worthless little frou-frou dog. God, I feel horrible."

"Why?" Hawkshaw asked. "For not liking her dog?"

She shot him a quelling look. "Of course not. I feel awful that this happened to her. I feel responsible."

"Why?" he said. "You didn't set the fire. You didn't want the fire set. Don't wallow in misplaced guilt. It's self-indulgent and stupid."

Her head jerked up. How insensitive was this oaf, calling her stupid at a time like this? But then she read the calculation in his cool eyes. She realized he *wanted* her angry, if only to keep her from slipping into a morass of self-blame.

Hawkshaw said, "You'd better think about yourself. Your place was damaged. You couldn't go back there if you wanted to."

She held his gaze as steadily as she could. "Damaged how badly?"

He turned and looked out over the water. "Most of the furniture's ruined. Charlie's toys. Your books."

She flinched as if he'd struck her. "Charlie's toys? My books?" she repeated numbly. "All of them?"

"All of them," he said. "I'm sorry, Kate."

Kate put her fist to her chin to keep her jaw from trembling. She muttered a swear word against her knuckles. Tears, hot, filled her eyes, but she blinked them back. "Who would do such a thing?" she begged. "And *why?*"

He sighed, turned back to her. "His name is Kyle Johnson. Do you know him?"

She shook her head in dismay. "I never heard of him. Is—is he the stalker?"

"The police are checking it out. They don't know much yet. Except he has a prior conviction for arson. Sometimes arsonists are kinky. It's not unusual."

She gazed up hopefully at his shadowed face. "So he might be the one?"

"He might," he said.

Her hope rose higher. It was such an unfamiliar sensation, it made her feel light-headed, almost giddy. "If he set this fire, he's in big trouble, isn't he? Arson's a major crime, and he's got a previous conviction. They'd send him away for a long time—wouldn't they?"

"Yes. They would."

"That means—" her voice quavered, almost broke "—that Charlie and I *could* go back. Not to the condo, not to our things. But we could go home again, back to our old lives."

"Maybe," he said quietly.

"But if he's the one—"

"*If*, Kate," he emphasized. "If. He may be. He may not."

She felt too heady with hope to be brought down again. "He has to be," she protested. "How could he not be? What sort of unbelievable coincidence—"

"Unbelievable coincidences happen all the time," he countered. "That's why truth is stranger than fiction. In law enforcement, you see it all too often. The suspect looks perfect. Circumstances point straight at him. There's only one thing wrong. He didn't do it. Circumstances can't always be trusted."

"No," she argued. "He *has* to be the one."

He put his hand on her shoulder again. "They have to check him out, Kate. Until they're sure, Corbett wants you to stay here."

"No!" she cried. "I want to go home. I want to take my child and go."

His grip tightened. "The good news is that they have a suspect, a good one. The bad news is that Corbett's not sure it's the right one. He says he's had suspicions—"

She stiffened. "About what?"

"He's not ready to say."

"Not ready?" she mocked. "For God's sake, why? Our whole future's at stake here."

He leaned nearer. She could see his eyes reflect the glitter of the moonstruck water. "If he's got reasons, they're legitimate. Maybe he doesn't want you to suspect somebody unjustly."

"Good lord," she said with a bitter laugh, "As if I haven't already suspected everybody under the sun? Do you know what it's like, looking at every man you meet and wondering if he's the one?"

"A little," he said. "I understand a little. Looking at the faces in a crowd and wondering if one belongs to an assassin. I've lived it. So has Corbett. It makes a man cautious.''

The water lapped against the shore.

"Very cautious," he said. He leaned nearer still.

"I can't stay here," she breathed. "I don't want to. And you don't want me to, either."

"We don't always get what we want," he said.

For the space of three heartbeats, they looked at each other, his face poised inches from hers.

My God, she thought. *I think he wants to kiss me. And I think I might let him.*

But the spell broke. He gave her shoulder a fraternal pat and drew away. "Sleep on it," he said, rising. "But Corbett's right, and you know it. You can't take Charlie back there until it's safe. And you're one hundred percent sure."

He stepped back, his manner clearly putting more than physical distance between them. "You should go inside. You still have to catch up on some sleep. Me, I'll just stay out here."

He slapped his bare chest, and the sound echoed over the water and resonated into the darkness. He turned his back on her and gazed up at the stars.

She knew she was being dismissed, and she cursed herself for feeling even a moment's tenderness toward him. She stood in one brisk motion. "Good night," she said.

"Good night," he said. He kept his attention on the sky.

Her heart stormy, she stalked away, up the stairs and into the house. Later, she lay in bed, sleepless, her emotions churning.

Kyle Johnson, a man of whom she'd never heard, had destroyed her home and all of her and Charlie's possessions. He had to be the stalker; he simply had to be.

Corbett was being careful to a fault, that was all. It was his nature. She didn't want to stay here, yet she knew Hawkshaw was right. She couldn't take Charlie back until she was certain the stalker was in custody and the nightmare was officially over.

But Charlie's toys, which he loved so much, were gone. How would she ever explain? And her books, her precious books. She allowed herself a few futile, angry tears over the toys and books.

Then she wiped her eyes and got up to wash her face. For no reason she could articulate, she was drawn to the window. She parted the curtains and peered out.

Hawkshaw, still bare-chested, stood in the moonlight on the dock. A beer can glittered on the boards beside his naked feet.

He held the snapshots she had given him in his left hand and something else in the other.

He stared for a long time at the top photograph, then suddenly a small flame flared from his right hand—a lighter. He set the edge of the photo ablaze, watched the fire grow, and then, just before the flames touched his fingertips, dropped the burning picture into the moving water.

She caught her lower lip between her teeth and watched as he went through the pictures, setting them afire one by one and letting the river bear each away.

Three he saved. He looked at them again in the moonlight, then stowed them in his back pocket. He picked up his beer, sipped it, and gazed into the darkness.

You've got your own demons, haven't you, Hawkshaw? And you guard them just as zealously as you guard everything else.

THE NEXT MORNING, Hawkshaw rose and showered and slipped into a pair of faded cutoffs. He intended to wear nothing else except the stone amulet on the thong around his neck.

But he caught a glimpse of his half-naked body in the mirror and remembered the kid would want to imitate him and go bare-chested, too. He forced himself to pull on a T-shirt. The cloth's snowy whiteness looked alien against his dark skin.

If he went barefoot, the kid would want to go barefoot. If he wore thongs, the kid would want to wear thongs but had none. With a sigh of resignation, Hawkshaw sat on the bed's edge and laced up the skanky running shoes he'd nearly worn out in Washington.

For some reason he didn't care to explore, he shaved.

He went into the kitchen. It seemed so foreign to him, no longer comfortable. It was as if a familiar and raffish old dog had suddenly been gussied up, a bow tied in its hair.

He missed the kite hanging from the cupboard door. He hadn't remembered that the tiled floor was such a pale green. He was used to it being the color of marsh grime and old dust.

He made coffee in a pot so well-scrubbed that he felt guilty using it. The window over the sink had been washed, which allowed him to see too clearly that the dock needed resealing and restaining.

Damn, he thought sourly. To see one part of the house tended and orderly forced him to admit just how neglected and disorderly the rest was. He'd grown used to it that way. He didn't particularly like it, he was used to it, that was all.

He poured coffee into a mug that seemed unnaturally clean. *The goddess of goddamn soap,* he griped mentally, and at that moment, the goddess herself came into the living room.

She wore white denim shorts and a shirt whose color reminded him of fresh apricots. Her hair was pulled neatly back and fastened with some sort of clip. In one hand, she carried a pair of white sandals.

She stopped dead when she saw him, her eyes, wary, fastened on his. In a rush last night came back to him, the moonlight, her nearness, his face poised so close to hers. A tingling stirred his groin.

Then he remembered the pictures he'd burned, and even more sharply he remembered the three he'd saved and put away, facedown, in the dresser drawer.

He looked away from her and frowned. "You're up early," he said, his voice even gruffer than he'd intended.

"I—" she hesitated "—thought you'd be outside by now."

He shrugged. "I'm on my way. Help yourself to the coffee."

"I've been thinking," she said in a tight-sounding voice. "About what Corbett said. About staying here until we're sure this Johnson man is the stalker. I suppose he's right. It would be foolish to go back before we're certain."

He picked up his coffee mug. "Yes. It would."

He started for the front door so he could watch the morning sun burn the mists off the water. But she stepped into his path, deliberately blocking his exit.

"I know you don't want us here," she said. "That you'd rather be alone."

The set of her mouth was determined, almost defiant. He felt a muscle twitch in his cheek. He made no reply, only gazed down at her as if to say, *so?*

She crossed her arms. "We'll be gone as soon as possible. In the meantime, I'll keep cleaning. I thought I'd start on the living room today. Where's all this fishing stuff supposed to be?"

Right where it's at, thought Hawkshaw. Then, with a wave of empty resignation, he thought, *Oh, hell. Sell this run-down place. Buy the boat. Sail for the wild meridian.*

"Set it on the deck," he said. "I'll lock it in the dock shed."

"Is the kitchen done to your satisfaction?" she asked. "You didn't say anything."

"It'll do," he said.

He saw a spark of temper in her eyes, and he rather liked it. He allowed himself the slightest of smiles.

"I've been pretty ruthless about throwing things out," she said. "Is that all right?"

His smile died. She threw things out easily because she saw them as junk. He had avoided the job because he saw the same objects forming an insurmountable wall of memories.

"It'll do," he repeated. "Are we through talking now? My coffee's getting cold."

"We're not through," she said. "And your coffee's still steaming. I appreciate your kindness to Charlie. But I meant what I said last night. Please don't spoil him or let him get too excited."

A sarcastic answer hovered temptingly on his lips. Instead he said, "Are you going to tell him about the fire?"

That damned hunted look came into her face. "Not yet. Not until I know Johnson's the one. I'll tell him then."

If Johnson's the one, thought Hawkshaw. But he merely nodded. "I'll try to keep his mind off things," he said. "That's all."

She stepped out of his way. A sad smile hovered on her lips. "That's a lot," she said. "Thanks."

He looked into her brown eyes and for a second seemed nearly to fall into them, a steep, dizzying fall. Desire, sudden and unwanted, swelled in him, cutting off his breath.

He said nothing. He went out the door into the quiet of the morning. He escaped her. *By the goddamn skin of my teeth,* he thought.

CHARLIE WAS WAKENED by a hand on his arm, Mama's warm hand that let him know he was safe.

He opened his eyes and saw her pretty face hovering over him, smiling. "Good morning, glory," she said. "Ready for breakfast?"

Charlie blinked sleepily and inhaled. The air was warm and it smelled of salt and marsh.

I'm in Florida, he thought with a surge of almost unspeakable joy.

He stared at the curtains. The curtains were brown, and they had blue-and-white fish on them—because this was Florida, and the sea was all around them, full of fish.

Mama was talking and asking questions, but he hardly heard her. Images cascaded through his mind: the salt river winding by the house, the low, mysterious mangrove islands all around, the palms, the wonderfully dangerous poisonwood tree.

Mama shepherded him into the bathroom, but he was so excited he almost danced away from her; she had to hold him tightly by the shoulders.

The bathroom's green wallpaper enchanted him; it was alive with pictures of pink-and-yellow fish, and he wanted to fall into the greenness and swim with them, swim in the Florida waters forever.

He thought of the sea at Bahia Hondo, so blue it dazzled his eyes. He thought of how it moved and changed and frothed white and cold around his ankles, the sand smooth beneath his feet.

He thought of the birds cruising in the impossibly blue sky: the gulls, the terns, the egrets, the pelicans, cormorants, plovers, skimmers. Hawkshaw knew all their names because Hawkshaw knew everything.

"Where's Hawkshaw?" Charlie demanded, trying to twist away from Mama.

"Stop squirming," Mama ordered, and she wiped a damp washcloth over his face.

"Blah! Gah!" spat Charlie and squirmed harder.

She dried his face with a towel, and Charlie thought, *She's smothering me, help, help!* He bet Hawkshaw never had to wash his face.

"Hawkshaw's taking me in the kayak today," said Charlie, desperate to escape Mama. "He hasn't left yet, has he?"

"No. Stop wiggling. Put on your shirt."

"Hawkshaw doesn't wear a—"

The shirt coming over his head cut off his words. *Help,* he thought, *she's got me captured!*

"He's got on a shirt today," she said.

"He does?" Charlie asked, taken aback.

"Yes. Put on your shoes."

"Hawkshaw doesn't wear shoes," he said contemptuously.

"He's got them on today," she said grimly, and made him sit on the bathtub's edge while she laced up his tennis shoes.

Charlie wriggled and twitched. "Where is Hawkshaw?" he asked. "Is he fishing without me?"

"He's on the deck," she said. She didn't seem pleased, and Charlie couldn't understand why. She was here in this magic house on this magic island with Hawkshaw, who was the purest magic of all. Why wasn't she happy?

"I don't ever want to go home," said Charlie.

"We can't stay here forever," Mama said, tying his other shoe.

"Why not?" Charlie asked.

"Just because," said Mama, doubling the knot.

An idea that had drifted through Charlie's mind before suddenly took root and bloomed like a great tropical flower. "Yes, we could," he said. "You could marry him. He could be my daddy. 'Cause I don't have one now."

His mother's jaw dropped. She stared at him as if he'd said a bad word. "Don't even *think* that," she warned him. "And don't you *dare* say such a thing to him. I mean it."

But her words barely registered.

Charlie slid off the bathtub's edge and darted out the door and across the bedroom into the hall. He half ran, half hopped away, toward the deck and Hawkshaw.

"I mean it, Charlie," his mother cried after him.

But he hardly heard her. His head was too full of potential miracles.

CHAPTER SEVEN

HAWKSHAW HAD TO DEFUSE the situation carefully.

"I don't want to get married," he said, throwing out the fishing line.

"Why not?" Charlie asked. "She's pretty. She cooks good. She can whistle on two fingers like a guy, really loud."

"People have to love each other to get married. I love somebody else."

Charlie looked crestfallen. "Who?"

"Just somebody else."

"Are you going to marry her?"

Hawkshaw knew the truth was too complicated for a child to understand. He took the easy way out. "Yes," he said.

Disappointment stamped the boy's expression. "When?"

"One of these days."

"Soon?"

"Pretty soon."

Charlie looked around, at the dock, the stairs, the house. Maybelline was stretched out on the deck, sleeping in the sun. "Will she live here?" he asked, a plaintive note in his voice.

Sandra would live in a place like this when hell froze over and the devil got saved, Hawkshaw thought bleakly.

"No," he said. "I'm selling it. That's why your mother's cleaning it up. To get it ready to sell."

"You'll *sell* it?"

"Yes."

"But where will you live?"

"Someplace else. On a boat, I think."

"In Florida?"

"No. In a boat, you can go anywhere. I'll go to Mexico, maybe."

"Not live in *Florida?*" Charlie said in disbelief.

"There are other places."

"Not as good," said Charlie with conviction.

"There are lots of places, just as good," said Hawkshaw. "You'll see for yourself someday."

Charlie shook his head and looked sad. He pulled down the bill of the Secret Service cap and stared out at the water. "I don't want to see them. I like this place."

"There are other places," Hawkshaw repeated.

Then Charlie had a tug on his line, and Hawkshaw helped him reel in the fish. It was only a silver jenny, about six inches long, but Charlie grinned as if he'd landed Godzilla. Hawkshaw found himself smiling, too. He unhooked the fish. "We can use him for bait or set him free," he told the boy. "What do you want to do?"

Charlie didn't hesitate. "He's a real nice fish. Let's let him go."

"Okay. Let him go."

He handed Charlie the squirming fish, and Charlie squatted by the water's edge and set it free. With a silvery flash, it disappeared into the dark water. Charlie, squinting against the sunlight, gazed up at Hawkshaw.

"What's her name?" he asked. "The lady you're going to marry?"

"Sandra," Hawkshaw said, and the name gave him a sick, hollow feeling in his chest. "Her name is Sandra."

KATE LOOKED UP at the man and the boy. She was on her knees, scrubbing the living room's tile floor. "I don't think I really want to get into a kayak," she said dubiously. "I think scrubbing might be more fun—really."

"Mama," Charlie cried. Pained frustration crackled in his voice. "Mama, come *on.*"

"I don't much like the water," Kate said, turning back to her scrub brush. She particularly didn't like dark, brackish water that contained sharks and eels and manta rays.

She said, "Go without me. I'll stay here."

"You can't stay here," said Hawkshaw. "I can't leave you alone. We all go, or nobody goes."

"Mama," Charlie begged. "Ple-e-e-ease."

I don't want to go out into a swamp full of slimy things. Haven't I got enough troubles?

"I'd rather stay here and work," Kate said stubbornly. "Go ahead. I've got Maybelline, and I'll keep the door locked. I'll be fine."

"Mama, you're no fun," Charlie accused, and turned his back on her.

Hawkshaw gripped the boy's shoulder, shook it slightly. "Don't talk that way to your mother, or you're never getting into that kayak."

Charlie shrugged, but he muttered, "I'm sorry."

"Go out on the deck and wait," Hawkshaw told him, and, to Kate's chagrin, Charlie obeyed without a peep of protest.

Hawkshaw hunkered down in front of her, and she was uncomfortably aware of the powerful muscles flexing in his bare legs. He smelled of sunshine and salt air and afternoon heat. She smelled of soapsuds and disinfectant.

He tried to take the scrub brush from her wet fingers, but she held on to it.

"Kate," he said, warning in his voice. "Get off your knees. You've been working since you got up. Take a break."

"No," she said, clutching the brush more tightly. "This is my part of the bargain."

"And I said take a break. It's my house, dammit. You're getting it too damn clean. It makes me nervous. Slow down."

She sat back on her heels and blew an errant strand of hair out of her eyes. "Let go of my scrub brush."

"You forget. It's my scrub brush," he said between his teeth. He pried it from her grasp, his fingers irresistibly strong. He stood, hooking one hand under her right elbow and drawing her, resisting, to her feet.

Her legs were unsteady from so much crouching and kneeling, causing her to sway to get her balance. He kept his grip firm on her arm, steadying her.

"I'm fine," she said, pulling away, but her elbow prickled where he'd touched her, as if sparks shot through her flesh.

She stared at the floor. The clean part was pale gray, the rest a much darker, mottled gray. She was almost half done and wanted to finish it.

She'd scrubbed and worried, mourning over her burned books and Charlie's lost toys and their few possessions. Work had kept her from feeling sorry for herself.

"Come on," Hawkshaw said, crossing his arms. "You need a change of scene. I can practically see the cloud of gloom forming over your head. Put on old shoes, a hat and some sunscreen. The fresh air'll do you good."

Kate looked at him numbly. She'd brought no old shoes, no hat. Any such things that she'd left behind in the condo had now turned to ashes.

He must have realized what was going through her mind. He went to a closet, threw out a white-billed hat with the word Hawaii embroidered on it in rainbow-colored script.

The hat sailed through the air and landed on the worn couch. "It's adjustable," he said, still digging in the closet. "You can wear it—you can have it."

He tossed out one ancient rubber thong, then another. "Take these," he said. "I don't know whose they were. They look like they might fit."

He turned to her, raised one brow critically. "You bring sunglasses?"

She nodded. She'd brought a cheap pair of sunglasses. Her good pair she'd left at home. She supposed they were broken and melted into rubble. She slipped on the thongs and tried not to think that what used to be her home was a ruin.

"I don't know why you two can't just go without me," she said, adjusting the band on the hat.

"I want you always within earshot," he said. "Both of you."

She wanted to say, "They have Kyle Johnson, the danger's over—it's got to be." But she knew Hawkshaw would say pessimistic things and fill her with doubts when she needed hope.

"Come on," he urged. "Who knows, you might break down and actually enjoy it."

Ha! she thought.

But she pulled on the hat. She took her old sunglasses out of her purse and thrust them on her nose. She raised her arm to Hawkshaw as in military greeting. "Take me to your swamp," she said.

He gave her the barest of smiles. "It awaits you," he said, "with open, wiggling arms."

Kate shuddered.

HAWKSHAW MOVED with the sureness and ease of a man who'd been around boats all his life.

He'd dragged two aqua-blue kayaks to the water's edge, and to Kate they looked like crude toy boats. She would as soon paddle around the mangrove islands in a Styrofoam ice cooler.

But Hawkshaw seemed to have perfect confidence in them, and Charlie, of course, showed neither doubt nor fear. He never did when he was afire with enthusiasm.

Hawkshaw had donned the wide-brimmed Aussie hat for the trip. "Just sit in the front," Hawkshaw told her. "Be the lookout. Charlie, you get in back. You can be the pilot."

"Oh, wow," Charlie breathed in delight. "*Way* cool."

The boy clambered eagerly into the long, open depression that served as the kayak's back seat. The kayaks, Hawkshaw said, were the light, recreational kind called sit-on-tops, molded of plastic foam.

Hawkshaw adjusted the boy's life jacket, then nodded for Kate to get in, as well. Gingerly she climbed into the thing. He handed her a two-bladed oar that was surprisingly light and gave one to Charlie, too.

Hawkshaw pulled their kayak into the water. Keeping the rope in hand so they wouldn't drift away, he splashed back to shore, pulled in the second craft, and lowered himself into the seat.

He'd shown them on shore how to paddle—even Kate had to admit it didn't look hard—and told them to follow

him. He set out with surprising speed down the widest
arm of the tidal river.

Kate swallowed hard and began to paddle. Charlie paddled, too, although he had trouble getting a rhythm. Kate
realized that Hawkshaw had put him in the back seat only
on the pretense of making him captain.

Her strokes were stronger and surer than the boy's, her
position more crucial. It was she who was in charge of
this silly little boat.

Yet once the boat took to the current, it no longer
seemed silly. It moved with swiftness, silence, and enormous grace. Even her beginner's strokes carried them
along with ease.

Charlie was chattering happily in the back. Other than
his voice, the only sound was the rush of the water, the
splash of their paddles, the faint rustle of wind in mangroves. By the time the house was out of sight, Kate felt
that they had entered a different world, mysterious and
untouched.

Hawkshaw slowed and let their boat catch up with his.
He tilted the brim of his hat lower. "What do you think,
Charlie?" he asked.

"Radical," Charlie said. "But where is everything? I
don't see animals or fish or hardly even any birds."

Kate looked about, half in apprehension, half in awe.
Charlie was right. Except for them, the backcountry
seemed deserted.

"There's plenty of life here," Hawkshaw said. "You
just have to look for it. Most of it's down here." He
nodded at the rippling water.

The water was not blue, but a dark brownish-green.
Kate saw nothing but small riffs of foam swirling by.

"I can't see anything," Charlie protested. "At home,
from my bedroom, I can see this squirrel. Sometimes he

sits right on the window. I draw his picture. You should see all the pictures I drawed of him."

Kate bit her lip and said nothing.

"I got a bank shaped like a squirrel, too," Charlie said. "It's got a real dollar bill in it. My daddy gave me that dollar. I'm going to save it forever."

Kate's heart twisted. The plastic bank was gone now, she knew, the dollar bill, too. The childish drawings were lost forever. She and Hawkshaw met each other's eyes guiltily. A silent message passed between them. *He doesn't know yet. It's best he doesn't.* Then each of them looked away.

Hawkshaw took up a net and with a quick scoop, brought something out of the water. "Maybe you'll draw me a picture of this," he said.

It was a crab, larger than a man's fist. It was gray, with bright-blue legs and enormous red claws.

"Gah!" Charlie said in wonder. "He's a giant."

"We'll find bigger," Hawkshaw said, taking the crab from the net and holding it carefully. The big scarlet claws snapped frantically, clacking at the air.

Hawkshaw let his kayak slide alongside theirs. "You've got to be careful with these guys. They can really pinch. Want to hold him?"

"Oh, yeah," Charlie said and reached.

"Charlie, be careful," Kate said, alarmed at the crab's waving claws.

Hawkshaw gave her an unsmiling look. "Here, kid. Like this."

Kate caught her breath as Hawkshaw guided Charlie's hand to grip the crab correctly. But the boy held it exactly as told and stared at the crab in amazement.

He wanted to keep the animal as a pet, but Hawkshaw said the crab looked pretty young, that they'd wait and catch another one. Reluctantly Charlie put the crab back into the water and released it. In a split second, it vanished.

Then, as if to reward Charlie for his kindness to the crab, an enormous blue-gray bird appeared, walking on a sandy strip of shore. Slender and long-legged, it moved with all the aplomb of a king.

Hawkshaw put his finger to his lips. Charlie was transfixed, and Kate herself was awed. The bird was tall, taller even than Charlie, but graceful as some creature out of a dream ballet.

It stopped and stretched its long neck higher, the better to study them. They were close enough to see the long feathers of its throat ruff and the markings on its face like a highwayman's mask.

As the kayaks glided closer, the heron turned, lifting his wings. He rose from the ground, soaring low and following the tidal river until he disappeared around a curve.

Charlie spun around to look at Hawkshaw. "Did you see it? What *was* it?"

"It was a great blue heron," Hawkshaw said, trying not to smile at the boy's wonder.

"It must have been the biggest bird in the world."

Hawkshaw explained about herons, and Charlie hung on his every word. He was so enchanted that Kate could not begrudge him his hero worship.

She watched as Hawkshaw pointed out another, much smaller bird he called a green heron. Charlie listened avidly. He had a dozen questions. Hawkshaw answered them all.

If she and Charlie were lucky, Kate thought, this—moments such as these—would be what he remembered from their time on the run. The fear and confusion created by the stalker would fade, and perhaps Charlie would never know how truly terrifying it had been.

When they went home—and she prayed it would be soon—few material goods would await them.

But Charlie would have this, these few days. They would be a small island in time, where he had enjoyed the greatest happiness of his young life. He would always have the memory of the backcountry.

Nobody could take that from him.

But, she realized with a helpless sense of irony, only Hawkshaw could give it.

HAWKSHAW PADDLED down a smaller, more winding channel. It narrowed until there seemed barely enough water to float the kayaks.

The mangroves closed over them on either side, a long, dark cave of vegetation. These narrow passages were shadowy and spooky, and Charlie was almost afraid, except Hawkshaw led the way.

Charlie supposed Mama was scared half to death. Girls would not like such a place. This, of course, helped him feel braver.

On either side the long, naked roots of the young mangroves thrust into the water like thousands of fingers. Hawkshaw said the mangrove used these long root-fingers to grasp a place in the sandy shallows to make its watery home.

Each mangrove, said Hawkshaw, had dozens and dozens of prop roots to anchor it, so the trees looked as if they stood on millions of slender crooked legs. Sometimes the trees stood so thickly together, it seemed only the smallest fish might swim through that great tangle of roots.

The corridor narrowed to such a cramped space, they

could not paddle. The big people could not even sit up straight.

Hawkshaw showed Charlie and Mama how to propel the boat forward by clinging to roots and branches above and pulling, hand over hand like Tarzan.

"Yuck," Mama said. She said it with a great deal of feeling.

Charlie kept on going, hand over hand. He was Tarzan, king of the backcountry.

"If you think you see a big spider in the mangroves," Hawkshaw called over his shoulder, "don't panic. It's just a mangrove crab."

"Double yuck," said Mama with more passion than before. But she didn't say they had to back up and stop. She didn't say they had to go home. If a guy had to take a mama on such a trip, she was a pretty good mama to take.

Then the cave opened to wide water, and the kayaks were floating in a big sort of bay, a still, open place. Charlie was almost disappointed. He'd grown to like the secrecy of the mangrove passage.

"Can we go back through it again?" he asked Hawkshaw. "Can we, huh?"

"There's hundreds of them," Hawkshaw said. "We'll see more."

Hawkshaw gave Mama a funny look. "You all right?" he asked.

"I'm just dandy," Mama said, but her voice was not her normal voice. "I'm just happy as a swamp rat."

A smile quirked the corner of Hawkshaw's mouth, just barely. He turned his attention to Charlie.

"We just went between two islands of red mangrove. They call them red mangroves because of the reddish roots."

Red mangrove. Charlie burned the name into his memory so he could know the things that Hawkshaw did. He studied the long pinkish roots snaking down into the water. He studied the dark, shiny leaves.

"The red mangrove's a special plant," Hawkshaw said. "It's doing a special job."

Charlie stared at the trees in perplexity. They didn't seem to do anything at all, except dangle their roots in the water and rustle their leaves in the breeze.

"What?" he demanded. "What do they do?"

Hawkshaw regarded the trees as if they were very special indeed. "They're creating more land. Yessir, right before your eyes. They're performing a miracle."

Charlie frowned. "But how? They're just standing still, and water's all around them."

"That's the first part of the miracle," said Hawkshaw. "The red mangrove's the only tree strong enough to grow in water this salty. An island can start with just two or three mangroves."

"Like a little family," Charlie said brightly.

Hawkshaw's expression was strange for a moment. "Yes," he said. "Well. Yes. That's a good comparison. A very well-rooted family. And the little family gets bigger."

Charlie nodded, pleased with himself. "Just like human families do."

Again Hawkshaw looked slightly uncomfortable. Then he said, "All those roots catch particles. The particles turn the sand to mud. Leaves fall and the mud gets thicker. Soon there's a little island. And the mangroves created it."

"Did mangroves make all Florida?"

"No," Hawkshaw said. "Just some of it. But when they make an island, other plants come. The black mangrove grows better where there's land. But the red mangrove likes living at the edge. And it sends its seeds out to sea. To start the whole process over.''

Charlie cocked his head and looked at the trees with growing respect. The mangroves seemed magic, like spirit-trees who could talk among themselves when no humans were near.

He imagined the mangroves whispering at night about sending their young ones abroad, to explore new waters and create new islands.

His mother's voice interrupted his pleasant daydream. ''Oh—what's that *thing?*''

Charlie turned and saw a small oblong thing bobbing in the ripples. It was almost transparent and made him think of a balloon filled partly with water, partly with air. It was an eerie iridescent blue.

''It's a man-of-war jellyfish,'' Hawkshaw said. ''Be careful. It's poisonous.''

Charlie stared at it, charmed.

''Ugh!'' exclaimed Mama, and she began to push it farther from the kayak with the edge of her paddle.

''Don't do that,'' snapped Hawkshaw. ''I've got to handle that paddle when we get back. I don't want to get burned.''

Mama jerked the paddle away from the jellyfish. ''Well, ex-cuuuse me,'' she said frostily. ''How was I to know?''

Hawkshaw didn't know that nobody snapped at Mama and got away with it. It must be one of the few things in the world that he didn't know.

Charlie shrugged at Hawkshaw as if to say, *Women, how do you deal with them?*

KATE SAT ON THE EDGE of a small, uninhabited island while Charlie explored with Hawkshaw. She stared across the open water at more islands in the distance. She was strangely perplexed.

It was as if Hawkshaw were a wizard, and he had cast a spell on Charlie. With each hour the spell grew stronger. She knew she should be grateful to the man, and in a way she was, but still...

She sighed and watched a large white bird fly across the sky. What kind of bird, she did not know—but Hawkshaw, of course, would.

She looked about her with a critical eye. This island, Hawkshaw had said, was not as large as a city block. This shore was barren and stony, for reasons she didn't understand (but Hawkshaw, of course, did and was probably explaining to Charlie at this very moment).

She didn't find the island enchanting. It looked, in fact, scraggly and poor. The trees behind her were not mangroves; they were other sorts for which she had no names, and a scrawny lot they seemed.

Wild weeds and grass grew from the sorry-looking soil, and Hawkshaw had said no mammals or reptiles really lived here because there was no fresh water. It seemed untouched for a good reason. It was a desolate place.

All she had seen of the backcountry had an air of loneliness about it. Grudgingly, she admitted it had a rather austere, almost haunted beauty. It might even have a certain peculiar grandeur.

But the narrow tunnels through the mangroves had made her feel claustrophobic. Hawkshaw had led them through half a dozen to get to this place, and their route had twisted and turned so many times, she was completely lost. Alone, she might never find her way back to the house.

The briny water that surrounded the island was full of

bizarre and often hostile life. Once there had been a splash and a great stirring of sand in the water, and Hawkshaw said it was probably a barracuda. Such creatures gave her the shudders, but Charlie was bewitched by it all.

She desperately wanted Charlie to be happy. She was glad he was gathering a rich store of memories. And yet—

Charlie's voice broke her reverie. "Mama! Look what we found!"

She turned and saw Charlie running out of a stand of trees toward her. Behind him strode Hawkshaw, his face impassive as usual.

Charlie came at her so fast he nearly stumbled, but he caught himself. He squatted by her side and opened his left fist. "Look!"

His rather grubby palm held a weathered chunk of thick amber glass, its edges worn smooth.

"Oh," she said brightly. "It's pretty."

"It's really, really old glass," Charlie said excitedly. "From the sea. The sea's been tumbling it around for years. That's why it's so smooth. Hawkshaw says I can keep it.

"And look at *this,*" Charlie said, opening his right hand.

Kate stared down at what appeared to be a small, flattish rock, gray and crumbly.

"It's a piece of Indian pottery," Charlie said, eyes wide. "Indians used to live in the Keys. Hawkshaw says maybe a hunting or fishing party left this behind. This is *ancient.*"

Kate smiled at the humble little piece of clay. "That'll make a wonderful souvenir for you."

"Oh, no," Charlie said, shaking his head. "Hawkshaw leaves all the Indian stuff on the island. In a cairn."

"A cairn?" Kate repeated.

"It's a heap of rocks or stuff," Charlie said. "A mem-mem-memorial to the Indians. I get to put this on the cairn."

She looked up at Hawkshaw. He stood, one hip cocked, his long legs hard and ropy with muscles. His arms were crossed. "I don't like to take Indian things. It doesn't seem right. Over here, Charlie."

He tilted his head toward a small mound of pottery shards lying beside a fallen tree. Kate would have taken the little heap for nothing more than a haphazard pile of rocks.

Charlie went to the cairn and reverently set his shard atop the others. He turned toward Hawkshaw, who nodded his approval. Hawkshaw said, "You want to go swimming, kid?"

"Yes!" Charlie cried.

"No!" Kate said almost simultaneously. Then she added, "There are jellyfish in there. And barracudas—even sharks, you said so."

"They won't bother us. And I'll keep an eye out. It gets hot out there, and it's a long trip. I want to cool off."

He took off his hat and cast it carelessly on the ground. He kicked off his tattered shoes. Then he stripped off the white T-shirt and tossed it to hang on a bush. The stone amulet lay nestled just beneath the bare hollow of his throat.

His shoulders were wide and the same deep bronze as his chest and legs. Kate felt the stirring of purely sexual appreciation and almost winced at the force of it. She had to pretend not to notice.

He said to Kate, "You should come in, too. You look hot."

"I don't swim well enough," Kate objected.

"The water's not deep here. It won't even be up to Charlie's chin."

"I'm not going in that—that animal soup," she said.

Hawkshaw shook his head as if he thought she was foolish. Charlie handed Kate the Secret Service cap. "Here," he said. "Hold this for me."

He struggled out of his own shirt. "Charlie," she warned, but he didn't seem to hear her. He sat down and tugged at his shoelaces.

When his feet were free, he sprang to his feet, hitching up his shorts. "Let's go in," he said to Hawkshaw.

"The footing's a little tricky," Hawkshaw said. "And your feet aren't used to it. I'll carry you in."

He swept the boy into his arms. Charlie whooped in joy. Hawkshaw looked down at Kate. "Okay?"

She gave up. She didn't want to be the wicked witch of Parentland. "Okay," she said unhappily.

She watched as Hawkshaw waded into the water. The boy's thin little chest seemed so white against the man's brown one.

"He'll get sunburned," she called after Hawkshaw.

"The sun's past its zenith," Hawkshaw shouted back. "Let him get used to it a little at a time."

He turned from her to face the open water as he waded deeper. Then he faced her again and put Charlie down. The boy squealed and splashed, the water almost to his shoulders.

"Charlie," Kate called, "be careful out there. Do you hear?"

"He's safe," Hawkshaw said above the splashing. "He's with me."

CHAPTER EIGHT

THAT NIGHT, Charlie seemed both bewitched and exhausted by the day's events. Kate stood, arms crossed, supervising him as he washed his face and brushed his teeth.

"Oh," he said suddenly, his mouth full of toothpaste foam, "Hawkshaw can't marry you."

"*What?*"

"He says he can't marry you," Charlie said around his toothbrush. "He's gotta marry somebody else. Her name is Sandra."

Kate was appalled. "You asked him to marry me?"

Charlie spit into the sink. "Sort of," he said. He rinsed his mouth, and spit again.

Kate put her hand firmly on his shoulder and turned him around to face her. "Didn't I tell you not to even think of such a thing?"

"I must have forgot." He yawned widely.

"Cover your mouth," she ordered and he did. "Don't ever mention an idea like that to him again. I don't want a husband. You're the man in my life."

Charlie yawned again, even more lavishly.

"I mean it," she warned. "If you ever talk about it again—" she searched her mind for the worst possible threat "—no more fishing for you. And no more kayak trips."

"Aww, Mama," he whined.

"I mean it," she said sternly. "No arguing. Now, into bed. You're dead on your feet."

Charlie protested feebly, but she guided him to bed. He was already starting to nod. He flopped down limply, and his eyes fell shut almost before Kate had tucked the sheet around him.

She studied him affectionately. His face against the pillow was no longer pale, but lightly tanned. A constellation of freckles stretched across his nose and cheeks.

Beside him, on the ancient night table were his treasures: the Secret Service cap, a heap of whitened sea shells, and the sea-smoothed chunk of amber glass.

She bent and softly kissed his cheek. "Good night, champ," she whispered. "I'll find you a home soon. I promise."

But not a stepfather, she thought grimly. The stalker had frozen her feelings about sex and intimacy, made her frightened of them.

She turned off the bedroom light, leaving the one in the bathroom to cast its soft glow. She went down the hall to the living room to clean up Charlie's papers and crayons, which littered the floor.

There were books strewn about, as well, tattered old nature guides belonging to Hawkshaw. Charlie had been copying pictures from them. Maybelline lay beside the mess, snoring softly.

Hawkshaw stood in the kitchen, opening a can of beer. "Is he asleep?" he asked.

"Yes," she said, kneeling to gather Charlie's scattered drawings.

"I walked the dog," he said. "She seemed a little restless."

"Thank you," she said, not looking at him. She began to stack the papers. She had expected him to be outside, brooding on the deck and guarding his privacy. His presence made her uneasy.

She allowed herself a glance around the living room. She'd cleaned only half of it, and it resembled a divided country, with a clear border between the tended and untended territory.

Hawkshaw strolled to the edge of the living room, stared over the beer at her. He wore khaki shorts and a white T-shirt and thongs. Somehow the muted light in the living room made his green eyes seem greener.

He said, "Corbett called."

She drew in her breath sharply. "Corbett? Why didn't you tell me?"

"You were putting Charlie to bed," Hawkshaw said. "You told me he needs his routine."

"He does, but I really wanted to talk to Corbett. Does he know any more about this Kyle Johnson?"

"No. Johnson's no help. He claims he's innocent of everything, including the arson. The police are having a tough time putting the pieces together."

"Excuse me?" Kate challenged. "This is the information age, the era of computers. All the knowledge you want is supposed to be at your fingertips—but they can't check out one small-time arsonist?"

"They're trying to reconstruct his last two years. The time you were being stalked. They know he's been in Columbia off and on. But he's a loner. His answers are vague and convoluted. His alibis are hard to confirm. Corbett's got a mug shot from the police. He's going to fax it to you, see if you recognize the face."

She stacked the nature guides and tried not to think of her own books, lost in the fire. "Why would he burn my place if he wasn't the stalker?"

Hawkshaw shrugged one shoulder. "Maybe he had the

wrong place. Maybe he didn't like the building. Maybe little voices in his head told him to do it.''

"I'm going to have little voices in my head, if this doesn't clear up soon,'' she said, putting the books on the coffee table.

"Look,'' he said, not unkindly, "nobody knows when a case like this'll break. It may take a day, it may take a week.''

She picked up the crayons and set them beside the guidebooks. "In the meantime, we're stuck here. And you're stuck with us.''

He shrugged again, as if the matter were beneath his notice.

She took the drawings, neatly stacked now, and set them beside the crayons. She rose, moved to the screen door, and looked out. The mangrove islands were black against the luminous sky, the water shimmering.

Her back was to Hawkshaw. She didn't see him move closer to her, nor did she hear him, but she somehow sensed it. "I'll keep my end of the bargain,'' she said. "The living room—I'm not finished yet. But is it done to your satisfaction so far? You need to say if it's not.''

"Don't throw out my boating magazines,'' he said. "That's all.''

"What about that awful shark on the wall?''

"I like the shark. The shark stays,'' he said.

She stared at the moonlight glittering on the live water. She took a deep breath. "I'll try to stay out of your way. Charlie says you're getting married. This must be very awkward for you and your fiancée—a strange woman and child moving in on you.''

He was at her side. He seemed too near, much too near, and she fought against flinching away from him.

She said, "Tell your fiancée I'm sorry. That I certainly

don't want a personal relationship any more than you do.''

He said nothing. She felt him looking at her, and it gave her a funny, tingling feeling.

"Would you tell her that?'' she asked. "That the last thing I want to do is intrude. That I want to go away from here as much as you want me gone.''

He still said nothing. His silence seemed to stroke her like hands, to caress and explore her.

Don't be ridiculous, she told herself, but a discomfort surged through her that was as embarrassing as it was exciting.

"Am I blocking your way?'' she asked uneasily. "Do you want to go out?''

"When I want to go out, I'll go out,'' he said.

"I should go to bed,'' she said. "Let you have your privacy.''

But she didn't move. Neither did he.

"Privacy,'' he said in such a low voice it made her feel shivery.

"Yes,'' she breathed, feeling hot and prickly all over.

"Well,'' she said, not looking at him, "good night. Come on, Maybelline. Let's go to bed.''

For a dizzying second, she thought Hawkshaw might reach out and touch her. Quickly she moved away and again called the dog. "Bedtime, Maybelline.''

As she left the living room, Maybelline sleepily following her, she was conscious of Hawkshaw's eyes on her. Awareness of him throbbed through her veins. She was relieved to shut the bedroom door behind her, to shut away his troubling presence.

She put on the oversize T-shirt she wore as a nightgown and got into bed. She lay there, sleepless, the sheet pulled up primly over her chest.

After a while, she recognized what was coursing through her, the restlessness that seemed so foreign, so unnatural. She was shocked to put a name to it. For the first time in what seemed an eternity, she felt the simple, elemental burning of desire.

She rolled over and put the pillow over her head.

Oh, no, she thought. *Not him. Oh, no. Oh, no. Oh, no.*

HAWKSHAW STAYED UP LATE, sitting on the deck, drinking beer, and staring at the glittering water. He'd meant to brood on Sandra. Instead, he kept thinking of Kate Kanaday.

This displeased him, but he couldn't help it. At last, he stood, crumpled the beer can, and yawned. Reluctantly he went to bed.

Early that morning, he had a bittersweet dream about trying to make love to Sandra. She didn't want him. She turned away from him. She told him to leave her alone, that she was through with him, that she loved someone else.

His heart felt like an empty shell, and he was overwhelmed by self-loathing for having lost her. He hurt all over from wanting her.

Then she turned back to him, forgiveness in her sapphire-blue eyes. "I can't leave you. Not really," she said.

He went to her. He wrapped his arms around her and kissed her in a way to tell her she was the only woman for him, now and forever.

She kissed him back, just as passionately. But somehow, in the middle of the kissing, she turned from Sandra into Kate Kanaday, and somehow, although he was disappointed, he couldn't stop the sexual excitement threatening to boil over within him.

He woke up in a sweat, aroused and confused. He

cursed himself and took an ice-cold shower. He made a pot of coffee. He sat on the deck and watched the flights of birds lacing the dawn sky.

He thought about Sandra in Hawaii. She was probably asleep. She was probably not sleeping alone. Unlike him. And unlike Kate Kanaday.

He should have known Sandra would remarry. She hated being alone. She was the kind of woman who always needed company, needed attention. He, like a fool, had not given her enough of either.

The sun was barely up, but the phone rang. Hawkshaw rose quickly to answer it, not wanting it to wake the woman and the boy. The morning was peaceful, even if his mind wasn't, and he was in a mood to guard his solitude.

But the seeming calm of the morning split apart when Corbett delivered a terse message.

"Damn," Hawkshaw said in disbelief. *"Damn."*

"Yeah, it's so rank, it stinks," said Corbett. "Break it to her easy, will you?"

Hawkshaw thought of Kate's face, so spirited yet so often shadowed by worry. He thought of his dream and set his jaw. "I'll try," he said between his teeth.

"Tell her I'll call her later in the morning," Corbett said.

"Will do."

"Sorry to call you so early. I just got the news myself."

"It's okay," said Hawkshaw, glancing out the door at the paling sky. "I wasn't asleep."

When he hung up the phone, he ran his hand through his hair in frustration. He moved restlessly to the coffee table and picked up Charlie's drawings. They were good, surprisingly good.

Hawkshaw shook his head. *I'm sorry, kid,* he thought. *I'm sure as hell sorry.*

KATE SOFTLY SHUT the bedroom door behind her and tiptoed down the hall into the living room. She had slipped into a pair of denim shorts and a lavender T-shirt and had left her hair loose, spilling over her shoulders.

Hawkshaw stood by the front door, staring out moodily. He didn't look at her.

"You're up early," he said.

"I heard the phone."

"It was Corbett."

She looked at him, waiting for him to say more. For no reason, she felt apprehensive and her heart beat faster.

Hawkshaw moved to the kitchen counter, took down a mug from the cupboard. "Can I pour you some coffee?"

"Yes, please," she said. Her heart beat harder still.

On the wall between the kitchen and living room was the plastic clock shaped like a cat. The cat's round cartoonish eyes darted back and forth with each *tick* and each *tock.* It seemed to be looking nervously from Kate to Hawkshaw and back again.

Hawkshaw's body seemed taut, as if ready for trouble. A frown line had etched itself between his eyes. He poured the coffee and pushed the mug across the counter. "Here," he said.

She didn't move. An ominous flutter sickened her stomach. "Something's wrong," she said. "Isn't it?"

He nodded, and her muscles stiffened in anxiety. *Tick. Tock. Tick. Tock.* The cat looked at Kate, then Hawkshaw, at Kate, then Hawkshaw.

"What is it?" she demanded. "Is it about Johnson?"

"Yes," he said in his low voice. "There's a complication," he said.

She stood, clenching and unclenching her fists. "Complication?" she echoed.

His frown deepened. "Kate—" he began, then paused. Then he said, "There's no easy way to say this. Johnson's dead."

All air and heat seemed to vanish from the room. She felt chokingly breathless and cold. "Dead?" she repeated.

"Columbia's county jail is crowded," he said, watching her reaction. "Too crowded. He was in a cell with five other men. There was some kind of argument. Somebody stabbed him in the heart. With a knife filed out of a spoon. He died almost instantly."

A feeling of unreality stole over Kate. She made a helpless gesture. "I—I don't understand. What does it mean?"

"It means he died without ever talking," Hawkshaw said. "The police are still trying to piece his story together. To see if he could be your stalker. Or not."

"But—" she stammered "—but—if he's the one, and he's dead, then it's over. I never wanted anyone dead. I just want this to be *over*. I want to take Charlie and go *home*."

"Corbett wants you to wait," he said. "He's still not convinced that Johnson's the man."

Tears welled in her eyes, hot and humiliating. She blinked them back. But her jaw was shaking with emotion, and she pressed her hands to the sides of her jaw to steady herself.

"The police are overworked," Hawkshaw told her. "They're checking out Johnson, but so far they haven't found much of a trail. It may take a week, ten days, maybe longer. You've got to be patient."

"Patient?" Her jaw shook harder.

She could not say more. A man was dead. He had

burned her home, and now he was dead. It was beyond reason. She put both hands over her mouth for a moment, as if holding back a cry.

"Are you all right?" he asked.

Get hold of yourself, she scolded.

He came to her, put his hands on her upper arms. "Are you all right?" he repeated, his eyes intent on hers.

"Yes," she lied. But she had started to tremble and could not stop.

"Come here," he said, and drew her into his arms. He held her tight. He put one hand behind her head and gently pressed her face to his chest. Against her cheek, she felt the beating of his heart, galloping as hard as her own.

THERE HAD BEEN NOTHING rational or logical in Hawkshaw's decision to draw Kate close to him. It was not even a decision. It just happened.

He knew immediately he was in trouble. He had wrapped one arm around her waist, pulling her against him. Her body was taut and shuddering, so he pressed her closer still. His other hand was laced in the cascade of her hair, cradling her head against his chest.

The warmth and softness of her body ignited him. She drew in her breath, half a gasp, half a sob, and he sucked in his own and held it, unsure what to do next.

He bent his face, another mistake. Her hair tickled his chin; its clean, spicy scent tingled. He stood perfectly still then, trying not to move at all.

He wanted to press his lips against the silk of her hair. To move his hand beneath her chin, to draw back slightly, tilt her face toward his. To kiss her, his hands moving slowly, sensuously over her body.

His heart thudded in his chest, echoed in the swift

pounding of his pulses. He hadn't touched a woman this way for over a year, and suddenly he wanted this one very badly.

He thought of his dream, ground his teeth. She trembled against him again, and the motion sent fire whipping through his blood.

Her hands rested against his chest lightly, but not easily. They were motionless, knotted uncertainly into fists.

She did not resist him, but she was almost as still as he was. He thought, *If she looks at me, then I'll know she wants me to kiss her. And I will.*

But she did not lift her face. She kept it buried against his chest. He could feel its heat through the thin cloth of his shirt. He could feel the uneven rise and fall of her breath.

He liked the curve of her waist beneath his hand. He resisted the desire to spread his fingers, savor the sensation. He yearned to move his hand up her back, to bring her upper body closer to his. He wanted to move it farther down, to press her pelvis more temptingly against his own.

He felt dizzied with lust, but he kept his hand where it was. He thought feverishly of Sandra. He had often held Sandra with such hunger—was it greater than this? It must have been, and yet—

He fought a small war with himself about dipping his head to kiss her ear, just the tip of it. He was losing.

"I think I'm all right now," Kate whispered. Her breath seemed to nuzzle the flesh over his heart.

She drew back from him. He wanted her to turn her face up to his, to give him a look that said, *Yes. I know. I want it, too.*

She did not. "Are you all right?" he asked. He heard the huskiness of desire in his voice and forced himself to release her, but could not do so completely. He kept his hands on her shoulders, willing her not to pull away from him completely.

But she stepped away, moving to the counter that separated the living room from the kitchen. "I'm sorry," she said. "The news about Johnson—it was a shock. I didn't mean to weaken."

Hawkshaw watched her, his heart still slamming at his ribs. "Everybody weakens sometime," he said.

"It's a jolt, a man being dead because of this. For a moment, I felt—responsible."

"He was in jail because he set a fire," Hawkshaw said. "It was his own fault. He got into a fight. It was his fight, not yours. Don't waste your guilt or your sympathy."

She shrugged sadly.

"Save your strength for Charlie," he said.

"You're right," she whispered.

He moved to the counter, lifted her mug. It was growing cool. He picked up his own mug, now cold as well, and emptied the untouched coffee into the sink. He refilled the mugs.

He set one down before her. Still she didn't meet his eyes. "Don't let this gnaw at you," he said gruffly. "And until you know more, pretend Johnson was the stalker. It'll make you feel better."

Her cheeks, he noted, were flushed. It became her, dammit. She nodded as if assuring herself. "We don't know that it *isn't* him."

"Right," he said. "In the meantime, be like the mangroves. Make an island of peace for yourself here. Where you don't have to worry. At least not for the time being. Because worry isn't going to help. Not a bit."

She picked up her mug and stared at the dark surface of the coffee. "I know."

"I'll see that Charlie has a good time," he said. "Try to look on it as kind of a vacation."

She gave him a brief glance, a wry smile. "A working vacation." She cast a significant look at the half-cleaned living room.

"Fine," Hawkshaw said with a careless shrug. "A working vacation."

They stood in awkward silence, and he wondered what she was thinking. His own mind was so jumbled he was unsure what he thought himself.

They heard the door of the back bedroom creak open, sigh shut. Maybelline came plodding down the hall.

"Charlie must be up," Kate said. "I'll have to make him sit down and eat breakfast. He starts out the day full throttle, he's so afraid he's going to miss something."

Maybelline stopped in the middle of the living room and began to chew on her hip with an air of resignation.

"That poor dog," Kate said with a shake of her head. "Her hip is acting up. Oh, God, there's so many things to tend to."

"I'll take her out," said Hawkshaw, glad for a chance to escape, "make myself scarce for a while."

She gave him another brief glance, another smile, this time grateful. He did not allow himself to smile back. He turned and left her.

CHAPTER NINE

As KATE DID the breakfast dishes, she watched Hawkshaw and Charlie through the kitchen window. The man was teaching the boy how to cast with a fishing rod.

Hawkshaw wore a Miami Dolphins cap, the bill backwards, so Charlie wore the Secret Service cap with the bill backwards. Hawkshaw wore a white T-shirt, so Charlie did, too. Hawkshaw's shorts were cutoff jeans, so Charlie had insisted on the same, and he wore no socks with his shoes because Hawkshaw didn't.

They made an odd pair, out there in the strong morning sunlight. Hawkshaw was tall and bronzed and thickly muscled. Charlie was small for his age and still had a child's almost fragile thinness. His tan was only a few days old.

Hawkshaw's patience with the boy amazed her, and the man himself puzzled her more deeply the longer she knew him. He'd stunned her when he'd taken her in his arms.

He'd been surprisingly compassionate, a perfect gentleman. He'd comforted her, that was all. He'd made no untoward move toward her, none.

Yet a strong jolt of sexual awareness had surged between them, and it troubled her. She knew she'd felt it, she was almost certain he had, too, yet neither had acknowledged it.

If they were wise, she thought, neither of them would. He was engaged, and she was not ready for either a romance or fling, especially a seamy little fling with another woman's fiancé.

She dried her hands, gathered up her cleaning implements and moved into the living room. She and Hawkshaw were cooped up here in this small house on an island where they never saw anyone except each other and Charlie. Perhaps it was inevitable that the idea of sex would begin to smolder.

Well, let it smolder and burn out and die for good. That part of her life was set aside, glassed in, roped off, a museum exhibit she didn't want to visit, even in memory.

She poured her energies into trying to clean and tame the other half of the living room. She tried not to think of the dead man, Johnson. She didn't want to contemplate the possibility that Johnson wasn't the stalker. And she tried to keep her mind away from any thought of Hawkshaw.

When the phone rang, she stiffened in apprehension, knowing she wasn't supposed to answer it. Hawkshaw came bounding up the stairs with that alacrity she thought must be second nature to him.

He picked up the receiver before the third ring. "Hawkshaw here," he said, leaning against the counter. "Yes, I told her. Any more news? Yeah, she's right here."

He held the phone toward her. "It's Corbett. No more news on Johnson. Sorry."

Numbly Kate took the phone from him, careful not to let her fingers brush his. "Hello?" she said.

She watched Hawkshaw ease out the back door, leaving her alone.

"Kate, it's me," Corbett said. "I'm sorry about this Johnson bombshell. It's a complication we didn't need."

Johnson probably didn't care much for it, either, Kate

thought with atypical cynicism. But all she said was, "I know."

"The police are trying to trace his life the past two years. It's not an easy job."

Kate's hand tightened on the receiver. "Tell me honestly, Corbett, do you think he's the one?"

"He could be, Kate. But I want you to stay put until we're sure. You understand?"

She fought back a sigh. "I understand."

"I'm letting the police handle that. They've got more resources. I'll check out the other loose ends."

She frowned, not understanding. "What other loose ends?"

"Just anything else that might have bearing," Corbett said vaguely.

"I'm so tired of imposing on you and—your friend. And I'd like to call Chuck's brother, Trevor, in Minneapolis. I haven't been in touch for almost a week. He'll be getting worried about us."

"No," Corbett said with a sharpness that surprised her. "I don't want you contacting anybody, and I don't want anybody even guessing where you're at. It's better to be safe—"

"—than sorry," Kate finished in chorus. Lord, she was tired of that weary proverb.

"Is Hawkshaw treating you okay?"

Kate tensed. "He's all right. I don't have much to do with him. And vice versa."

"Well, I'll bet he's got Charlie tagging along at his heels, eh?"

"Yes," she admitted. "You could say that."

Corbett chuckled. "Oh, yeah. When my kids were younger, I practically had to scrape them off him. He's got a magic touch. Shy with adults, but dynamite with kids.''

Kate lifted an eyebrow. Shy? Hawkshaw was *shy?* Such a thing had never occurred to her.

"Tell Charlie to enjoy himself," Corbett said. "As for you, try to relax. If we're lucky, Kate, maybe this thing is over for good."

"Yes," she said softly, "I hope so."

"I've faxed a mug shot of Kyle Johnson down there, in care of that motel. It's waiting for you. See if you can recognize him."

Kate swallowed down her distaste. "I'll do my best."

"And Kate?"

"Yes?"

"You'll need to start making a list of what was in your condo and what it cost. For the insurance company. They can't reimburse you without it. I've got a man coming to evaluate the damage on the structure itself."

"I—I'll do my best," Kate said.

But how do you put a cost on things like Charlie's baby pictures? And the only photos you had of your parents? And the books you'd loved since you were a child?

"In the meantime, take care of yourself and Charlie. I'll be in touch."

"Corbett?"

"Yes?"

She took a deep breath. "You talked about 'loose ends.' Is there still somebody you suspect? Somebody besides Johnson?"

He was silent a moment. Then, gently, he said, "Kate, it's my business to suspect. It's what you pay me for. But at this point, let's just hope it's Johnson, all right?"

"All right," she agreed reluctantly, but she wished he'd tell her the whole truth.

After she hung up the phone, she went outside. Hawk-shaw and Charlie were waiting for her.

Hawkshaw drove them in the Thunderbird to the Fla-mingo Motel to pick up Corbett's fax.

But Kate did not recognize Kyle Johnson from his pic-ture. The blurry reproduction of Johnson's photograph showed her only a stranger. He had an unremarkable face with a rather weak chin. He wore glasses, his mouth was primly set, and his hair was receding.

She and Hawkshaw showed the picture to Charlie, but did not tell him why. Charlie shook his head. He did not recognize Johnson. He began to ask questions about her-ons instead.

Kate let Hawkshaw answer him. She stared at Kyle Johnson's bland, almost prudish face. He was dead now—was it somehow because of her?

She prayed it was not so, but dead or alive, the man didn't seem quite real to her. And she didn't want him to.

Not to her, and especially not to Charlie.

KATE DIDN'T LIKE CLEANING, but when she did it, she went all out. She lost herself in the work.

Late that afternoon when Hawkshaw and Charlie came inside, she was standing on the couch, scrubbing vigor-ously at the shark.

"You're brushing my shark's *teeth?*" Hawkshaw de-manded in disbelief.

"They were dingy," Kate said. "He'd lost the whiter-than-white brightness of his smile."

Charlie giggled, but she kept on lathering the teeth with foam.

Hawkshaw shook his head. "Whose toothbrush?" he asked suspiciously.

"It's an old one I found in a kitchen drawer yesterday. I kept it for hard to clean spots," said Kate. "Like this."

She squirted water at the shark's jaws with a squeeze bottle. "Rinse, please," she said to the shark.

Charlie giggled again.

"Are you going to floss him, too?" Hawkshaw asked sarcastically.

"Maybe," said Kate. "His oral hygiene's pathetic. He had a dead bug and a gum wrapper in his mouth."

"Look," Hawkshaw said, "stop buffing the shark. It's a nice afternoon. I thought we'd go out in the kayaks. Give the kid some more practice."

"You men go by yourself," Kate said, wiping the shark's mouth dry. Its teeth sparkled.

"We men don't leave you alone," Hawkshaw said. "You can't work all the time."

"I can try," she said. She spritzed spray cleaner straight onto the shark's dusty face. She polished his eyes; she burnished his cheeks.

But in the end, she relented and let Hawkshaw bear her off again into the strange waters of the backcountry. Today the mangrove islands and tidal channels seemed more familiar, less forbidding and eerie.

With Hawkshaw in the lead, again they wended through the narrow mangrove corridors. Sometimes the shadowy passages would bring them to another swiftly flowing channel, sometimes to an isolated bay.

This network of bays and channels and mangrove caves reminded Kate of a great maze. Hawkshaw knew his way through the maze by heart, and he knew its secrets.

Yesterday the place had frightened her. Today, almost against her will, she began to find an odd peace in it. The plashing of the paddles sounded as natural as the sighing of the wind, the whisper of the water.

They stopped at the same uninhabited island with its stony shore and low trees. Once again she stayed on the bank and watched as Hawkshaw and Charlie peeled off their shirts and waded into the salt water.

Her other life seemed light-years away, as if the stalker were a man in a fading nightmare. Here, under a flawless sky, with her son and Hawkshaw the only other humans in sight, Johnson and his violent death seemed to belong to another, less real universe.

At last Charlie and Hawkshaw came slogging back to shore. They pulled the kayaks back into the water and Hawkshaw helped Charlie into his seat.

Suddenly Hawkshaw pointed high up into the shimmering sky. "Hey," he said, "a frigate bird. Can you see him, kid?"

Charlie threw his head back, narrowed his eyes. "Oh, yeah," he breathed. "The *magnificent* frigate bird."

"That's right," said Hawkshaw.

Kate, too, stared. At first she could see nothing. Then she focused on a black speck on the horizon. How could Hawkshaw see these things before anyone else did, how could he identify them so surely?

"How do you know?" she asked.

Hawkshaw turned his gaze to her. "You'll just have to trust me," he said.

Trust, she thought, with a plummeting feeling. She'd almost forgotten how to trust. Trust made you dependent, it made you vulnerable.

"Trust is something I no longer trust," she said.

Hawkshaw stood in the water, and she still stood at the stony edge of the shore. He reached his hand out to her. "You trust Corbett," he said.

"That's different," she said, knowing it was true without knowing why. But she took his hand.

THAT EVENING, Hawkshaw got an unexpected phone call from a neighbor who had long been absent, Aggie Hamilton.

"Aggie," he said with real pleasure. "I thought you'd gone north for good."

"Nope," Aggie said. "Too much traffic, too much noise, too damn much everything. I got the homesick blues."

"You're home for good?" he asked dubiously. Aggie had been hell-bent on moving. Her brother had left her the property that bordered Hawkshaw's, half a mile away.

Like Hawkshaw, Aggie had a ramshackle, out-of-the-way house, only it was in even worse shape than his own. Like him, she threatened to sell off the sorry place and move on. And like him, she'd somehow procrastinated well over a year, putting it off.

"Home for good? I don't know," Aggie said with a rueful laugh. "Maybe I been an old swamp wampus so long I'm past civilizing. The boys come home with me. Gonna fix this old place up. Maybe I'll stay. Maybe I won't."

"Boys? Which of the boys?" Hawkshaw asked. Aggie, twice divorced, had come to the Keys twenty years ago to help her brother raise his six sons.

"Burt and Ozzie and Gator," Aggie said. "They're taking their vacation time to do it. I said, 'You damn fools, who wants to work on vacation?' But you can't talk no sense into their heads."

Hawkshaw smiled. Before coming to the Keys, Aggie had been a barmaid in the backwoods of Wisconsin, used to dealing with rough-hewn men. Her brother's wife had been stricken by heart disease, and it was Aggie, no-nonsense and with the bark of a drill sergeant, who'd moved in and taken the household in hand.

"When'd you get back?" Hawkshaw asked.

"This afternoon," Aggie said. "And we bought a couple of quarts of chili and two Key lime pies at that Cuban place up in Islamorada. How 'bout you come over and help us eat it up? The boys'd like to see you."

These days Hawkshaw made it a rule to avoid the rest of humanity as much as possible. But he was tempted to break the rule for Aggie. Her manner was briery, but her heart was soft as a marshmallow, and she'd been good to his father. If his father had had any working brain cells in his head, Hawkshaw had often thought, he would have married Aggie Hamilton.

"I can't," he apologized. "I've got—company."

"You?" Aggie asked. "Company? Who?"

Anyone else he would not have bothered to answer. But this was Aggie, forthright as sunshine and so blunt it stopped being a flaw and turned into a virtue.

"Some people who need to be out of sight for a while," he said. "It's kind of a legacy."

"Hmmph," said Aggie, "from all that Secret Service stuff?"

"Indirectly, yes."

"Well, hell, bring 'em," Aggie ordered. "We got plenty."

"I'd better keep them under wraps. Sorry, Aggie."

"Under wraps?" squawked Aggie. "From *me?* Like I'm gonna get a megaphone and announce your business to the world? I don't care if you got the Sultan of Twerpistan over there. Bring him on. I ain't shy."

Hawkshaw would like to see her. But he said, "Sorry, Aggie. Another time."

"Now you've gone and ruined my surprise," she said gruffly. "Now I gotta tell you. I got somebody else over here, too, and he can't stay but the night. Dwight's here. Him and his oldest son. And he really wants to see you.''

Dwight. Hawkshaw wavered, weakened. Dwight was the oldest of the six brothers, the only one near his own age, the closest to a friend he'd had in his youth. Together he and Dwight had explored every corner of the back-country.

Dwight was ailing now, stricken with the same disease that had wasted away the boys' mother.

''He's not doing well,'' Aggie said with unexpected seriousness. ''He really hoped you'd come.''

Hawkshaw's loyalties fought within him, but the grave-ness in her voice tipped the balance.

''I'll be there,'' he told her.

She sighed, as if in relief. ''Good. And bring this mys-terious company of yours. Tell 'em their secret's safe with us. You know it's true.''

Hawkshaw smiled. Yes. He knew it was true.

AGGIE HAMILTON'S little kitchen was dusty and musty, yet in spite of its neglect, it somehow seemed homey, as if it were still permeated by past love and still cheered by the echo of all the laughter that had bounced off its walls.

Now laughter, in sporadic bursts, filled the evening air again as the men sat on the listing deck, reminiscing. Charlie sat among them, clearly happy to be included in all this masculinity.

Aggie's relatives were mostly big men, dark and ro-bust, with deep chests and booming voices. Two were bearded, and one had arms covered with blue and red tattoos. Only Dwight, Hawkshaw's childhood friend, was not strapping and exuberant.

Like his brothers, Dwight was tall and dark, but his body had an almost frail leanness. His black eyes sparkled with alertness as he listened to the others, but he seldom spoke. When he did, his voice was breathless.

Inside Kate helped Aggie with the few supper dishes, a mismatched collection of bowls, saucers, spoons and forks. Through the kitchen window, they could see the men and Charlie sitting in an equally mismatched collection of chairs.

Aggie rinsed the last dish and put her considerable energies into mopping the counter. "This place is filthy. You must think I'm a pig, inviting you to such a sty."

"It's just been shut up a while," Kate said diplomatically. "You've been gone—how long?"

"Nearly a year and a half," Aggie muttered, scrubbing at a stubborn spot of mildew. "One by one the boys had gone up north. Miami, Orlando. They'd tell me, 'Come on. Come on up and join us.' But I'd say, 'Somebody's got to hold down the old homestead.'"

Aggie assaulted a spider skulking under a cabinet and routed it. She nodded at the window, toward where Hawkshaw sat with Dwight.

"Then Hawkshaw's daddy died. The heart kind of went out of me. I needed a change of scene."

"Oh," Kate said, wondering what the relationship had been. Aggie was not a beautiful woman. She was big and rawboned and sunburned and wind-roughened. But she had a frank, guileless manner and obviously a generous heart.

"Then Dwight, he got sick," Aggie said. "And one thing led to another, and I stayed up there and stayed and stayed. Then one morning I woke up and said, 'It's time to go home now, Aggie. Pack your things.' But the boys come to help me settle in. To fix what needs fixin'. They're good boys."

"They seem like fine men," Kate said with sincerity.

"They are fine men," Aggie said. She began to scour the sink, her movements vigorous and swift. "Down here it's easy for boys to drift into trouble. The drug trade, smuggling, and such. They never done that. They make an honest dollar. They's good to their families. They don't fool around. They don't drink."

Aggie furiously polished the faucets and spigot. "I know you got some kind of trouble," she said without looking at Kate. "Hawkshaw don't want me to ask you questions about yourself, and I won't. But I want to ask you about him. Is he doing it? Is he drinking?"

She shot Kate a look that demanded the truth and no less.

Kate stopped short, the dish towel poised over a half-dried bowl. "A little," she said. "He's drinking a little."

Aggie turned away and swore under her breath. "He'll be just like his father. I was afraid of it. I have nightmares about it."

Kate felt both traitorous and curious. "I haven't seen him drink *much*," she said.

"House still a mess?" Aggie asked. "Trash full of beer cans?"

"Well…yes," Kate admitted.

"Oh, hellfire," Aggie said in disgust and threw down the scouring pad. She put one freckled hand on her hip and looked Kate in the eyes. "Gonna be just like his daddy if he ain't careful. What a waste. Maybe I'll turn around and go back north. I can't stand to watch it happen twice."

Tears rose in Aggie's blue eyes, and she dashed them away with her knuckle, sniffed, and squared her shoulders. "Hellfire," she said again. "Him, of all people. A hero. With the medal to prove it."

Kate stared at her in bewilderment.

"Didn't he tell you he's a hero?" Aggie asked, wiping her eyes again. "No. Of course. He wouldn't. Well, you seen that scar on his right arm?"

"Yes?" Kate said.

"You remember when that crazy fool shot at the Secretary of State five years ago? And two Secret Service agents was shot instead?"

Kate remembered. The Secretary of State had been coming out of a Washington hotel where he'd made a brief speech at some sort of conference.

A small crowd of spectators and media people had clustered outside the hotel waiting for his appearance. The Secretary had been only a few feet from the door of his limousine when, from the crowd, a troubled young man named Ronald Sarton opened fire.

The agent directly behind the Secretary had pushed the Secretary into the car, then whirled toward the shooter, using his body to shield the official, but he'd already been shot in the arm. The agent holding the door had turned to counter the attack and protect the wounded man.

The second agent was hit more severely, in the chest. The Secretary was unhurt except for a stubbed toe and scratched hand. Other agents wrestled Sarton to the ground and subdued him.

Kate could still see the news footage in her mind. One moment the Secretary was waving and smiling at the camera. But the next, the agent behind him cried out something incoherent, and shots were popping like firecrackers. Then two men lay bleeding on the sidewalk.

"That was Hawkshaw?" she breathed, feeling sick for his danger, his pain.

"That was him, all right," Aggie said. "He was the one pushed the Secretary to safety. Took a bullet in the arm. If you could get him to talk about it, he'd tell you his friend took the brunt of it, that his friend saved him and was the *real* hero."

A realization stole over Kate, chilling her. "His friend," she said hesitantly, "the other agent who was shot. Was his name Corbett?"

"It was," Aggie said. "He retired afterward, I think."

"He was the more seriously hurt," Kate said. "Wasn't he?"

"Oh, Hawkshaw claimed to Dwight he didn't do anything at all. It was Corbett that saved the day, Corbett just sensed something was wrong and that was what saved them," Aggie said with disdain. "But it was the both of them was heroes, and that's God's truth."

Kate's head buzzed oddly. Again the news footage played, ghostly, through her mind. A tall, still-youngish agent in a suit, throwing himself between the Secretary and the gunfire. That was Hawkshaw. And the older agent, Corbett, trying to shield the younger.

Now she understood why Hawkshaw had taken them in, her and Charlie. She knew what he thought he owed to Corbett—his life.

"I got the newspaper stories all pasted in my scrapbook," said Aggie. "I'd show you, but it's packed away."

The woman began putting the dried dishes into the cupboard, moving with speed and military precision. "So—" she said "—Hawkshaw claims he's gonna sell his place? Or that's what he's saying this week?"

"That's what I understand," Kate said uneasily. She thought of what Charlie had said, that Hawkshaw was buying a boat and getting married and sailing off to Mexico with his bride.

"I'd hoped he'd stay," Aggie said, setting the silverware into its drawer with a clatter. "His daddy had a good business here once. Hawkshaw grew up with it. Started leading those trips when he was fourteen years old.''

She sighed, put her hand on her hip again. ''Dwight worked there, too, during tourist season. After him, the other boys. But…things just fell apart. And there was nothing I could do to stop it. Not one damn thing.''

A series of emotions passed over her open, weathered face. Then she shrugged philosophically, as if none of what she thought mattered.

She tweaked the kitchen curtains, which were dingy. ''I'll have to wash and iron these. So many things to do. The phone ain't even hooked up yet. I had to call y'all from the motel pay phone. Well, I couldn't go without calling him first thing. Not Hawkshaw.''

''You've known him since he was young, but you still call him Hawkshaw?'' Kate said. She didn't want to ask outright, but she hoped Aggie would solve at least this minor puzzle about the man.

''Hmph,'' said Aggie. ''Well, he doesn't have any other name, you know. Just initials. W.W. It's easier to say Hawkshaw.''

''Just initials?''

''His parents couldn't agree on a name. But they both had daddies whose initials were W.W. So that's what they put on the birth certificate.''

Aggie shook her head at the foolishness of it. ''I always told his daddy it wasn't proper. Giving a child nothing but initials. But by then it was too late.''

Kate smiled and nodded and said nothing. She could see that Aggie's concern for Hawkshaw was long-standing and affectionate.

''I wish you could have seen the medal he got,'' Aggie said pensively. ''It's one of the highest the Secret Service gives. It was a beaut. Well, what's gone is gone.''

Kate gave her a questioning look. "Gone? You mean he doesn't have it anymore?"

"No," said Aggie. "He doesn't." And then, as if she knew she had said too much, she drifted into cryptic silence.

CHAPTER TEN

CORBETT CALLED the next morning. Hawkshaw answered, as usual, and Kate waited for him to hand over the phone and go back outside.

After the screen door closed and he'd descended the back stairs, she said, "Corbett, I've got a question for you."

"I'll answer if I can."

"When that man tried to kill the Secretary of State five years ago, two agents were shot. It was you and Hawkshaw, wasn't it?"

Corbett was silent a moment. "I'm surprised he told you that."

"He didn't. Let's just say something jogged my memory. You left the Service after that?"

"I reached retirement age when I was still in the hospital," Corbett said. "I had a wife, two kids. Nothing gives you a sense of your own mortality like a bullet hole through your middle."

"Did you save Hawkshaw's life?"

"No," Corbett said irritably. "He likes to *think* I took a bullet for him. It was nothing but chance."

Kate suspected he was being overly modest. "Would you swear to that?"

Corbett sighed. "It's yesterday's news, Kate. Let's talk about you instead. Hawkshaw said neither you nor Charlie recognized Kyle Johnson's picture."

"No. Not at all. Do you know any more about him yet?"

"Not yet. Sorry. In the meantime, you need to make out that list for the insurance company. The contents of your condo. What was lost."

Lost, thought Kate in dismay. *Gone forever.* The emotional wound of it stayed open and painfully throbbing. Corbett had said her car, in the underground parking garage, was untouched. But now the only other possessions she and Charlie had were Maybelline and the contents of a few hastily packed bags.

"I'll make the list," she managed to say.

"And I'll keep in touch," Corbett vowed. "Count on it."

He kept his promise. For the next three days he called each morning and each night. But he could never give Kate the news for which she waited so anxiously.

"I'm sorry," he'd say. "The police haven't gotten any further. Kyle Johnson's still a mystery."

To make time pass and keep her mind occupied, Kate forged on cleaning the house. At least, that's what she did mornings and early afternoons.

In the late afternoon Hawkshaw insisted she stop. Then the three of them set out in the kayaks, exploring deeper and deeper into the backcountry.

The afternoons stretched out in a deceptively lazy rhythm. Although Kate still became confused and lost in the maze of mangrove passages, Charlie, with his own brand of passion, was learning his way.

During these three days and nights, Hawkshaw took care to keep his distance from Kate, and she from him. They treated each other gingerly, and they avoided being alone together.

Aggie Hamilton sent Ozzie over with two loaves of

freshly baked bread. Twice she invited them to come again to her house. But Hawkshaw didn't accept her invitations. "Later," he told her.

Kate thought, *He means he'll see her after we're gone.* She was disappointed, for she liked Aggie. But instinctively she understood that Hawkshaw didn't want her talking to the other woman. Aggie knew far too much about him. Her knowledge was like a door into the past, and Hawkshaw intended to keep Kate locked out.

ON THE FOURTH MORNING of this mock tranquillity, conflict erupted.

Kate thought of it as the Great Comic War. It started when Kate cleaned out the big front closet. In its depths she discovered a pair of heavy, dust-covered cardboard boxes. With difficulty, she tugged them out.

She was opening the first when Hawkshaw came inside. He stopped in his tracks and stared down. "Wow," he said with a rare show of enthusiasm. "My *comics.*"

He crouched beside her and began to shuffle through the box's contents. Kate would have edged farther away from him, but there was nowhere to edge; her back was literally against the wall.

He touched the box with something akin to reverence. "I thought my father'd thrown these out years ago."

"That privilege is going to be mine," Kate said. "Or so I hope."

He stared at her as if she were insane. "My comics?" he asked, aghast. "Are you kidding? These are valuable."

Kate shrugged and tried to be less conscious of him. Fresh from the morning sunshine, Hawkshaw seemed to radiate more heat and life than any ordinary man ought.

"Look at this," he said in obvious delight, "*Superman. Spiderman.* And *Sergeant Steelarm*—my favorite."

Kate wrinkled her nose. Of all comic books, she most disapproved of war adventures. They were macho, garish, and violent.

"Sergeant Steelarm and the Combat Commandos," he said, flipping open a comic. "Lord, how I loved these."

At that moment Charlie burst in the door. "Hawkshaw, there's a great big wasp out—hey, what's this?"

Charlie skidded to a stop, the wasp forgotten. He eyed the box of comic books as if it were a trunk full of gold.

"Totally cool," he said in awe.

He flung himself down to sit beside Hawkshaw. He snatched up an issue of *Sergeant Steelarm* and leafed through it greedily.

"Charlie—" Kate warned.

He didn't hear her. "*Totally* cool," he repeated. "Were these yours?" he asked Hawkshaw.

Hawkshaw nodded. "Yep."

"Can we look at them?" Charlie asked. "Can *I* look at them?"

Kate winced. But before she could say anything, Hawkshaw replied, "Sure. Why not?"

"I'll tell you why not—" Kate began.

But her words didn't register with Charlie. "Wow," he said. "Can we look at them while we fish? Nothing's biting today."

"Go ahead," said Hawkshaw. "But treat them with respect. These are antiques."

"Awesome," said Charlie, grabbing up a thick stack. "*Ancient* comic books."

Hawkshaw glanced at Kate's face and frowned. In his low voice he told Charlie, "Take them outside, kid. Be careful of the wasp. Don't bother him, he won't bother you."

Charlie sprang to his feet, clutching the comics to his chest. He bulleted outside, banging the door behind him.

"Now you've done it," Kate said to Hawkshaw.

"Done what?" he demanded. "I thought you wanted him to be interested in reading."

"I want him to read classics," she said and tossed the box a malevolent look. "Not that stuff."

"This stuff *is* classic," Hawkshaw retorted. "Look at this—*Sergeant Steelarm and the Bullion of Borneo*—this was a masterpiece."

"I don't like Charlie wasting his time on such—"

"If he enjoys it, it's not a waste of time. Reading's reading."

"I want him to read *real* books—"

"Comic books are a start."

She managed to stand up. He stood with her. Her back was still against the wall. "You should have asked my permission before you let him have them."

"I'm sorry," he said, but he didn't sound sorry. "Want me to go out and tell him he can't look at them? That they offend your elite sensibilities?"

"No," she said. "I'm not going to play the villain of the piece. But I don't want him to get in the habit of—"

He leaned closer. "For crying out loud, Kate. He's a kid. Let him act like one."

Animosity crackled between them. She held his stare without wavering, determined to be as stubborn as he. But the atmosphere between them warped dizzily. The mutual tension transmuted into another sort, even more powerful.

For the first time, Hawkshaw seemed to realize how closely he stood to her. His gaze fell to her mouth, lingered there.

She stirred uncomfortably, and her skin hummed with

awareness of him. Her breathing had become uneven, shallow.

His face tautened, and the frown line appeared between his brows. He stepped backward, slowly, as if he were reluctant to do so.

"Sorry," he said and moved farther away still.

He shook his head as if to clear it. He gestured brusquely in the direction of the comic books. "I'll put these out of sight," he said. "Who knows? They may bore him in no time."

She nodded. Her heart beat unaccountably hard. "I certainly hope so," she said, her throat tight. "Then we can forget about them."

But Charlie didn't grow bored with the comics, and Kate and Hawkshaw weren't allowed to forget. Sergeant Steelarm had come to live with them, like a brawny, ever-present ghost.

CHARLIE WANTED TO READ more comic books that night, but Mama said, "No."

So he'd gone back to copying pictures out of Hawkshaw's bird book. He was drawing a great blue heron. Then he had an idea—what an idea! But how to do it?

He would ask Hawkshaw. Mama was frowning over some sort of list she was trying to make. Hawkshaw was outside on the deck.

Charlie grabbed his paper and crayons and went out on the deck. Hawkshaw was lying in the hammock, barefoot, reading a boat magazine that he had propped on his chest. He didn't look up, but he said, "Hello, kid. What's up?"

Charlie decided to plead for the comic books one last time. "Can't I look at another comic?"

"Three a day, that's the limit," Hawkshaw said, not

moving his eyes from his magazine. "Your mother says so. Her word's law."

Charlie sighed in frustration and went back to Plan A. "Then will you help me put names on my pictures? Will you do the writing?"

Hawkshaw tossed him a brief glance. "You do the writing, kid. I'll help you spell."

"Hawkshaw," Charlie said in his finest whine, *"please."*

Hawkshaw, as usual, was impervious to whines. "I have spoken."

Disappointed but still determined, Charlie plodded to the picnic table and sat down on the bench. He went through his drawings and picked out his best heron picture.

He took out a blue crayon and frowned. He didn't know how to do the next thing. "Hawkshaw," he said. "How do you spell 'great blue heron'?"

Hawkshaw got out of the hammock and left it swinging empty and lazy. He came and sat beside Charlie. Patiently, he said what letters to put down and when to put spaces between the words.

At last Charlie finished the printing. He looked on his work with satisfaction. The letters weren't all the same size, and they ran uphill, but they looked nice under the picture. GReAt BLUe HerON. He thought the words looked very official.

"Boy," he said, still admiring the job. "That's *work.*"

"Yeah," said Hawkshaw. "I may have to get back in the hammock and rest."

"Wait," Charlie said, riffling through his pictures. He pulled out another drawing. "I want to do this one. How do you spell 'little blue heron'?"

Hawkshaw put his elbow on the table. He stared at the

drawing and rubbed his upper lip thoughtfully. "Well, there's a secret to that," he said. "I could teach you, I guess. If you really wanted to know."

"A secret?" Charlie asked. "What?"

Hawkshaw explained. Charlie listened, his brow creased in concentration. By the time the sky was getting dark, he had labeled three kinds of herons and two kinds of egrets.

Then Mama called from the house. "Charlie? It's eight o'clock. Time for your bath. Come in now."

"Awww, Mama," Charlie complained.

He turned to Hawkshaw. "I don't want to go in," he blurted. "I like it out here with you. You don't yell at me like my daddy did. He was always getting mad at me. And Mama, too."

Hawkshaw registered no surprise, but he stared at him. "What?" he said.

"They talked about a divorce," Charlie said, peeling paper from a magenta crayon. "If you marry Sandra, you might get a divorce. Then you might think about my Mama again. You know?"

"Charlie?" called Kate.

"You heard your mother," Hawkshaw said tonelessly. "It's eight o'clock."

Charlie almost balked, except he *was* tired. But his mind, though weary, was fertile. He had another sudden inspiration.

He shoved the labeled pictures toward Hawkshaw. "Keep these for me," he said. "Don't show my mama. I want to surprise her. Okay?"

Hawkshaw nodded solemnly. He took the pictures and concealed them inside his magazine just as Kate came out on the deck to usher Charlie inside.

She locked her hand around the boy's. "Bathtime," she said. "You can pretend you're a fish."

"I don't want to be a fish," Charlie protested. "I want to be Sergeant Steelarm. Hawkshaw, does Sergeant Steelarm have to take baths?"

"Yes," Hawkshaw said calmly. "Whenever his mother tells him to."

"I'm Sergeant Steelarm," Charlie cried as Kate led him inside. "I've been captured by the cannibals of Borneo. They're going to put me in a big pot of hot water!"

"Tough it out," Hawkshaw said. "Take it like a man. You'll make it."

Reluctantly Charlie let himself be drawn in to the house. "I'm going to be boiled alive," he told Maybelline, who was lying beside the hallway. "Maybe they'll shrink my head."

Maybelline was not impressed. She yawned widely, closed her eyes, and left him to his fate.

HAWKSHAW SAT on the tattered couch, sorting through a carton of his father's old diving equipment. Kate had found the box in the back of the hall closet and said she hardly knew what it was, let alone if any of it was salvageable.

He was glad Kate was off behind the closed door, tucking in Charlie. The woman got to him; she made him edgy so that his nerves crawled with unwanted excitement.

This excitement, he knew, was only lust, and he'd despised himself for it. He'd sworn off other women in hopes Sandra would come back to him. She still might come back—it wasn't totally impossible, he told himself.

The phone rang. Hawkshaw rose from the couch and hustled to the counter to grab the receiver. He suddenly wished with all his heart it was Corbett—Corbett saying that all was well, that Johnson was the stalker and Kate could go safely back to Columbia. To live happily ever after and far from him.

"Hello?" he said.

"Hello," said a husky voice. It was Sandra.

His heart contracted sickly. "What is it?" he asked.

"I was thinking of you," she said. "So I called."

Blood drummed in his ears. "Thinking of me?"

"Yes," she said. "I'm going to do it here. Get married. A week from today."

The room tilted dizzily. "Married?" he repeated.

"Yes," she said. "As soon as my contract at the club is up. I thought I should tell you."

Still dazed, he spread his free hand over his forehead, as if holding his skull together.

"Aren't you going to wish me happiness?" she asked.

"I've always wished you happiness," he said tightly. "I never wished you anything else."

"He's not like you," she said. "He's very different."

Different. Yeah. Well he would have to be, wouldn't he? He could think of nothing to say that would not betray his bitterness.

"We have a lot in common. We both love theater, opera, art galleries. Things like that. He's like me—he wouldn't know one end of a fishing pole from another."

"Yeah," said Hawkshaw. "Well."

She laughed again. "It's so different from us. You and I—we never had anything in common. Except sex."

"Yeah," he said. "There was that, wasn't there?"

"Wasn't there?" she said, her voice almost a whisper. "That was one thing we got right. For a while, at least."

Hawkshaw moved his shoulders restlessly. "So this Hawaiian gig's going to be your honeymoon, is it?"

"Yes," she said. "It's very beautiful here. We're in Maui. I love it—the beaches, the shops—it's adorable. We may buy a time-share place here."

"Sandra," he said wearily, "where's your fiancé? Should you be calling me up like this?"

"He's playing golf," she said lightly. She herself did not play golf or tennis or any other sport. She kept in shape by dieting and some sort of exotic exercise he couldn't pronounce.

"Does he know you're phoning me?" Hawkshaw asked.

"We don't have secrets from each other," she said in the same light tone. "I thought I should tell you my plans. No matter how often I tell you otherwise, you have this sad, crazy idea that we'll get back together. I called to tell you that it's impossible now. I'm setting you free."

Free. The word was like a knife, and she was twisting it, expertly.

She said, "I've told you to find someone else. I really wish you would. I worry about you down in that dreary place."

He smiled grimly to himself. Sandra had hated the backcountry. "You worry about me," he said. "You expect me to believe that?"

"We were—close—for a time," she said. "In spite of what you did, I have some feeling for you."

He suppressed a sigh of bone-deep frustration. "You still have some feeling for me. Besides resentment and contempt?"

"Oh, really," she said, sounding wounded. "Once I thought I loved you. Then I thought I hated you. The truth is somewhere in between."

"It was never in between for me," he said. "You know

how I felt about you. How I still feel. I'd cut off my arm to change what happened. I never meant to—''

"You can't change what happened," she said, ice coming into her voice. "I have to live with it forever. Forever."

And so do I, he thought fatalistically. Mentally, he swore, cursing himself for the ten thousandth time.

"As for how you still feel about me," she said, "it's time to get over it. Get me out of your mind. You know what you're like? A stalker or something. You just won't let go."

"A stalker," he said in disgust. Is that how she saw him? A sicko like the man obsessed with Kate?

"Do you want to give me a wedding gift?" Sandra asked, her voice quiet and breathy.

Not particularly, he thought. His mood grew blacker by the second.

"I'll tell you what I'd like from you," she went on. "I'd like you to find yourself another woman. Just get involved with someone—anyone."

"Oh, hell," he said with distaste.

"It doesn't have to be meaningful," Sandra said. "You don't have to love her. It can be the first woman who comes along. Just get on with your life. Without me. Because what you and I had has to end. For good. I told you—I'm setting you free."

He shook his head. "You're enjoying this, aren't you?"

"No, I'm not," she answered. "I truly wish you'd take up with somebody. You're a highly sexed man. I should know. But I belong to someone else now. I suggest you learn to enjoy what you can get."

He thought of telling her that at this moment there was

a woman in the back bedroom. A pretty woman and spirited, one he might quite enjoy seducing.

"Oh, God," Sandra said in a hasty whisper. "He's coming back. I've got to get off the phone. I meant what I said. For your own good. Goodbye."

There was a sharp click in his ear, and the line went dead. He slammed the receiver down. His heart drummed and his head seemed full of heat and darkness.

She'd done it. She'd done it. Sandra was marrying another man, it was happening within the week. A sick, sour emptiness opened up inside him like a chasm.

Because of him a terrible thing had happened to Sandra's sister. Sandra blamed him. Sandra had left him, and he must bear the weight of it to the grave.

He had not meant for her sister to die, not wanted it, God knew. But what did his good intentions matter? Daisy was dead; his marriage was destroyed, and now Sandra belonged to someone else.

TWO HOURS LATER, Kate eased the bedroom door closed behind her and softly made her way down the hall. She hoped Hawkshaw was out on his precious deck, staying out of her way as usual. Better yet, she hoped he was asleep.

She'd tried to sleep herself, but couldn't. Now she felt compelled to take another stab at the troublesome insurance list. She and Charlie would be even more strapped for money if she didn't.

She was surprised to see Hawkshaw standing at the kitchen counter. He'd washed some of the old diving equipment and was examining it with a critical eye.

He acted as if he didn't see her. He opened the refrigerator door and took out a beer. Two empties already stood on the counter. The can made a hissing sound when he pulled off the tab.

He came strolling into the living room. "Ah," he said, "the little list maker. Making her little list."

His tone was sarcastic, and when she looked up, he had a mocking twist to his mouth.

"I didn't know you were here," she said. "I didn't mean to intrude." She picked up her notebook and pencil.

He moved to her side. Her muscles tightened, and she found her teeth were on edge.

With an easy, catlike movement, he positioned himself in front of her so she couldn't reach the bedroom without forcing her way past him.

He looked her up and down, one eyebrow cocked critically. "Charlie says his father used to get mad at you and him. To yell. That you talked about divorce."

Kate gave a sigh of disgust. "Oh, did he blurt *that* out? I'm sorry. I tell him to keep our private business private, but he—he's impulsive. He forgets."

"He's a kid," Hawkshaw said. He set the beer aside and crossed his arms. The stance made Kate nervous.

"Pay him no mind," she said uneasily.

He cocked his head. "And all this time I thought you were a poor, bereaved widow. You had me fooled."

"I didn't try to fool anybody," she said, her chin rising. "You made assumptions. They were wrong. Would you step aside, please. I wouldn't mind some privacy myself."

He held his ground. "Did you let Corbett make the same assumptions?"

She took a sidelong glance at the beer can on the lamp table. He seemed to know what she was thinking.

"I'm not drunk," he said sarcastically. "I've had a few beers, that's all."

She believed him, but he was making her uncomfortable. She stepped backward, edging up against the counter.

"Did you tell Corbett you and your husband were having trouble? That you'd talked of divorce?"

She gripped her notebook more tightly to her chest. He seemed to note the action with interest. She said, "I said the marriage had a few problems, that's all."

Hawkshaw took a step nearer. "But you didn't tell him the nature or extent of those problems?"

"What business is it of yours?" she challenged. "I think that's between Corbett and me."

"Corbett pulled me into your business," he said. "Now I'm wondering how well he understood it. Couldn't this have bearing on your 'situation'? Precisely what *were* the problems between you and your husband?"

Kate felt trapped between defiance and guilt. Chuck was dead; he could not defend himself, and she did not want to dwell on the bad things in her marriage. Chuck was Charlie's father, after all. But Hawkshaw was right: she had not told Corbett the whole truth.

She shrugged as if the past no longer hurt. "Chuck— could be impatient with Charlie. He didn't want to admit that Charlie had a—a condition. He said whatever was wrong with Charlie was my fault. Because I was a bad mother."

"I think there's more than that," Hawkshaw said. His voice was quiet, yet somehow she perceived a danger in that quiet.

Kate turned from him, facing the counter and gripping its edge. "We were mismatched," she said miserably. "It's that simple. We didn't know each other well enough when we married."

"People do that sometimes," he said.

She swallowed. "My mother and father had died within a year of each other. I felt so—unattached to life. Then I met him. I was a senior in college. He was studying for his doctorate. I was dazzled. I thought he was so intelligent, so accomplished, so centered, so mature."

"And what did he think you were?" Hawkshaw asked in that same unnervingly quiet voice.

She smiled ironically to herself. "He thought I was someone who'd stay dazzled forever. And never think he was less than perfect."

"And that's what split the marriage?" he asked. "That neither one of you was flawless, and you quarreled about Charlie?"

"Mostly," she said vaguely.

"Mostly," he echoed. He'd moved closer. She could feel his breath on her ear. "There was more. What was it?"

She gripped the countertop more tightly. She inhaled sharply, held it. "He was—jealous," she admitted.

"Did he have reason?"

Her body stiffened. "No," she retorted. "Not at all."

"Tell the truth, Kate. Was there somebody else? A lover? More than one?"

She whirled to face him. "I ought to slap your face."

He leaned nearer. "You're an attractive woman. You must have had your—admirers."

"There was nobody," she insisted.

He was too close, and she felt trapped against the counter.

"Then why was your husband jealous?" he asked.

Tears of rage rose in her eyes. "I told you—it's none of your business."

"And I told you that it is," he countered. "Why was he jealous? What haven't you told Corbett?"

She glared at him as if she would kill him if she could. "He was impotent," she said. "Ever since Charlie was little. There—are you satisfied?"

He blinked in apparent surprise. Then his face went blank.

Indignantly she dashed the tears from her eyes. "Damn you," she said. "You've got the whole story now. Does it make you happy? He was so ashamed. He didn't want anybody to know. It wasn't his fault."

"I'm sorry," Hawkshaw said, but he did not draw away from her.

She pressed the heel of her hand hard against her cheek. "It must have had something to do with—with his health. But I didn't know he was sick. *He* didn't know. He had— this problem. Then he started having mood swings. Then—he had that terrible seizure. And he was dead. I shouldn't have fought with him. I should have understood. I should have—"

She could not go on. Guilt and regret overwhelmed her. She could not remember the last time she'd cried; it was a luxury she no longer allowed herself, but she cried now. Bitterly and helplessly.

"My God," he said, his forehead furrowed. "I'm sorry."

Slowly, almost with an air of reluctance, he put his arms around her, drew her close.

She should have struggled. She no longer had the strength.

"Kate," he whispered and pulled her tighter. "Oh, Kate."

CHAPTER ELEVEN

HAWKSHAW GATHERED HER closer still. He rested his cheek against the top of her head. Her face, pressed against his chest, was hot and wet, and her body heaved with silent sobs.

He didn't know why he had done this to her, taunted her and stripped her of her secrets. She'd walked into the room, and he, still shaken by Sandra's call, had felt a score of emotions tumble through him. He'd resented Kate, and he'd wanted her, and he'd resented himself for wanting her.

"I'm sorry," he repeated. "I didn't mean to..."

He could say no more.

I didn't mean to hurt you, he thought. He kissed the top of her head, felt her silky hair beneath his lips.

Slowly her sobbing ebbed, but he realized he did not want to let her go. And she did not move away from him.

They stood, heart beating against heart. She had gone absolutely still in his arms. Her hands had at first gripped his shoulders almost spasmodically. Now they felt tense upon his flesh, but tentative, unsure, as if she was thinking of drawing away.

He was conscious of the warmth of her body against his. Beneath his hands she felt as if she were poising herself to flee, yet she did not.

He drew in a shuddering breath. So did she. Then he kissed her hair again, sighing silently against it.

His hand moved up her back, exploring its sculpted curvature. She sighed, too, as silently as he. She shivered.

He pulled back so he could put his other hand beneath her chin and raise her face to his. Her eyes were closed. She shook her head, and the tracks of her tears glistened in the lamplight.

"No," she whispered. "Don't."

"Shhh," he breathed.

She ducked her head, shook it again. "I'm sorry," she said. "I didn't mean to cry. But when I think about it all, I feel so—guilty."

"Don't," he said. "You shouldn't."

He reached into his back pocket, took out his handkerchief. He dried her closed eyes, wiped away the streaks of tears as gently as if she were a child.

"He died so young," she said. "It doesn't seem fair to talk about—things he wanted secret."

"Shhh," he repeated.

He lifted her face to his again. "Open your eyes," he said.

She did. Her lashes were still starred with moisture. She looked up at him with an expression that seemed half frightened, half desirous.

He thought, *And now I kiss her.*

He did. Her lips were hot and soft beneath his. They tasted of salt.

His heart tumbled as if it were falling down a steep hill. He kissed her harder. His heart seemed to reach the bottom of the hill and plunge off a cliff.

Slowly, hesitantly, she began to kiss him back. Her mouth moved against his with a shy hunger. Her hands tightened, ever so slightly, on his shoulders.

The movement, small as it was, filled him with a kind of craziness. He drew her against him possessively. His hands began to move over her body. He touched her breast, claimed it.

She sucked in her breath, but she didn't try to wrest away. She did not move his hand, but she drew her face back from his.

"We can't do this," she said shakily. "There's Sandra."

"Shhh," he said for the third time, bringing his lips so close they nearly touched hers. "There is no Sandra."

"But—" she said, her breath warm against his mouth "—but…"

"There is no Sandra," he said. "She left me. She isn't coming back."

He kissed her again. He undid the top button of her blouse. He undid the second button. And the third.

IT WAS THE FIRST TIME she had been with a man in years. It felt strange and inevitable, both right and wrong. It felt wonderful.

Somehow she and Hawkshaw had made their way into his bedroom. He had stripped away first her clothes, then his own. He molded his naked body against hers.

His hands skimmed over her, strong, yet maddeningly gentle. His mouth was like a sweet weapon, taking her prisoner. Hot, it explored the curve of her throat, then moved to her breast.

She gasped at the exquisite eroticism, laced her fingers in his hair, and held him more tightly to her.

"Touch me," he whispered, guiding her hand to his erection.

He touched her in return until she was wild with wanting him.

He half pulled, half ripped the spread from the bed and lowered her to the sheets. He had knocked the pillow aside, but now, his body atop hers, he paused to recover it, to place it beneath her head. That simple gesture of kindness almost overwhelmed her with emotion for him.

He kissed her breasts again. Then his mouth was against hers. "I don't think I can wait," he whispered.

"I don't want you to wait," she said.

She opened herself to him, felt the exciting thrust of his hardness deep inside her. Their bodies locked together, her need as great, as urgent and undeniable as his.

KATE FELL INTO a drowse nestled against Hawkshaw, her cheek on his bare shoulder. His arm was around her, his legs still entwined with hers.

An hour later her eyes fluttered open. When she realized where she was and how she'd got there, she went hot with embarrassment. Hawkshaw was asleep; she was fairly certain from the sound of his breathing.

His arm was still around her, his fingers resting lightly against her naked breast.

Well, thought Kate unhappily, *I was completely shameless. How much will I hate myself in the morning?*

But at least, she thought, he had produced a condom from the drawer of a night table. They hadn't been quite that crazy, to have unprotected sex.

She knew she should slip away silently and go to the chaste confines of the back bedroom. But still she couldn't bring herself to move away from Hawkshaw. Not quite. Not yet.

She fought down the desire to touch him, to trail her fingers down the long, warm musculature of his arm, to lay her hand over his chest to feel the beating of his heart. She had the foolish urge to nuzzle his shoulder, to feel his flesh against her lips again, to taste it.

She was not sure what her emotions were about Hawkshaw. But she was both awed and dismayed by how eagerly, how completely, her body had responded to his.

If he had cast a mental spell over Charlie, he had cast a physical one over her. Sex with her husband had been swift, infrequent, and often awkward. Then it had become nonexistent. But Hawkshaw knew how to make love to a woman. He knew how exactly.

She had found a wildness and sheer, physical joy with him that she had never before felt. Ruefully she remembered the cliché: *I didn't know it could be like that.* Now she knew.

She could not resist. She turned, softly kissed his shoulder.

He stirred. His arm tightened around her. "What?" he said in a sleepy voice. He shifted position, brought his face close to hers.

"I have to go," she whispered. "If Charlie wakes up and I'm not there, he'll be upset."

"Not yet," Hawkshaw said. He stroked her tumbled hair back from her face.

"I have to," she repeated. She touched the amulet that hung against his chest.

"Not yet," he said again, bringing his lips against hers. He kissed her so deeply she grew dizzy with it, and then he began to make love to her again.

"SEE," HAWKSHAW TOLD Sandra, drawing her close. He ran his lips along her neck. "I told you it'd be better than ever. And it was." He kissed her shoulder. "It was."

He awoke with a start, disoriented.

The illusion of Sandra's nearness vanished, so did the phantom warmth of her skin. Hawkshaw lay in his rumpled bed, his eyes narrowed against the first rays of sun slitting through the blinds.

He raised himself on his elbow, looking at the tangled sheets. He was alone. But he hadn't been.

He swore to himself and raked a hand through his hair in self-disgust. He fell back against the bed.

On the sheets and on his skin was not the scent of Sandra, but of another woman. He swore again. He had taken Kate Kanaday into his bed last night, and made love to her not once, but twice. Was he insane?

Yes, he damn sure was. Vaguely he remembered Kate rising from the bed, slipping into his bathroom. He'd heard the sound of the shower pattering like spring rain. He'd heard her move softly back into the bedroom.

Then, lightly fragrant with soap, she kissed his mouth. "I have to go back to my own room," she'd whispered. "Thank you."

Thank you. He groaned and rolled over, put the pillow over his head. It smelled like Kate's lemony shampoo, so he flung it away.

Last night, overcome by testosterone, he'd nearly ravished the woman. Why? Bleakly, he remembered Sandra's words: *Find yourself another woman... get involved with someone—anyone,* she had said. *I'm setting you free.*

He sat up, rubbed his unshaven chin. Well, he'd made love, or what passed for it, all right. Had he done it out of spite, despair, or simple lust? He didn't know.

And he knew he wasn't free of Sandra. Sometimes he thought the sort of love he had for her was a disease that ate at the soul, and he would never be cured of it.

So he'd used Kate. And he hoped she had sense enough to understand it and know that she'd used him, as well. He'd been working on a nice, simple life. He didn't want her emotions complicating it.

He would have to tell her that, up front.

He heaved himself out of bed, stalked into the shower,

and twisted on the water, ice-cold and full, sharp blast. He didn't shave, because he didn't want to look like he was going into courting mode.

He pulled on a pair of denim shorts and unearthed a clean T-shirt. He strode barefoot into the kitchen. He snatched up the coffeepot and started to fill it.

Down the hall, he heard the bedroom door open. He fought against wincing. He knew it was Kate; she was an early bird. He didn't allow himself to look up.

"Good morning," she said in a quiet voice. "It's a little cloudy out. Think it'll rain?"

He shrugged, kept busy with the coffee. "It might."

"We're starting to run low on groceries," she said. He heard her move closer, stop on the other side of the counter. "Could we go shopping soon?"

"Yeah, sure," he said, switching on the coffee machine. "Later. After Charlie's up. Right now I guess I'll go out. There's an old boat motor in the shed I might work on."

"Hawkshaw?" she said, and he didn't like the note in her voice. It said, *Let's talk. Let's get personal.* He didn't want to do either.

"I'd like to talk to you for a minute."

This was the moment he had dreaded, of course. He shot her a furtive look and was surprised by two things: how pretty she looked and how she wasn't trying to. Her face was bare of makeup except for a touch of pink lipstick.

He felt a surge of sexual awareness. *Hell,* he thought with a stab of irony, *I might not love her, but I already want her again.*

She gave him a wary look that made him wonder if she might be thinking the same thing about him.

She cleared her throat self-consciously, but she held his gaze. "About last night..." she began.

Hawkshaw groaned inwardly. Some of the world's worst conversations began with those words.

He tried to cut her off. "About last night," he said, "I was wrong to push you the way I did. About your husband. Charlie had implied that you hadn't been happy..."

"You were in a strange mood," she said.

He thought of Sandra. "Yeah. Sorry about that." *Don't ask about it,* he mentally warned.

"I won't ask you about it," she said, surprising him again. She raised her chin. "I guess I made a scene. Crying and all, I mean. It's not my style. I'm sorry."

Hawkshaw was suddenly ashamed of himself. "No," he said with a shake of his head. "I'm sorry. The fault was mine."

He stared, unseeing, at the coffee dripping in the coffeemaker. He crossed his arms. "Everything that happened last night, the fault was mine."

"It was mine, too," she said. "I just want to know one thing."

He nodded curtly, waited.

"This engagement—it's just something you told Charlie, to fend him off?"

"Yeah," he said uncomfortably. "More or less."

"I understand," she said. "I wanted to be sure."

"She left me. She's marrying someone else." He was surprised to hear the words come out of his mouth. Speaking them made their reality seem more final.

He got out two mugs, filled each with coffee. He pushed one across the counter to Kate. He raised his gaze to meet hers, which was both shy and frank.

She put her hand on the mug, clasping it, but she did not lift it. When she spoke, she sounded almost painfully businesslike. "What happened with us then," she said, "happened between two free, consenting adults. We hurt no one."

Unless it was you, he thought. He realized he very much did not want to hurt this woman. But she did not seem hurt. Only tense, yet self-possessed.

"Once," she said, "you told me not to get personal with you. I haven't forgotten. So about last night—" she lifted her mug and clinked it against his "—let's consider what happened not personal. Agreed?"

Hawkshaw stared at her, slightly stunned. He had expected to say that to her, not the other way around. She raised her brows, waiting for his reply.

"Agreed," he said. "Nothing personal."

Together they raised their mugs and drank to it.

KATE SAT ON THE COUCH, sipping her coffee without tasting it and staring at her list without seeing it. She had not felt as cool and in control with Hawkshaw as she'd pretended.

Last night his lovemaking had shaken her. Never had she reacted to a man with such passion; never had she *imagined* such passion.

Back in her own bed, she had lain thinking of him. Her body still tingled from his touch, but her mind was perplexed.

Hawkshaw had been a generous and exciting lover, yet she had sensed a kind of desperation in him. He had said he was not engaged, that there was "no Sandra," that Sandra had left him. He had said this with a resignation that was tinged with both bitterness and futility.

Kate remembered the wedding snapshots and how Hawkshaw stood in the darkness, setting them afire and dropping them one by one into the water. She remembered that Corbett had said something cryptic about Hawkshaw being "completely married."

Sandra had been his wife, and he still wanted her. She was the reason he closed himself off from the world. He had not told Kate this, but she knew. Hawkshaw had taken her to bed because his body had wanted gratification, but his emotions could find none.

Kate had known as soon as she'd seen his face this morning: he regretted what had happened between them, and he feared she would make a claim on him. Intense physical hunger was one thing, and he had yielded to it. An emotional relationship was another thing, and he was incapable of it.

So be it. But she knew the physical hunger was still there for both of them. She had promised herself not to fall in love with him. She hadn't promised not to sleep with him again.

It would happen, she knew. And so did he.

CORBETT CALLED at ten o'clock. He told Kate that facts were beginning to dribble in about Kyle Johnson, but slowly.

"He was the classic quiet loner, Kate. He lived mostly on a disability allowance—had a history of schizophrenic episodes. Worked off and on at various jobs in electronics."

Kate's heartbeat took an excited skip. "Electronics?"

"Worked at a number of places. Midwest Electronics, Dover Repair, Radio Hut—the list goes on."

"That's promising, isn't it?" Kate asked. "He'd be the sort who'd know how to tap into a phone. Or even a computer. Wouldn't he?"

"He might," Corbett said, but he didn't sound convinced. "He was a bright guy. Moved to Columbia about four years ago. Changed places frequently. Didn't make friends. Didn't leave much of a trail. The puzzle's missing a lot of pieces. We don't know where he was living at the end.''

"Still, he sounds likely," Kate said, hope rising. "The only question would be, 'Why me?' Why would he fixate on me?"

"Why not?" Corbett said. "Who knows what goes on in these guys' heads? And we don't even know if he's our man. You're still sure you don't recognize his picture?"

Kate thought of the picture of the man with the glasses and prim mouth. The image gave her a small, creepy shudder. "No. I'm sorry."

"Lately he'd been getting his mail delivered to a post office box. We don't know where he was staying before he was arrested. We don't know if he had anything that relates to you—pictures, tapes, computer files. We just don't know."

"You'll find it soon—I know you will."

"Maybe, Kate. In the meantime, I'm still checking other possibilities."

"What other possibilities?" she demanded. "You keep saying that, but you're never specific. I want to know."

But Corbett stayed vague and changed the subject. "How's Hawkshaw treating you?"

She thought of how erotically Hawkshaw had treated her, and she blushed. "Fine," she said. Then she added, "But I'm ready to get out of here."

He laughed. "A lot of women in Washington would have loved to be where you are now. Try to enjoy it. He's a lovely guy when you really know him."

Kate could think of many words to describe Hawkshaw, but "lovely" wasn't one of them.

"Anything you need from me?" asked Corbett.

She thought of Maybelline resignedly gnawing at her haunch. "The dog's hip is acting up. She needs a cortisone shot and she needs it soon. I'll have to have a copy of her records and X rays from the vet. Could you have him send them to me?"

"I'll pick them up and send them myself. I'm still not giving anyone your address. Today's Sunday. I'll send them by express tomorrow," he promised.

"I'd appreciate it. And so would Maybelline."

"Hawkshaw said he wanted to talk to me," Corbett told her. "Put him on, will you?"

"Just a second."

She set the phone aside and went to the kitchen door. Charlie and Hawkshaw were stretched out in two ancient lawn chairs, and Hawkshaw was pointing out something in a comic.

"Hawkshaw," she called. "You wanted to talk to Corbett?"

He uncoiled himself from the chair and came loping up the stairs. He gave her an unreadable look. "I'd like this to be private."

She stiffened in apprehension. "What I told you last night, that's not to be repeated."

"Corbett should know," he said.

"No. He doesn't need—" she began, but he cut her off.

"He should know," he repeated.

She glared resentfully. "I won't talk to him about it," she said. "That's final."

He ignored both the glare and the statement, held the door open for her to go outside. Reluctantly she went out into the bright sunlight.

Charlie was frowning in concentration over the comic book. She gazed down at him.

He was turning brown as a berry, she thought, and the sun was bleaching light streaks in his dark hair. He looked healthier and more relaxed than she could ever remember.

She sighed and thought of Hawkshaw telling Corbett about her husband's sexual problems. She felt the guilt of betraying Chuck's deepest secret.

It was true their sex life had not been satisfying, and finally had become nonexistent. But she had one wonderful gift from it—Charlie. She watched the breeze ruffle his hair, and her heart filled with a poignant love for the boy.

"I CAN'T BELIEVE she didn't tell me," Corbett said irritably.

"She didn't want to talk about it. Didn't want 'to speak ill of the dead.' She's on a guilt trip about it."

"Guilt," Corbett grumbled. "She keeps things too locked up inside her. She's like you."

Hawkshaw ignored the comparison. "It raises some questions. Did he have reason to be jealous? She swears he didn't."

"I believe her," Corbett said. "But what her husband *thought* is something else. Could he have accused somebody, put the idea into their mind? Planted it?"

Hawkshaw had wondered the same thing himself. "Stranger things have happened," he said. "But she doesn't want to talk anymore about it. She's emphatic on that point."

"Then make her change her mind," Corbett said. "Find out what you can. I'll tell you something, Hawkshaw, I don't like the feel of this Johnson thing. He sounds crazy enough. But there's just not enough to prove he's the one.''

''Then Kate's question is a good one. If it wasn't him, why'd he burn her place?''

''They're checking. Maybe we'll know soon. Let's hope so.''

''Yeah,'' said Hawkshaw. ''Let's hope.''

''Take good care of her,'' Corbett said. ''And the boy. I know you will.''

Hawkshaw flinched. Bedding the woman he was guarding was a betrayal of the code he'd once lived to serve. Did it make any difference now? These days he felt a strange hollowness where his honor used to be.

CHAPTER TWELVE

KATE TRIED TO KEEP from thinking by working. She took down the living room curtains and loaded them in the ancient, clattering washer. Then she was ready to pit her strength against the clutter in the guest bedroom. She knew it was Sunday, a day of rest, but she wanted activity.

The bedroom could keep her busy for hours, even days. Hawkshaw's father had stacks of old newspapers and magazines, boxes full of moldering clothes and corroded tools and mismatched crockery.

She found boxes of canceled checks that went back for thirty years. There were several decades' worth of mildewing tax forms and warranties for appliances that must have been consigned to the junk heap years ago.

By early afternoon, she was ready to take on the big closet, which was stuffed with clutter. But Charlie came for her, grabbing her hand, pretending to try to drag her from the room. It was time for the kayaks again.

"Just a minute, Charlie," she told him, "let me clean up. I'm all dusty. Run outside. I'll be right there."

When she came into the living room, Hawkshaw stood as if waiting for her. "Charlie's been running at top speed today," he said. "I haven't had much chance to talk to you since Corbett called. He wants to know more about your husband's jealousy. Will you talk about it?"

"I wish you hadn't said anything to him," she said shortly. "I didn't want you to. You knew that."

Hawkshaw rubbed his unshaven jaw. "He's right. It could have bearing on your case. And that affects not only you, but Charlie."

"I don't see how," she said miserably. "It was something that was just between us."

"Nobody else knew about it?"

To Kate's dismay, she felt fresh tears of guilt and sadness welling in her eyes. She blinked them back furiously. She didn't want to look at Hawkshaw, so she gazed out the screen door at Charlie, who played beside the kayaks.

Hawkshaw persisted. "He told nobody?"

"No. He was—ashamed. He hated talking about it. I hate it, too."

"So you never told anyone, either?"

She felt a wave of self-disgust. "Not until last night. And I shouldn't have."

His voice became unexpectedly gentle. "I'm glad you did."

She said nothing. She bit her lip and watched Charlie. He sat in the kayak on dry land, pretending to paddle. He wore Hawkshaw's black Aussie hat.

Hawkshaw said, "You shouldn't have had to keep the truth to yourself. It's cost you."

She shot him a look of rebuke. "You, of all people, ought to understand the need for privacy. We all have our secrets, Hawkshaw."

"Yeah," he drawled. "We do."

She let her eyes rove back to Charlie playing beside the tidal river.

"We'll discuss this again," Hawkshaw said.

She didn't answer. She stared at the river. Beyond

where her son played, the channels stretched out like watery paths leading into the heart of a great, living maze.

CHARLIE COULD FIND his way to the island now.

That he could learn such a thing pleased and amazed her. Letters and numbers might confound him, but he was learning to read the difficult book of the backcountry's waterways.

She did not think she could master the task herself. The forking streams and the overwhelming sameness of the mangrove tunnels would always confuse her. Charlie's accomplishment filled her with happy pride.

But when they returned to the house, a new crisis arose, and Kate's fragile sense of joy vanished. They were getting ready to go into Key West to shop, when it happened. Maybelline disappeared.

Kate, inside, was putting in a last load of laundry before they left. Charlie was engrossed in stealing a few minutes to fish from the dock.

Hawkshaw was stowing the life jackets and paddles in the shed when Kate came running down the deck's back stairs. She seized Charlie by the shoulders.

"Charlie—did you let Maybelline outside?"

The boy was clearly startled. "No," he said. "I thought she was in the house."

"She was," Kate said. "But the front door was ajar, and she's gone. I thought maybe she was with you, but when I didn't see her—"

"I didn't open the door," Charlie protested. "I wasn't near it."

Kate looked about, a frantic expression on her face. "Didn't I close the screen door tight enough? Oh, God."

Charlie looked stricken. He began to whistle for Maybelline, and Kate called. But the dog did not come. There was no sign of her.

Hawkshaw closed the shed's door, snapped shut the padlock. Charlie had dropped the Cuban reel, and Hawkshaw went to the boy's side, picked up the reel and began swiftly to wind the line.

"Hawkshaw," Charlie said, "Mama left the screen door open. And Maybelline's *gone*. I didn't do it—honest."

Hawkshaw figured that Kate didn't need to take any more blame on herself. "I might have left it open myself," he said. "It doesn't matter. The important thing is to find her."

"But how?" Charlie pleaded. He looked around in despair. Except for the river side, the yard was hemmed in by growth that seemed impenetrable.

Hawkshaw knew that there were things in those forested depths that would find a basset hound tasty. Alligators, for instance. There were still a few good-sized ones around Cobia.

"What if she falls in the water and a shark eats her?" Charlie cried.

Kate's face paled.

"That's not too likely," Hawkshaw said, although sharks could haunt the saltwater channels. And barracudas were said to be particularly fond of dog.

He put his hand on the boy's shoulder to calm him. "She probably sniffed out a rabbit, that's all. Bassett hounds have good noses. They were bred to catch rabbits, weren't they?"

"I don't know," Charlie said in a small voice.

"Yes." Kate nodded. Her voice sounded calm although her face was strained. "Rabbits and—and deer."

"See?" Hawkshaw said, giving Charlie an encouraging

pat on the back. "She probably picked up the scent of a marsh rabbit or one of the Key deer."

But Charlie was not comforted. "What if she gets lost? And can't find her way back? She'll starve—or a snake'll bite her. And she'll die."

"She'll find her way back," Hawkshaw assured him. "She's got a good nose. I told you."

But his heart was sinking. He knew they weren't getting into the car and heading for Key West and leaving the dog loose. He could tell by the quaver in Charlie's voice and the worry in Kate's dark eyes.

Maybelline, he thought hopelessly, *why can't you be good?*

He held back a sigh, but he made his tone confident, even hearty. "We'll look for her," he said. "There's a freshwater spring back in the woods. And paths that go to it. That's probably where she headed."

Kate looked nervous about going among the shadowy trees, so thick with vines and scrub. But Charlie brightened. "You really think she just followed a deer or rabbit?"

"Sure," Hawkshaw said. "We'll find her in no time."

Hawkshaw wasn't really sure what in hell a city dog like Maybelline might chase. In truth, marsh rabbits were rare and so were the Key deer, which were mostly nocturnal. And it did not take "no time" to find the basset hound. It took well over an hour.

Her heavy, low-slung body left a trail that was not difficult for Hawkshaw to read. But it was a complex trail, frequently doubling back upon itself, then heading off abruptly in a strange direction. Charlie got tired of tripping through the vines and low-hanging branches. Hawkshaw knew that either the three of them would have to turn back in failure or he would have to carry the boy. He carried him.

Kate stumbled sometimes in the overgrowth. She fought her way through the tangled copses. Miserably she slapped at mosquitoes, but she kept up with Hawkshaw and never uttered a word of complaint, not one.

At last, well past the spring, as they neared a small bay, Hawkshaw thought he heard a dog's growl. He stopped and listened. Charlie tensed in his arms and stared into the thick growth. Beside him Kate stopped, wiping back a loose strand of hair from her face.

He heard it again, almost drowned in the sighing rush of the water: a dog's low growl, then a bark.

"Come on," he said to Kate. "We've found her."

He made his way to the water's edge, trying to keep Charlie shielded from grasping vines and slapping branches. Kate struggled gamely behind him.

At last the trees opened to where the river flowed into the bay. "Maybelline!" Charlie cried happily.

Maybelline was a few yards upstream from them. She stood on the trunk of a dead tree that had fallen half on shore, half over the water. She was hunkered down, growling and trying to crawl farther out.

"Oh, good grief," Kate said, clutching at Hawkshaw's elbow. "What's she got there? What *is* it?"

The dog had backed an animal out on the fallen log, Hawkshaw saw, but it was merely a large pack rat, which looked more dangerous than it really was. The pack rat had something glittering in its jaws, some treasure it must have stolen for its nest.

"A pack rat," he said in disgust.

"A rat?" Kate echoed, horrified.

"It's not a real rat," Hawkshaw said. "They just call it that."

"Here, Maybelline," cried Charlie. "Here, girl!"

But Maybelline ignored him. Instead she snarled and feinted at the pack rat, which danced, skittering out to the far end of the broken tree trunk. The smaller animal was well over the water, and Maybelline, if she slipped, would plunge in.

"She'll fall," Charlie quavered. He tried to call her again. "Maybelline—come *here!*"

Instead the dog took another unsteady step toward the cringing pack rat. The pack rat scrambled to hang on to the end of the broken tree trunk. Its silvery plunder still gleamed from its jaws as its hind feet began to slip from beneath it.

"Here," Hawkshaw said, thrusting Charlie into Kate's arms. If he moved quickly and surely, he could still reach the dog by snatching at her from the shore. He ran, vaulting over a fallen limb draped with briers.

Maybelline feinted again toward the pack rat. Just at that moment, Hawkshaw lunged for her, seizing her collar. The rat sprang away and plummeted into the current.

Hawkshaw swayed for a second—the dog weighed a good sixty pounds. At first she was too shocked to react, then she began to struggle. But Hawkshaw regained his balance and imprisoned her against his chest. He started to carry her back to Kate, who had the leash.

"The rat!" Charlie said excitedly, for the pack rat was swimming past Kate and the boy now, paddling desperately with the current.

A light splash broke the waves, along with a sudden surge of mud from the bottom. Then there was only half a pack rat in the water. Its tail, its hindquarters were gone. Dark blood bloomed around it like a flower.

Kate screamed and hugged Charlie more tightly. Hawkshaw swore.

What was left of the pack rat's body went limp. Its bright little treasure dropped from its jaws and disappeared in the depths. The current bore the little animal's remains away.

"Wow," Charlie said, staring after it, half frightened, half mesmerized.

"Oh, my God," Kate said, turning her face away. "What *was* it?"

"Barracuda," Hawkshaw said tonelessly.

"It could have got Maybelline," she said, her voice shaking. "If you'd slipped, it could have got *you*."

"Naw," he said. "Not me. They don't attack humans that often."

"Maybelline," Charlie said, his eyes wide, "you almost got ate by a barracuda."

Maybelline whined and wrenched to escape, but Hawkshaw held her fast. He hardly noticed the dog's weight. He stared at Kate, who was struggling not to show Charlie how appalled she'd been by the barracuda's attack.

"It was so fast," she whispered.

"Yes," Hawkshaw said. "They're fast. They usually strike once, and that's it."

"The pack rat—it was carrying something," Charlie said. "What?"

"I don't know," Hawkshaw said. "They collect shiny things. It's their way. Maybe that's what the 'cuda saw. They're attracted to bright things in the water."

Kate said, "The poor thing. The poor thing."

"There are predators. There's prey. That's the way it is," he said.

She flinched slightly. He wished he could take his words back. She understood too well what it meant to be prey.

THEY TOOK MAYBELLINE back, locked her safely in the house. They went to the outskirts of Key West to grocery shop and to pick up a few extra clothes and a pair of beach thongs for Charlie. Kate was glad for the distraction.

She was glad again, after dinner, when Aggie called and asked if she and Ozzie could come by and bring a sweet potato pie.

When they arrived, Ozzie immediately noticed the dismantled motor on the dock, and wanted to look at it. Hawkshaw said he could use the advice. As dusk approached, the men and Charlie squatted on the dock, deep in the discussion of mechanical mysteries.

Aggie joined Kate at the counter for a glass of iced tea. Aggie cast an approving gaze around the kitchen and living room. "You've cleaned this place up spick and span," she said. "I wouldn't have thought it could be done."

"All it took was a forklift and three cubic acres of elbow grease," joked Kate.

Aggie shook her head. "I won't argue with that. Hawkshaw's come down with a bad case of Keys Disease."

"Keys Disease? What's that?"

"Letting things just drift along. It can happen down here." She shook her head again. "I watched it happen with his father. This place went further and further downhill. I offered to help. I wanted to. Harry—Hawkshaw's father—he wouldn't take help. Not that way."

A fleeting look of unhappiness passed over Aggie's face.

"It's too bad," Kate said. "It could be a pretty little house."

"It was once," said Aggie. "But two alone, man and

boy, they never took to keeping up the place. Then, in the last years, things went from bad to worse.''

Kate's curiosity got the best of her. ''The two of them alone? Hawkshaw said his mother was alive—she left them?''

''Umm,'' Aggie said noncommittally, but she gave the barest of nods. She took a sip of tea.

Kate thought she'd blundered and wished she hadn't asked. But Aggie seemed to gaze far off, as if she could see a long-gone time. Then she spoke.

''She left *him* first, when they lived in Orlando. Her husband, I mean, Harry. She took the boy. Harry moved back here. It was where his people was from. Then she met another man, and he didn't want the boy, so she brought him here. She dropped him off and never looked back. I never understood how a woman could do that.''

Kate didn't either. She would let her heart be torn out before she would abandon Charlie.

''She was beautiful,'' Aggie said, as if that explained everything. ''She was very beautiful.''

She turned to face Kate. She gave her a crooked, half-pensive smile. ''But the memories aren't all bad. Dwight hung out over here. He was three years younger than Hawkshaw, and he idolized him. Hawkshaw, sometimes when his daddy was in the hospital, he stayed at our house. He was quiet, but he was like a big brother to my boys. He was good to the little ones, even. Always patient. We had some good times, we did.''

''Good grief,'' Kate said, ''you played mother hen to *seven* boys?''

''I enjoyed it,'' Aggie said simply. She looked at her work-roughened hands. ''He wasn't no trouble. Like I say, he was a quiet boy. He thought more than most. And he felt more than he let on.''

She smiled a crooked smile. "And don't think I was no saint, taking on all those kids. I've had me a good life. Some people might think not having children of my own, I got only the hard work and none of the joy. But that's not true. I've had a fine, fine life. Fuller than most."

She stroked the polished countertop. "I wish Hawkshaw would keep this place. But the other night he told Dwight he intends to move on. Buy a *boat*," she said with a fillip of gentle mockery. "Sail off to *Mexico*."

"Yes," Kate said, pouring more tea into Aggie's glass. "That's what he told Charlie."

"It won't work," Aggie said.

"What won't work?"

"He won't outrun what bedevils him," Aggie said. "Like father, like son." She gave Kate a long look. "There's some men, you know, they only let themselves love once in a lifetime. It's almost like they're punishing themselves."

"I suppose there are," Kate said lightly. "Well, it takes all kinds to make a world, doesn't it?"

But suddenly, she realized that Aggie understood she was attracted to Hawkshaw and that she was giving her a warning that was kindly but clear: *Some men...only let themselves love once.*

AFTER AGGIE AND OZZIE left, Kate stayed alone in the living room, working on her insurance list. Hawkshaw and Charlie sat out on the deck at the picnic table, drawing pictures and talking by the light of the citronella torches.

Eight o'clock came, and Corbett still had not called. Kate told Charlie it was bedtime, conscious that bedtime would mean she and Hawkshaw would again be alone together.

Charlie was tired but keyed up; once in bed, he took a long time to get to sleep. Kate was almost grateful. But at last his small body was motionless, his breathing even.

She rose and went into the living room. It was empty, only one lamp burning.

"Come out on the deck," said Hawkshaw's voice.

Now, she thought, *what do I say to him?* She had thanked him repeatedly for saving Maybelline, and she knew he wanted to hear no more about it. She feared what he would want to discuss.

But she straightened her back, opened the door, and slipped outside. Hawkshaw had extinguished all the torches but the one at the far end of the deck. The breeze carried its strong, lemony scent.

He stood in the shadows at the deck's other corner, one bare foot on the railing. His silhouette sharp against the star-bright sky.

The dusk's last light shimmered on the water's surface. Kate heard the whisper of the salt tide. Somewhere a night bird cried, the echo trembling on the air.

"Night heron," Hawkshaw said, almost absently. "Wish Charlie could see one."

The evening was warm, but she crossed her arms as if she were chilled. "Corbett didn't call," she said, knowing Hawkshaw would mention it if she did not.

He stared off at the dark profile of the mangroves. "It's not like him," he said.

She leaned against the door frame. "Maybe he changed his mind. Maybe he decided it wasn't important."

"He doesn't change his mind about things like that," said Hawkshaw.

She said nothing. The night heron shrilled again, and she hugged herself more tightly. Hawkshaw turned to her. She couldn't see his face clearly.

He, too, was silent for a moment. They both seemed to be waiting for something, she was not sure what.

At last he said, "He wants you to talk to me. About your husband."

She shook her head and stared down at the deck's shadowy floor. "You're not the easiest person in the world to talk to, you know?"

"So I've been told," he said. He turned to her. "But why don't you be brave and try?"

There was sarcasm in his voice, but a strange, harsh intimacy, as well. When she didn't answer, he moved away from the railing and came to her side. She found she was holding her breath.

Slowly he raised his hand and touched her arm. His fingers closed around her wrist lightly, with surprising gentleness. "Kate," he said.

Her heart bounded like a startled animal. "I'm sorry," she said. "It's just very hard for me to talk about."

His thumb stroked the inside of her wrist, up and down, over the racing pulse. "Tell me why."

She shook her head helplessly. "He's Charlie's father. He was my husband."

"He'd want you safe. Not running. I'm supposed to take care of you."

His thumb stopped stroking her wrist, but it rested where the vein jumped.

She closed her eyes. "Not like this," she said. "Not this way."

Quickly she drew away from him, walked to the far end of the deck. The torch flared like a small, fiery flag on the night. She rubbed her arm where his hand had rested and stared into the darkness.

"If not for your sake," Hawkshaw said, "for Charlie's. Your husband can't be hurt anymore. Charlie can."

She listened to the rush and ripple of the water. Moon-light glittered on its surface, and she raised her eyes to the moon, which had barely started to wane.

"All right, Hawkshaw," she said. "What do you want to know?"

"You say your husband wouldn't tell anyone about this problem between you. But if he *had* wanted advice, where would he have gone? If he was going to talk to somebody, who would it be?"

Kate shook her head stubbornly. "Nowhere. No one."

"Some people would see a priest or minister or rabbi. Would he? Is there any possibility?"

"None. Chuck wasn't religious."

"What about the family doctor? That would be a log-ical choice."

"No," she said. "I asked him to. He wouldn't. He refused. Absolutely."

"A family member? Would he have told anyone in his family?"

"No. He wasn't that close to anyone except his brother, Trevor. And Trevor had his own problems. Chuck wouldn't have added his own."

She sensed that Hawkshaw had moved behind her, that he was close to her again. But he didn't reach for her, and she was glad.

"What about work?" he asked. "Did he have any spe-cial friends at work, any colleague he trusted?"

"No," she said. "Chuck didn't make friends easily. And he didn't believe in palling around with the people he worked with."

"How about his department head? Could he have seen him as a father figure, gone to him in a crisis?"

"Dr. Barnard," she said with spirit, "was not a father

figure. He was cold as a robot. He didn't like emotions. Only computers.''

''I don't suppose,'' Hawkshaw said, ''your husband ever got close to any of his students.''

''You suppose correctly.'' She sighed. ''He considered it bad form to fraternize with students.''

Hawkshaw fell silent a few minutes. ''How about a shrink?'' he asked finally. ''A psychiatrist?''

''No,'' she said. ''I asked him that, too. He wouldn't.''

''You're sure?''

''As sure as I can be.''

She heard Hawkshaw sigh harshly. ''If he was going to go to somebody—anybody in all those people I mentioned—who would it have been?''

She put her hand to her forehead, ran her fingers through her bangs. ''I don't know. The doctor, maybe. Or a psychiatrist. He was a scientist. If he wanted help, he'd turn to a fellow scientist.''

''But he didn't. Not that you know of.''

''No. I've told you that from the start.''

''Still, it's *possible* that he saw someone without your knowledge.''

''Yes,'' she said, starting to feel dazed by the barrage of questions. ''It's possible.''

''But you looked through his papers, his bills, his checkbook. You found no evidence such a thing had happened.''

''No. None.''

''Nothing in his papers at the university, either.''

''No. Oh, stop it, please, Hawkshaw. Can't we drop it?''

She closed her eyes and put her hand over them. In her mind's eye, the little waves still twinkled, so happy, so mocking.

"Kate, you had to talk. We had to know. Even if it leads nowhere."

"I feel like I've failed him again."

"You haven't failed him. Your loyalties were split, that's all. And what do you mean, 'again'?"

"Something terrible was happening to him. I didn't understand."

"He couldn't understand it himself, Kate. How could you? You can't blame yourself."

"I can and I do," she said. "You don't know what it's like. To feel you've betrayed someone you could have helped. Someone it was your duty to help."

"Yes," he said. "I know."

You can't know, she thought bitterly.

He said, "It feels like hell."

His breath warmed her ear, feathered the nape of her neck. She kept her eyes shut and fought to suppress a shudder. "How?" she whispered. "How can you know?"

"I just do."

"That's not a real answer," she said.

"It's enough if you'll let it be."

"No," she said. "That's not fair."

"Kate…" His hand closed around her upper arm, and he gently forced her to turn to him.

"No," she repeated. "Why should I be the one to tell all my secrets?"

"Shhh," he soothed. "You had to. You know it. I know it."

His other hand traveled to her face. His thumb and forefinger framed her jaw, and he tilted her face to his. This time she shuddered.

"You shouldn't touch me like that," she said.

"Someone should," he said.

"No. No."

"Yes." She heard him draw in a breath. "Look at me."

Her eyes fluttered open. His face was burnished by the dancing gold of the torch, and the shadows under his cheekbones were deep.

His mouth descended on hers with an inevitability she found bittersweet.

CHAPTER THIRTEEN

THEY'D MADE LOVE, and she had slept in his arms, her naked body warm and silky against his. Now she was gone.

He had awakened alone and lay staring at the ceiling. He missed the touch of her more than he would have thought.

For a time, she had made him forget the past, the future. The universe had condensed into this darkened room, this bed, their pulsing bodies.

He remembered, and his heart gave a peculiar tug in his chest. She was giving and sweet in bed, and she had made him ache with wanting her.

She had been almost shy with him at first, but he'd kissed and stroked away the shyness, turning it into a hungry abandon that matched his own. Sex had become a kind of wild music playing through them. It built, driving more and more frantically. It flowed into complex sensual harmonies of mouths and lips and hands. It had possessed them.

He smiled at the irony of it; he and Kate were good together. Very good. But in a different way from Sandra. He and Kate were more natural, more primally attuned.

But it was Sandra that haunted him. He wondered if she'd made love to the man who was to be her new husband. Was the sex good between them? Did it turn into music?

I never want you to touch me again, she'd told him. He'd asked for her forgiveness; in the end, he'd begged for it. *What you've done is unforgivable,* she'd said.

Once he'd loved two things in the world, but they'd been incompatible: Sandra and his job. She'd had her own career; and it sometimes kept her on the road. He, too, had to be away, sometimes for weeks at a stretch. He'd thought they'd work it out.

But his job was the more demanding of the two, and she grew to hate it when she wasn't working, which was often. He traveled too much, she said. His hours were lousy and unpredictable, she said.

When another agent came down with flu, Hawkshaw was assigned at the last minute to go with the Vice President to Scotland. He'd been supposed to take Sandra to Martha's Vineyard for two weeks. She'd been angry, even jealous, when he had to go abroad.

But Hawkshaw had reasoned that she could go to the Vineyard without him. After all, she could still take her half sister.

Sandra's half sister, Daisy, came to stay with them for a few weeks each summer. Daisy was nineteen, but she had the mind of a six-year-old. A sweet kid, she could be hard to handle, but Hawkshaw never had trouble with her.

Sandra had resented taking on Daisy alone. Hawkshaw told her he'd be home in only a week and that the trip meant a lot to Daisy. He'd thought he was being kind.

The two women were at an inn on the island. Daisy had wanted to take out one of the inn's bicycles and ride by herself. Sandra had warned her not to. But Sandra got caught up in a conversation by the pool. Daisy stole away, took one of the forbidden bicycles. There was an accident, right on the cobbled street in front of the inn.

Daisy died. Sandra, hysterical, blamed him for not being there. And he blamed himself.

He, after all, was the expert in protecting people. If
he'd been there, Daisy would never have slipped away
undetected. Even if she had, he might have saved her.
He'd had emergency training; he might have stopped the
bleeding.

Sandra couldn't. She'd run to the street when she heard
the squeal of brakes, the clash of metal. Helpless, she'd
seen Daisy die before her eyes. While Hawkshaw was in
Scotland. Watching the goddamn Vice President play
goddamn golf.

Sandra had hated him for this, and Hawkshaw had
hated himself. He was supposed to be one of the best
qualified guardians in the world, but he had failed his own
family. Daisy was dead, Sandra had left him, and he
couldn't say he blamed her.

His friend Dwight heard the news and had come up to
D.C. to try to comfort him, but Hawkshaw wouldn't be
comforted. He'd gotten stinking drunk and thrown his
damned Medal of Valor into the Potomac.

Somehow, he'd gone on to finish his last year in the
Service. And then he'd come here. And he remembered.
And remembered. He had to stop remembering so much.
But when he'd burned the wedding snapshots the other
night, he hadn't been able to burn those with Daisy in
them. Not loving, innocent Daisy. Not that he needed
photos of her. Her image was forever burnt into his heart.

He rose and pulled on his clothes, made his way
through the darkness to the front deck. The last citronella
torch still burned in the holder's socket, growing weaker
and more unsteady.

He listened to the whisper and rush of the water, and
he thought of taking Kate Kanaday into his bed. He would

sleep with her again. He would do it as long as she stayed and as long as she was willing.

Wasn't it what Sandra had told him to do, to sleep with the first woman he found? Would Sandra be pleased by such a turn of events? Or jealous? Would she give a tinker's damn either way? Probably not.

He was on the rebound; so was Kate, in her way. They'd both gone without the physical act of love for too long. He was wary of relationships and so was she.

This affair was oddly satisfying. It was pragmatic. He needed it, she needed it. It meant nothing. It had arisen from nothing, and when she left, it would subside into nothing again.

He frowned, wondering why Corbett hadn't called. When Corbett said he was going to do a thing, he did it. Hawkshaw wondered what had come up. Perhaps, at last, there had been a break in Kate's case.

He hoped so. She deserved it.

And he hoped, after she was gone, that she would find someone. She was a woman who seemed formed for loving, in body and spirit. He would miss her—a bit. And he wished her well.

KATE SLEPT LATE, for once, and awoke only moments before Charlie. She helped him dress and made him wash his face and brush his teeth and comb his hair.

He fidgeted, but she insisted he sit at the kitchen counter long enough to eat half a bowl of cereal, drink most of a glass of orange juice. Then he ran outside, banging the door behind him, to join Hawkshaw. Hawkshaw was already out on the dock, working on the boat motor. He was hunkered over the oily parts, which were neatly arranged and glittered in the sunlight. He looked fit and masculine and starkly handsome.

He greeted Charlie and ruffled his hair. Kate's throat constricted a bit with emotion. He was so good with Charlie, and Charlie loved him. Hawkshaw could be an eminently lovable man if he would only allow it. *She* could love him, if circumstances were different.

Love him? The thought astonished and appalled her. She rebuked herself for entertaining it, even for an instant. Circumstances were *not* different.

She heard Hawkshaw ask Charlie, "Is your mother up yet?"

"Yeah," Charlie said with disgust. "She's going to start cleaning the house again. Why does she do that all the time?"

Hawkshaw shrugged. She did not hear his answer. He did not so much as glance in the direction of the house.

And why should he? Kate thought, resenting her vague disappointment. Did she hope he would look this way in the romantic hope of catching sight of her? Did she think he would be yearning and moping for her?

She squared her shoulders and began to clean up Charlie's breakfast dishes. She and Hawkshaw had a makeshift work agreement. He provided temporary shelter. She provided the handy dandy home cleanup service.

Sex had entered into it because they were both adults, and they both wanted it and needed it. She was recovering from a disastrous marriage and a stalker. He was clearly still in love with his ex-wife.

They might be sleeping together, but there was no need to announce this to Charlie or for them to act as if the relationship was a love affair. It was not, and it would not become one.

Yet it was not that easy for Kate to separate emotion from sex. For her to be in Hawkshaw's arms at night, and in the daytime to pretend that nothing existed between them—this seemed hypocritical and confusing.

It was confusing because the sex didn't *seem* to be without attachment or emotion. When she and Hawkshaw were together that way, it seemed as if they were not merely having sex, they were making love.

He was gentle, yet exciting, and he made the act both wild and beautiful. She had been a wife for years, but it was as if she had never made love at all until she had done so with Hawkshaw.

She bit at her lower lip and furiously wiped the dishes dry. She set them back in the cupboard with a businesslike efficiency. But her mind whirled with contradictions.

She was marching down the hall, when the phone rang. She stopped, stiffening in apprehension. *Corbett,* she thought. *He'll want to know about Chuck.*

Her stomach pitched a bit sickly. She supposed the way she felt about Hawkshaw's lovemaking was yet another betrayal of Chuck. She turned, no longer understanding the Gordian knot of her own emotions.

Hawkshaw came up the stairs and through the door with his usual uncanny speed. He snatched up the receiver.

"Yes?" he said. "Yes, she did. Nothing. Nobody. She said maybe a doctor, maybe a psychiatrist. No. I'll ask."

Kate watched him uneasily. He was dressed in battered-looking shorts and running shoes, and his white T-shirt had a grease stain on the front. But he looked somehow official, and he looked in charge.

He threw a sharp glance in Kate's direction. "No," he said. "I'll tell her. Yeah. I'm sorry, too."

He hung up. From his face and from the coiled nervous energy in his stance, she knew there was trouble.

"Corbett?" she asked nervously.

He nodded, his eyes on hers. He said, ''Bad news, Kate. Johnson wasn't the man. He was in Peoria the first six months you were being stalked. He couldn't have been near you.''

She was stunned. ''But—but then why did he burn my place?''

''The police located his brother. He told them Johnson had a vendetta against a guy who used to own the townhouse across the street. He must have gotten the wrong address, that's all.''

''A mistake? He burned our home by *mistake?*''

''Johnson wasn't rational. The brother said they weren't close. He said Kyle imagined he'd been wronged by the owner of the townhouse. But the brother didn't want to get involved. He's got troubles of his own.''

She looked at him questioningly.

''The brother's deaf. He lives on disability payments, too. He'd been on a bus trip when Johnson got in trouble. He knew about none of it.''

''If it wasn't Johnson—'' Kate swallowed hard ''—then who's after me?''

''We still don't know. But Corbett thinks he may have a lead. He didn't say any more, doesn't want to raise false hopes. But he's got one. That's something.''

She could not speak.

''Kate,'' he said, ''are you all right?''

She was in shock, but her pride still functioned.

''I'm fine,'' she lied. ''I guess I'll be going to Denver after all. Well, it was the original plan, anyway. The mountains will be nice. Charlie will like the mountains.''

She wished he'd come to her, hold her in his arms. He only stood watching her, his face somber. *Of course, he wouldn't touch me in the light of day,* she thought. When they touched it was only under the cover of darkness.

"Denver's supposed to be a great city," she said, raising her chin. "And I'm ready to get on with my life. When's Corbett calling back? I need to tell him I want to move on."

Move on, she thought numbly. *That's it. Just move on.*

"I'll finish this back bedroom," she said with an air of finality. "Then I'll make arrangements. I can pack tonight, get a flight out of here tomorrow morning."

"Talk to Corbett first. He's calling back tonight," Hawkshaw said. "He won't want you leaving that soon. You can bank on it. You shouldn't try to make a decision like that right now. You're upset."

"I'm not upset," she insisted, keeping her voice steady. "Johnson's not the stalker. You both told me he might not be. I was prepared."

This was not the truth. She'd prayed that Johnson would be the one; she'd pinned all her slender hopes on it.

Now she felt sick with the old uncertainty. But she knew that feeling sorry for herself would only weaken her and give the stalker still more power over her.

She shrugged philosophically, then frowned. "Corbett should have told me himself. I could have talked this over with him."

"He offered to tell you. I said I would."

"You don't have to cushion me from the facts," she said. "I'm a big girl."

"I'm sorry," he said without emotion.

"You don't have to protect me."

"Yes," he said, "I do. That's why you're here."

"Well," she said with false lightness, "I won't be here much longer."

"We'll see about that," he said cryptically.

Outside, Charlie called for him. "Hawkshaw! Hawkshaw! Come see what I can do!"

He gave her a cool look, then pushed open the door and disappeared outside.

Her heart hammered in her chest. *Why? Why?* It banged out the same insistent question about the stalker, about Hawkshaw, about her life. *Why is this happening? Why?*

But she had no answer.

CHARLIE WAS LEARNING to read! He could not wait to show Hawkshaw. Letters were no longer frustrating squiggles on a page—they talked to him.

Charlie felt dizzy with triumph. He was like an explorer who has been long in the wilderness and now has discovered a fabled lost city.

"Look!" he told Hawkshaw, who'd squatted beside him on the dock. He pointed at the speech in a comic balloon.

"'Jim, you be the lookout,'" Charlie read, pronouncing each word emphatically, "'and keep that gun—re-re-re—'"

"Ready," coached Hawkshaw.

"Ready," Charlie said with relish. "Then Sergeant Steelarm says, 'Do you see what I see? Tracks! I got a feeling this is a trap.'"

Charlie took a deep breath, his chest tight with excitement. "And it *is* a trap. The ambush starts. All these words are about the gunfire—'Pow! Bang! Bratta-bratta-bratta!'"

Hawkshaw gave him a wise look, smiling slightly, one eyebrow raised. "That's pretty slick, Charlie. Can you do any more?"

"Yes," Charlie said, excited to show he could. Slowly, laboriously, he made his way through two pages. He stumbled over many words, and Hawkshaw had to help him with three big ones, but he read it all.

"'Great work, Steelarm,'" Charlie read, finishing the story. "'You saved the day—and the night!'"

He turned, grinning to Hawkshaw. "See? I learned 'great' and 'night' from writing the bird names. And I can read 'em in the bird book."

"Charlie," Hawkshaw said solemnly, "I'm impressed."

Charlie babbled on, explaining how he'd begun to recognize some words and sound out others. "Let's go tell Mama," he said. "I can read—now I won't have to go back to school."

"Whoa, hoss," Hawkshaw said, "not so fast. You've got to go back to school. That's not negotiable."

Charlie was crestfallen. "Awww," he said in a whiny voice.

"I myself went to school for years and years," Hawkshaw said. "It's what a man's got to do. Yes, you go back."

"I don't want to," Charlie complained. "I have to sit through all of first grade again. Because they think I'm dumb. *You* never had to sit through first grade twice."

"I sat through first grade three times," Hawkshaw said.

This not only surprised Charlie, it horrified him. "Three?"

Hawkshaw nodded. He counted on his fingers. "I did it once when I was your age. I did it again when Vice President Mills's oldest little girl went. I did it the next year when her little sister went. Three times."

"You had to sit through first grade when you were a grown-up?" Charlie asked, appalled.

"Yeah," Hawkshaw said, a frown line of disgust between his eyes. "I hated those little-bitty desks. Be glad you're doing it when you're the right size."

"But you didn't learn anything," Charlie argued. "You already knew it all."

"I did learn things," Hawkshaw countered mildly. "My printing improved. I print much better now. I learned some new history. And I finally learned how to read music." He shook his head at the memory. "That had been really hard for me."

Charlie digested this. If Hawkshaw had gone to first grade three times, it wasn't such a shame to go twice. And if even Hawkshaw, an *adult,* had learned from it, Charlie might, too. He didn't yet understand reading music, either.

Charlie shrugged off these complex thoughts. School was a million years off, anyway; he didn't have to worry about it now. But Mama was here—wait till she found out!

"Let's show my mama," he told Hawkshaw. "She'll be really glad. Hey, this is a big deal. You think we ought to go buy ice cream to celebrate?"

Hawkshaw's frown grew harder to read. "Your mama's not having a good day."

Charlie was puzzled. "Why? Did you have a fight?"

"No. She's got a lot on her mind. It's grown-up stuff."

"If she knows I can read, she'll be happy," Charlie reasoned. "That and some ice cream would really cheer her up."

"Look, champ," Hawkshaw said. "Why don't we wait—surprise her. We were going to surprise her anyway, with the pictures. Let's have a big surprise. I've got a plan."

"A plan?" Charlie asked, suspicious. "What?"

Hawkshaw explained, and Charlie listened. In a way,

the plan was good, but it involved patience and work, two things of which Charlie was not fond.

"If you'll do it," Hawkshaw said, "I'd not only buy you ice cream, but I'd take you to the beach. And you know what else? I'd give you that hat."

He nodded at the Secret Service cap that Charlie wore.

"*Give* it to me?" Charlie said in disbelief. "For keeps?"

"For keeps," Hawkshaw said. "And I'll give you the Sergeant Steelarm comics, too."

It was an offer so fiendishly tempting that Charlie could not have resisted to save his soul. He stared at Hawkshaw in awe. The cap *and* the comic books?

"Deal?" Hawkshaw asked and held out his hand.

Charlie clapped his small hand into the man's big one. "Deal," he said with conviction.

IN THE BACK of Kate's mind, she realized Hawkshaw and Charlie were acting strangely. But after Corbett's call, her thoughts were such a tangle, she had no time to wonder.

Charlie had a furtive, giggly air, as if he knew a secret it was killing him to keep. Hawkshaw, on the other hand, kept his face even more unreadable than usual. His air was so adroitly casual that she suspected it had to be studied.

That afternoon the rain came down in sheets, so there was no kayak excursion. Hawkshaw and Charlie stayed sheltered on the deck with their usual clutter of bird books and fish books and comic books and papers and crayons.

Kate was grateful for the downpour. It wasn't easy every day to watch Hawkshaw strip down to his shorts and take Charlie into the ocean.

Charlie was learning to swim like a little fish, which was good. But the sight of the tall, bronzed man teaching him filled her heart with confusion. Hawkshaw would have made a wonderful father, a perfect father.

He was also a wonderful lover, perhaps a perfect lover. Yesterday, she had watched him, as he stood waist-deep in the waves with Charlie. Hawkshaw had tossed the water out of his brown-gold hair. The sun had gleamed on his brown-gold skin.

Her stomach had fluttered, and her nerves had rippled with keen physical awareness of him. Hurriedly, she'd risen from the gray shore and turned from the sea, walking alone among the stunted trees and waving grass.

This afternoon, she was not on a sun-splashed island, cooled by the salty breeze, she was in a rather musty closet, with the sound of the washer chugging in the background. But the image of Hawkshaw still haunted her. She mentally damned Corbett for sending her here, triple-damned the stalker for sending her to Corbett for help.

She pushed the last box out into the open room and crawled out of the closet. She looked in dismay at the welter of boxes and brown paper bags and old bushel baskets spread across the floor. Hawkshaw's father must have stored things in this closet for years, one thing atop another, until he could get no more inside.

She stood, rubbing the small of her back and surveying the mess. Old grocery bags overflowed with collections of yellowed envelopes and moldering papers. Boxes bulged with a jumble of castoffs; Kate could see everything from a single shoe tree to worn paintbrushes, stiff and unsalvageable.

She sighed. The junk she could sort easily, but the papers would be a problem. She did not relish poking about in Hawkshaw Senior's records and correspondence. It did not seem a job for a stranger.

She would begin with the boxes, she thought, spanking

the dust from her hands. First, to make sure she'd cleared the closet, she rechecked it. Sure enough, she'd missed something.

In the shadows of the corner of the top shelf, sat an old overnight case. She stood on tiptoe to retrieve it. Its ancient leather was scuffed and mildewed, but the case was still sturdy. It was also heavy.

She set the case on the old bureau and tested the clasp. Unlocked, it sprang open. She hesitated, feeling oddly like Pandora. *Don't be silly,* she told herself. *You have to know what it is.*

She raised the lid. Inside were envelopes that obviously held letters. A dozen or so were of faded pastel and were addressed to Harry E. Hawkshaw. The handwriting was precise and feminine.

The return address read, Mrs. Sheila VanHook, 214 Rue du Chenes, Montreal, Quebec. Kate frowned. Was Sheila VanHook a lady friend of Harry Hawkshaw or a relative? Would Hawkshaw want these letters?

She riffled through the other envelopes. There were perhaps another two dozen slender ones, and the return address was W. W. Hawkshaw, Washington, D.C. They were letters from Hawkshaw to his father, Kate realized.

There were postcards from Hawkshaw, as well. Their gloss was fading, but the pictures were still clear: the Eiffel Tower, a Swiss chalet, an English double-decker bus, the Sydney Opera House, a kangaroo.

She read one without intending to; its message was so brief she'd taken it in at a glance. "Hi—In Australia for twelve days. Hope all is well. W. W. H."

The other cards bore greetings just as terse. Hawkshaw, Kate thought, was not a man who wasted words, even on his own kin. Yet she found something vaguely disturbing in the curt messages; it was as if Hawkshaw used them both to communicate and not to communicate with his father.

One envelope was blank and unsealed, the flap awry. She set the postcards aside and picked it up. She could see the edge of a photograph that had been torn, then mended with cellophane tape.

I shouldn't look, Kate thought, but curiosity tugged too strongly. She drew out a snapshot of a man, woman, and a boy of about five. They stood before this very back-country house, the man with his hands on the boy's shoulders.

The man was lean, leggy, and handsome, and at first glance, Kate thought he was Hawkshaw. But the clothing styles, the woman's hairstyle, the photo itself, all were too old for that. With a start, she realized Hawkshaw was not the man in the picture—he was the child.

He greatly resembled the man he was with; he had the same leanness and thick brown hair, the same prominent cheekbones. The woman was blond and delicate. She stood slightly apart from the man and boy. Her gaze was not on them and not on the camera. Her attention seemed to be caught by something that lay in another direction.

The snapshot had been ripped not once, but many times, almost to the point of mutilation. Then it had been painstakingly reassembled. On the back, in fading ink was written, Me, W.W., and Sheila.

Kate's heart dipped and took a small, nauseating leap. This was Hawkshaw with his mother and father, and his mother was Sheila—the same Sheila who had written the letters?

She looked in the envelope again and saw a single scrap of paper. She withdrew it and read the scrawled words.

This is the only picture left of me and W.W. and Sheila together. I thought W.W. might want it. The contents of this case is for W.W. to dispose of as he sees fit.

Harry Hawkshaw

Kate could not help herself. She picked up the envelopes from Sheila and studied the postmarks. These letters could not be love letters written when Sheila and Harry were courting. They were written years later, after Sheila must have married someone else.

Kate winced. Instinctively she understood that Hawkshaw didn't know these letters existed, or he never would have given her the chance to find them. Nor would he like them; they would unearth emotions he would sooner stayed buried.

Kate would give him the case anyway, she could not do otherwise. She burned to know what the letters said, but she knew it would be wrong for anyone to read them except Hawkshaw. And he might not read them. Perhaps he would destroy them without looking at them, consign them to fire as he had done with the wedding photographs.

There was only one thing left in the case, a flat, rectangular box that said STATIONERY. She lifted the lid gingerly, as if to make sure it did not contain a booby trap. Inside was a thin stack of papers. The top sheet was covered with Harry Hawkshaw's loose scrawl. Against Kate's better judgment, almost against her will, she found herself reading it.

Dear Son—
    You did not say much about your marriage except it is over but I can tell you are bothered. Well these

things happen.

To tell the truth I seen this coming. She only come here once with you and I knew then she would not be back. I looked into her eyes and I seen what I had seen before in my own life.

There are some women who

The sentence was unfinished. Kate lifted the page and looked at the one beneath. It was the start of a second letter.

Dear Son—

I know Im not the one to give advice about marriage and etc. Still although you did not say much in your letter I figure you are more broke up than you will say.

You and I was never very good at talking. I never told you much about what went wrong with your mother and me. I guess it is time to

This sentence, too, trailed off, unfinished. So did the letter. Beneath that incomplete letter lay another, and beneath that another.

Hurriedly, feeling like a spy, Kate put the lid back on the box. Her fingers were awkward with anxious emotion. Hawkshaw didn't know it, but he had half a dozen unfinished letters from a man now in his grave.

CHAPTER FOURTEEN

KATE WAITED UNTIL that night to tell Hawkshaw about the case with the photo and the letters. Both the snapshot and letters could be emotionally loaded for him; he would want to deal with them alone.

She tucked the sheet more firmly around Charlie and turned down the bedroom's air conditioner. She paused to look in the old wicker-framed mirror.

Her hair had tumbled from its makeshift bun and hung in fiery tendrils around her face. She had a dust smudge on her blouse, and her cheeks were a hectic pink.

She regarded her image with distaste. She thought, *I look like a kitchen wench expecting to get tumbled by the lord of the manor*. It was an unpleasant comparison and struck her as too close to the truth.

She changed her smudged shirt for her most modest one, high-necked and white. She unpinned her hair, brushed it, and skewed it back into an even tighter knot. She brushed a powder puff across her cheeks to pale them.

Now, she thought, *I look like a novice nun praying not to get tumbled by the lord of the manor.*

Perhaps she should hand the lord of the manor the overnight case and then go alone to her own bed and stay there. It would simplify life, and her life could certainly do with simplifying.

She took a deep breath, picked up the case by its handle, and hauled it into the living room. Hawkshaw stood next to the counter, drinking a glass of iced tea. Not a beer, she noted. Was that a good sign?

He drew one brow down in a frown and nodded at the case. "Where'd you find that? I haven't seen it for years."

"In the back closet," she said, setting it beside him on the counter. "Was it yours?"

His mouth took on a hard slant. "I—inherited it. But I never used it. My God, the old man saved everything."

She folded her arms primly over her chest. "He meant for you to have it. It's full of letters. Some from you. Some from a woman named Sheila. Some he started to write to you, but he didn't send."

His green eyes turned icy. "You *read* them?"

"No," she said. "I accidentally read a postcard from you. I didn't mean to. His letters weren't sealed. They're just in a box. I only looked enough to see what they were. There was a photo, too. In an open envelope. There was a note. I read that. It said the contents of the case were for you."

He regarded the case as if it contained a cobra.

"I waited till Charlie was asleep to give it to you," she said. "I figured you wouldn't need him clamoring to know what was in it."

Hawkshaw said nothing. He picked up the case and carried it to the kitchen trash can. He dropped it in.

Kate looked at him in shock. "You shouldn't do that. That photo—your father wrote it was the only one left of you and him and this—Sheila."

"For somebody who didn't read anything, you seem to have read a hell of a lot," he said.

"It was a *note*. I read it at a glance. I couldn't help it."

"Forget it," he said sourly.

"Sheila—she's your mother, isn't she?" Kate said. She knew she was plunging into forbidden territory, saying such a thing. She didn't care. She was sick of forbidden territory.

He made no reply.

"You might at least condescend to look," she shot at him. "You might find something in those letters that's important. After all, your father wanted you to have them, he put it all aside for—"

"Drop it, will you?" He picked up the tea and glowered at the glass as if he wanted something far stronger.

"Ah, the mysterious Mr. Hawkshaw," Kate taunted. "He doesn't wish to discuss his past. He doesn't even wish to *think* about it. But you know the truth? Mr. Hawkshaw thinks he's escaping his own history, but he's not. The past has its hooks so deep in him, I think it's got him for good."

Hawkshaw set down the glass so sharply that tea jumped out of it, splashing across the counter. "Are you done?" She saw danger flash in his eyes.

She didn't care. She'd held back long enough. "You're afraid of the past," she accused. "It's got so much power over you, you can't even talk about it. Some protector, Hawkshaw. You're frightened of a little suitcase."

He swore and hauled the case back out. He slammed it down on the counter with a crash. "What do you want?" he demanded. "I build a shrine to what's in here? It's an old man's garbage, like everything else in this house."

"He thought it was important," Kate countered. "He put it aside for you."

"He put aside every can and plastic container and old newspaper, too. You ought to know, babe."

Kate bristled. "You could at least show your father the respect to look inside."

He wrenched the lid open. He yanked out the blank envelope with the crumpled flap. He snatched the photo from it, along with the scrap of paper.

His face, already set in bitter lines, grew harder. He thrust the picture at Kate. "Want to see it again? It is my mother. That's probably the summer she left me here. Want to hear about it?"

"No," Kate said, "that's not what I meant. I only thought—"

He moved closer, holding up the snapshot so that she had to look at it. "She's beautiful. Did you notice that? She was very beautiful. She still is, I'm told. She should be, she's well-maintained. Money does that."

Kate moved her shoulders uncomfortably. "Hawkshaw, I didn't—"

"After the divorce, she worked at a motel in Orlando," he said. "But she wasn't born for a life like that. A rich man came along. She went with him. She didn't take anything with her. Not even—this."

He stroked the old overnight case. For the first time, Kate realized it had a cheap monogram stamped on the mottled leather of its front. The monogram said S.H.— Sheila Hawkshaw.

Kate felt a wave of dismay. "Hawkshaw, I'm sorry. I didn't—"

"Don't be sorry for me," he ordered. He pointed to his father's picture. "Save it for him. Because he's the poor son of a bitch who couldn't get over it. He's the one whose life was ruined. He started drinking hard. He was never a mean drunk. But he was a drunk, and it killed him."

He flung the picture back into the case. The scrap of

paper fluttered to the floor. He grabbed a handful of the pastel envelopes. He shook them in her face.

"And you know what these are?" he asked. "Letters from her, after she left. Telling us that she still loved us. She loved us, but she couldn't live this way, off in the backcountry. Oh, they really twisted the knife, these letters. Now you tell me, Kate, why in God's name would I want them? Why?"

She lowered her head, shook it. She wished now she hadn't been so reckless. Hawkshaw was angry, but the anger seemed to flow out of a wound too wide and deep to heal.

He hurled his mother's letters back into the case and drew out a handful of his own. He shoved them into her line of sight.

"My letters," he said with contempt. "You know what's in them? Nothing. 'Hi, Dad. I'm fine. How are you.' We didn't communicate too well, Dad and I. Here's the proof. Oh, yeah, a lot of happy memories here."

Kate's head snapped up. "If he kept them, he must have done it out of love. They must have meant something to him. And you might look at the letters he *tried* to write to you."

Hawkshaw pitched his own letters back into the case disgustedly. "He was probably drunk when he wrote them."

"How old were you," Kate asked softly, "when she left?"

"About Charlie's age," he said with no emotion.

He gave the lid of the case a dismissive flick with the back of his hand, and it fell shut. "It's over now," he said. "It's dead and buried. It doesn't need to be dug up."

He looked at the glass, sitting in a puddle of spilled tea. The tea dripped to the kitchen floor.

Then Hawkshaw's anger disappeared, as if he simply willed it away and consigned it to exile. "Sorry about the tea," he said. "I didn't mean to mess up your clean kitchen. I'll clean it up."

"No," Kate said, reaching for a dish towel. "I will."

He wouldn't let her. He took the towel and mopped the counter. "I get sick of watching you work all the time," he said. "It's like you're Cinderella. And I'm the lazy, evil stepbrother."

Kate looked at him in surprise, but he kept his attention focused on the spill.

He said, "You deserve better. The fancy dress, the glass slippers—the works. You should be taken to a ball. Sorry I can't oblige. But someday your prince will be along."

Something seemed to break slightly in Kate's heart, a thin little fracture that made her catch her breath. "I don't need a prince," she said.

He put the towel aside. "Yes," he said. "You do. I wish I was him. But I'm not."

"Yes," she said, the fracture splitting wider. "I know."

He came to her side, put his arm around her waist. He smoothed his free hand over her hair. "Does that bother you?" he asked, his voice husky. "That I can't be?"

"No," she lied.

"I shouldn't have taken things out on you," he said. "I'm sorry." He stroked her hair again.

"I—I was out of line," she murmured.

"No," he said, bending nearer. "Not you. You're right. I'm a coward about certain things. You're the brave one, Kate. You're not afraid of life at all. Not you."

She felt as if she were somehow falling upward into his eyes, and it gave her a swooping, giddy sensation.

It's going to happen again, and I'm going to let it, she thought. *Am I insane?* But when he lowered his lips to hers, she wound her arms around his neck and kissed him with abandon.

PERHAPS HAWKSHAW did not want to be her prince, but in bed, he seemed to forget this. Dizzied with pleasure, Kate felt not as if her body were being used, but as if it were celebrated and adored.

His hands held her face as if it were a flower. He kissed her temples, her eyelids, her lips. His tongue was hot and cunning against her own. His mouth explored the line of her jaw, nuzzled the pulses in her throat.

His hands closed possessively over her breasts, and his thumbs on her nipples teased them erect, then stroked them to even greater sensitivity. When he lowered his mouth to them, his touch sent quivers throughout her most sexual parts. She shuddered with wanting more, more, more.

His hands cradled her waist, holding her fast. His warm mouth traveled down to her navel. He kissed her inner thighs, and his hands moved to her hips.

She found she could not stop touching him. The angles and planes of his body had become familiar to her in the darkness. She knew the swell of his biceps, the complex musculature of his back.

His chest was like live sculpture beneath her fingers. She explored the hardness of his pectorals, the curve of his ribs. His skin was warm, its texture like velvet.

When at last he entered her, he lowered his mouth to hers and kissed her.

She twined her arms around his neck and held him tightly, wishing she could melt into his strength and warmth completely. And when it was over, she hid her face against his shoulder and held him more tightly still.

"Kate?" he said, concern in his voice. "What's wrong?"

"Nothing," she said, her eyes squeezed shut and pressed against his flesh.

"You're crying," he said. "Wasn't it good for you? Do you wish it hadn't happened? Oh, God, I'm sorry, Kate."

He tried to raise her face to him, but she resisted.

"No, no," she begged. "Don't. I'm fine. It was good. It was fine."

It was perfect, she thought. *Except he doesn't love me and he never will.*

"Then why are you crying?" he asked. "I can feel your tears."

"I—I got a hair in my eye," she lied. "It's out now. Just hold me for a while. Then I have to go."

He settled his body more intimately against hers, cradling her in his arms. Neither of them spoke for a long time. She laid her finger against the stone amulet he wore around his neck. It was warm with his body heat.

She said, "I want to ask you something personal. Just once."

She felt him tense. But he said, "What? About my parents?"

She hesitated. "No. About your wife. Your ex-wife. You're still in love with her, aren't you?"

At first she thought he wasn't going to answer. "Yes," he said at last. "I am."

A painful hollowness filled her. *He's not saying anything I hadn't guessed,* she told herself. *At least he's honest.*

But the illusion of closeness had faded, and only the hollowness remained.

SANDRA LEANED OVER the bed. She kissed his lips. She slipped her wedding ring into his hand.

"Goodbye," she said pleasantly. "I'm going to live with your mother. Neither of us wants you. We'll spend the rest of our lives not wanting you."

"No," he said and reached for her, but she had faded into the shadows. "Come back," he said, but she didn't answer and she didn't come back.

He looked down into his hand. Although the room was dark, he could see the wedding ring. It was broken in two. The edges were sharp enough to cut.

He touched one half of it. It sent out a shrill, urgent sound, like a rebuke or a warning.

Hawkshaw tensed. The sound jangled again. His sense that Sandra had been there vanished like the dream it was. He tumbled into wakefulness.

The phone had rung, it was ringing again. Suddenly alert, he sprang up, pulling on his shorts. He made it into the living room and grabbed the receiver.

"Hawkshaw here," he said, his heart beating unaccountably fast. He glanced at the clock shaped like the cat with shifting eyes. It was nearly five o'clock in the morning.

"Hawkshaw," said a woman's tearful voice. "This is Cherry Corbett. I—I'm worried about Bruce."

Alarm shot through Hawkshaw's system. Bruce was Corbett's given name. "What's wrong?"

"He's disappeared," she said in a quaver. "So's his car. I'm frightened."

"*What?*" Hawkshaw demanded, his body stiffening.

"He—he—said he was going to be home late," she

stammered. "We were supposed to go to a play at eight o'clock. He never—he never came home, Hawkshaw. He's run late before, but never like this."

"Have you called Bedlingham?" Bedlingham was Corbett's partner.

"Yes. He went straight to the office. Bruce wasn't there. There was no sign of him, Bedlingham said."

Hawkshaw's stomach pitched uneasily. "Have you called the police?"

"Yes," she said. "There's a pair of detectives here now. And Bedlingham. I shouldn't have called you, Hawkshaw. I know I shouldn't have brought your name into it all. But—but—I finally just broke down—I feel so desperate—"

She began to cry softly.

Hawkshaw swore to himself. "Cherry," he said firmly, "it's okay. Don't try to talk about it. Put somebody else on the phone, all right?"

He heard her weeping grow more distant, heard someone comforting her. He clenched his teeth. *Corbett, where are you? What in hell's happened?*

A man came on the line. "Hawkshaw? This is Bedlingham. When's the last time you heard from Corbett?"

Bedlingham had a smooth, ingratiating voice, but it had an edge of arrogance in it. Hawkshaw remembered that Corbett hadn't particularly liked Bedlingham, had talked of dissolving the partnership.

"He called yesterday morning," Hawkshaw said.

"What about?"

"Personal stuff mostly."

"He talks cases with you," Bedlingham said. It was more accusation than question.

Hawkshaw sounded casual. "Shop talk? Yeah. Sometimes."

"Was he supposed to call you back? After yesterday morning?"

Hawkshaw thought of Cherry crying in the background. He thought of Kate, sleeping safely in his arms.

"Yeah. He said he'd call back later last night, maybe."

"What about?"

Hawkshaw played for time. "Look, it's late. I'm still kind of foggy. And this is a shock."

"Was it about the Kanaday case?" Bedlingham challenged.

Hawkshaw thought of how much information it was politic to release. "He mentioned he was working a new angle on a case. I don't recall exactly what. He said he'd call if it worked out. He didn't call. End of story."

"Don't play cute with me," Bedlingham said with obvious distaste. "Did he tell you what this angle was?"

"No," Hawkshaw said. "Why should he tell me? You're his partner."

"The Kanaday case was obsessing him," Bedlingham said in the same displeased tone. "He wasn't talking. Not to anybody. Except you."

"He must have talked to somebody," Hawkshaw countered. "Or I wouldn't be getting this call at five in the morning."

"His wife," Bedlingham informed him. "He told his wife he'd been in touch with you. Not to worry about the Kanaday woman because you were involved. You are, aren't you?"

Hawkshaw's nerves were on full alert. "We talked, that's pretty much it," he said vaguely.

"Is she with you?" Bedlingham demanded.

"What's that got to do with you?" Hawkshaw asked.

"I'm concerned," Bedlingham said in his smooth

voice. "Corbett's missing. This client was taking a lot of his time lately. I want to make sure she's safe."

"And I want to make sure Corbett's safe," Hawkshaw countered. "Fill me in. What was his agenda yesterday?"

"There was a suspect in the Kanaday case. A man named Kyle Johnson. He found out that Johnson couldn't be the man. The time frame was wrong. But I think you know all this."

"I didn't ask about that. I asked about yesterday."

"I wasn't in the office a lot of the day," Bedlingham said. "I got my own workload, you know."

"And I didn't ask about your workload, I asked about his."

Bedlingham sighed, as if Hawkshaw's questions were both foolish and an imposition. "I didn't get in until close to four in the afternoon. Corbett was there. He was getting ready to take some records to the courier service. Something about a dog. He complained so much had been happening, he'd forgotten about the dog."

Maybelline, Hawkshaw thought. *He was taking Maybelline's veterinary records to be couriered.*

He said, "That's it? And then he was going home?"

"No," Bedlingham informed him. "*I* offered to take the records. He said, no thanks, he had another stop to make. It was on his way."

"Did he give details?" Hawkshaw challenged.

"No, Hawkshaw. That's why I've been asking you," Bedlingham said sarcastically. "My professional intuition tells me you know."

Hawkshaw had his own professional intuition. Corbett hadn't completely trusted Bedlingham, Kate didn't like him. And now the man was relentlessly trying to pinpoint Kate's whereabouts.

"What do you know?" Bedlingham persisted. "What can you tell us about Kate Kanaday?"

Hawkshaw considered his options. "Nothing," he said.

"If you know where she's at, I suggest you tell me immediately. I want to talk to her. And so, I imagine, will the police."

"I don't care what you imagine or why," Hawkshaw said. "I can't help you."

"Hawkshaw—" Bedlingham began, warning in his tone.

"Tell Cherry to stay strong. Corbett's a tough SOB. Tough and smart. Tell her I'll stay in touch. And that I love her."

"Damn well you stay in touch, Hawkshaw. If Corbett doesn't show up, and you're mixed up in this Kanaday thing, the police are going to want to talk to you. I suggest you stay put and cooperate."

"Actually, I was on my way to Disney World tomorrow," Hawkshaw lied. "If you want me, phone the Magic Kingdom. Tell them I'm the one who looks like a tourist."

"Don't get flip with me. The local police down there may be sent to interview you."

"Tell Cherry what I said. I'll phone her."

He hung up, his nerves swarming with apprehension. Corbett was missing; the news made him physically sick, not merely for Corbett, but Cherry, too. And Kate.

Kate, he thought with such force it wrenched him. *What in hell does this mean for Kate?*

Another, darker thought formed in Hawkshaw's mind: Bedlingham. He and Kate had worked in the same building before the stalking began, he in the detective agency, she in the bookstore. Had Bedlingham gone after Corbett because Corbett was getting too close to the truth?

Bedlingham had clearly fished to find out where Kate was, and Hawkshaw didn't like it. The man could be a dangerous adversary. But at least he was still a safe distance away, in Columbia.

But what if the stalker wasn't Bedlingham? What if someone else had gone after Corbett? Then what?

Does the stalker know where she is?

Hawkshaw looked at the foolish cat-shaped clock. The cat's eyes flicked back and forth, as if watching for something, waiting for something.

Hawkshaw swore. Over twelve hours had passed since Corbett had left his office and disappeared. He'd been carrying records for Kate, with her name on them as Maybelline's owner. And they'd been addressed to Hawkshaw, here on Cobia Key.

If someone had attacked Corbett, those records would be like an arrow pointing to Kate's whereabouts.

Twelve hours was enough time for a man in Columbia to board an airplane and make it as far as the Keys—or even to drive.

It was more than enough time.

CHAPTER FIFTEEN

OUTSIDE, IT WAS RAINING again, a fine, steady fall that rattled softly at the windows. The sky was still dark.

Kate sat at the counter, dressed only in her short white nightshirt. Her hair fell to her shoulders in a wild tumble. Hawkshaw had come into her room in the darkness, quietly insisting she get up.

Now he stood, wearing only his tattered shorts, his arms folded, his face solemn. He had news, he said. It wasn't good.

"I didn't want to alarm you," Hawkshaw said. "But I thought you should know."

She looked up at him. His mouth was set in a tight line. "You're worried about him, aren't you?"

He shook his head. "My job is to worry about you."

His words hardly registered. She was appalled by Corbett's disappearance and terrified for him. "Did you hear me?" Hawkshaw demanded. "I'm worried about you."

"This may not even be about me," she said, trying to think clearly. "Corbett had other cases besides mine."

"I'm aware of that," Hawkshaw said.

"He—could have stumbled onto something totally unrelated to me."

"I'm aware of that, too."

She stared at the mug, clenching it so tightly her knuckles whitened. "Whatever's happened—maybe it has nothing to do with me."

"And maybe it does."

"You don't *know* that."

"No. And neither do you."

She pushed the coffee mug away, stood up, went to the kitchen window. She could see nothing, only raindrops sliding down the surface, reflecting the kitchen's light.

She put her hand to her brow and rubbed it wearily. "I want Corbett to be safe. I want it more than anything."

"So do I," he said.

She reached out and touched the window glass. It was surprisingly cool. "I'll never forgive myself if this happened because of me, and he's hurt or—or—"

She could not finish the thought. She had liked and trusted Corbett from the first. He was a fine man, warm, smart, and honorable. He had a wife, children...

Hawkshaw moved behind her. He put his hand on her shoulder, and she could sense the tension in him. "Whatever happens—" he said in a low voice "—I mean that, *whatever* happens, it's not your fault. Do you understand me?"

"No," she said, letting her fingertips fall away from the window. "I don't understand. There's already one man dead—Kyle Johnson."

He wheeled her around to face him and gripped her upper arms. "Johnson crossed your path by mistake," he said from between his teeth. "He got killed by accident. You can't blame yourself."

He meant to comfort her, she knew, but comfort was impossible. "Hawkshaw, I mean it. I'm frightened for Corbett."

He drew her to him. "I am too," he said.

She lay her cheek against his chest, let her eyes close for a moment, to shut out the world. She could feel the beat of his heart beneath her ear, its steadfast rhythm.

"What can we do about him?" she asked.

"Nothing," he said. "Pray, if you're the praying sort."

Kate tried to pray, but her prayer was broken, incoherent. She offered it up anyway. *Please, God. Please, God. Please, please, please.*

"Kate?" Hawkshaw said. He smoothed her tangled hair.

"Yes?"

"We should think about moving."

She drew back, looked up at him in disbelief. "Moving?"

"Bedlingham believes you're here. The Columbia police must, too. And whoever Corbett ran into probably knows, too. He had records with your name on them, addressed to me, here. That's way too many who could know where you are. You may not be safe here."

Kate's muscles stiffened. Vaguely, in the back of her mind, she had realized this, but Corbett's disappearance had shocked away awareness of all else. It was Corbett, not she, who was clearly in danger.

"I—I—" she stuttered "—you're only guessing. There's no proof the stalker has anything to do with any of this."

Hawkshaw bent closer. "And no proof he doesn't."

Her fear surged, and she clutched at any reason that might prove Hawkshaw wrong. "Up till now the stalker's never actually hurt anyone—"

"Up till now," he said.

"He's done little things," she said frantically, "nothing violent."

"His 'little things' were violent enough to drive you here," said Hawkshaw. "They were violent enough for Corbett to send you."

"Oh...poor Corbett," she said in despair.

He grasped her upper arms again, holding her fast. "Listen to me. Maybe Corbett hinted to Cherry that you were with me *because* of something like this. In case something happened to him, we'd be warned."

"Warned?" Kate asked in horror.

"Yes," Hawkshaw said. "In the meantime, Bedlingham thinks you're here. He wants you to blow your cover and call him. I don't like that. And he warned me to stick around here. I don't like that, either."

Kate's head swam in confusion. "But Bedlingham's far away. You said—"

"Kate, I can't give you any more logic. I can only give you instinct. And instinct tells me to get you out of here."

"But—"

"I don't want to scare you."

"You *are* scaring me—"

"Then fight it, Kate. You're a fighter. You're brave. Be brave a while longer."

"Hawkshaw—"

"I know a place we can go," he insisted. "Farther up the Keys. We'll pack a car, rent a boat we can live on. We can get so far into the backcountry the devil himself can't find us. I know how. Trust me."

"But—"

"Don't tell Charlie. We'll pretend it's a vacation. I'll make sure we stay in touch with Aggie, with the police. When we're sure you're safe, we'll come back."

Kate was dizzied and breathless. "I'm not sure—" she began.

But Hawkshaw bent and kissed her with such urgency it blocked a thousand arguments. "Trust me," he whispered against her lips. "Do you trust me?"

She looked into his eyes. She nodded.

"Go pack and wake up Charlie," he whispered. "Hurry."

SWIFTLY SHE DRESSED and packed their clothes by the light of the small desk lamp. For the first time she was grateful that she and Charlie had so few possessions.

She packed Charlie's toys and books in his backpack with the picture of the Lion King. His crayons and tablet and drawings were elsewhere; she'd find them on the way out.

She bent and shook Charlie's shoulder gently. "Charlie," she whispered. "Wake up, Charlie."

He turned away from her, burrowing more deeply into the pillow. "Tired," he grumbled. "Tired."

At his feet, Maybelline grunted in sleepy sympathy. The rain still tapped at the window. No light came from between the curtains; the sky was still dark.

"Charlie, sweetie," Kate said, more insistently, "get up. We have to take a little trip." She gripped his shoulder again.

Charlie groaned and clutched his pillow more tightly. But then his shoulder tensed beneath her hand. "A trip?" he said in a muffled voice.

"Yes," Kate said with all the artificial cheer she could muster. "Hawkshaw's planned a trip. In a boat. It'll be a lot of fun. So rise and shine. We have to hurry."

She could almost see the relaxation evaporating out of the boy's body, the apprehension rushing in. He turned over to face her and opened his eyes, frowning with sleepy confusion. "A boat?" he asked. "The kayaks?"

"No," Kate said with the same relentless brightness. "A big boat. That we can live on for a while. You'll love it."

Charlie, still scowling, closed his eyes again. "I don't want to live on a boat," he protested. "I like it here."

She shook him harder. "Charlie, I'm sorry. There's no choice. We have to go. Now. Get up."

Charlie muttered and fretted, but Kate got him up, quickly washed his face and made him brush his teeth. "We'll have breakfast on the road," she said, quickly running the comb through his hair. "Won't that be fun?"

"I don't want to go," Charlie whined. But then he yawned so piteously it wrenched Kate's heart. He was a child who needed his sleep and who hated change. She hated uprooting him yet again. But she sat him down on the edge of the bed and began to lace his left shoe.

Hawkshaw knocked at the door. "Are you ready?"

Kate knotted the shoelace and began on the other. "Almost."

"Are you packed?"

"I haven't got Charlie's paper or crayons."

"I've got it all," said Hawkshaw. "Can I come in? I'll take the things to the van."

"I need Maybelline's leash," Kate said as she tied the second knot.

"I've got it."

"Come in," said Kate and stood. "I'm sorry," she told her son. "You'll feel better after you've had some breakfast."

The door swung open and Hawkshaw entered. He wore khaki shorts, a T-shirt and the wide-brimmed black hat. Oddly, he wore an army-green canvas vest that was fastened all the way up. He handed Kate the leash and looked at Charlie with a frown of concern.

"How you doing, kid?" he asked.

"This stinks," Charlie said miserably.

"You've got that right," said Hawkshaw.

Kate snapped Maybelline's leash onto her collar and coaxed her off the bed. The dog jumped to the floor with a heavy thump. She gave Kate a resentful look.

Hawkshaw took up the Secret Service cap from the nightstand and set it on Charlie's head. "Come on, kid," he said. "We're going to go stay on a boat. We'll live like pirates. Anybody comes near us, we'll scuttle them."

"I don't want to live like a pirate," said Charlie.

"Yes, you do," Hawkshaw said. He picked up Charlie and hoisted him into the crook of his right arm. He hefted one large suitcase under his left arm, picked up the other with the same hand.

"Heave-ho," he said. He turned to Kate. "Ready?"

She smiled weakly.

"Then let's go," said Hawkshaw.

Kate put on Charlie's backpack and picked up the smallest suitcase and Maybelline's leash. She clucked her tongue for the dog to follow.

"I'm thirsty," Charlie complained. "Can't I have a glass of orange juice?"

Kate and Hawkshaw exchanged glances. She did not know how long it would be before they could buy the boy breakfast.

"We could get you some orange juice, I guess," said Hawkshaw. He set down the suitcases by the front door and carried Charlie toward the kitchen.

At that moment, the lights went out, plummeting the house into blackness.

Kate stifled a cry of alarm. She stood motionless, staring in disbelief at the seamless dark. The rain tapped feebly at the windows.

In a small, frightened voice, Charlie said, "Hawkshaw? Mama? What's wrong?"

THE DARKNESS WAS featureless and thick as velvet.

Hawkshaw saw nothing but blackness, but his other senses leaped into a new dimension of keenness. He could feel the tension in Charlie's body, feel the faint warmth of the boy's uneven breathing.

He could smell the toothpaste, minty on the child's breath, the scent of his freshly washed face. He was sharply aware of the kitchen's lingering aroma of coffee and the ever-present saltiness in the air.

The rain clicked against the window. Somewhere, a board creaked, as if the house were huddling in tighter on itself because of the rain. He could hear the scrambling of an insect. He could hear his own heart.

"What's wrong?" Charlie asked again. His arms tightened around Hawkshaw's neck. "Turn the lights back on. It's scary."

"It's all right, kid," Hawkshaw said. "I've got you."

Hawkshaw edged through the darkness to the phone. He picked up the receiver. The line was dead.

Kate whispered, "Hawkshaw?" Uncertainty trembled in her voice.

"The phone's out, too," he said.

"Both at once?" Kate asked.

Hawkshaw listened to the rain. It was dying away. There was no wind. There had been no lightning, no thunder. Nothing to suddenly deaden both electricity and phone.

Reason whispered that the loss of power could be an accident, some central trunk or cable stricken. But instinct shrieked. *Be careful,* it cried.

The dog whined. He heard the snicking sound of her nails on the floor tile as she nervously shifted. "I want to go back to bed," Charlie quavered. "I don't like this."

"Kate," Hawkshaw said carefully, "there were candles

and matches and a flashlight in the kitchen. Where'd you put them?''

"In the top left-hand drawer," she said.

"Okay, Champ," Hawkshaw said to Charlie, patting his back. "Let's throw some light on the subject."

He moved into the lightless kitchen, groped for the drawer, opened it. He felt inside and found the flashlight.

He flicked it on, careful to keep its beam well away from the window. He took a candle, a book of matches. He seized a bottle out of the glass recycling bin and wedged the candle into it.

Charlie whimpered again and rubbed his eyes. Hawkshaw made his way to Kate. He handed Charlie over to her. "Take him," he said.

She wrapped her arms around the boy and watched, her eyes large, as he lit the candle and set it on the coffee table. He turned off the flashlight.

"What are you doing?" she asked.

"I'm going out," he said. "Stay in and stay away from the windows."

She clutched Charlie tighter. "Hawkshaw, be careful," she said. "If somebody's out there—"

He reached inside his vest and drew out his automatic. He had worn the vest to keep her and the boy from seeing he was armed. He handed her the gun.

"This is the safety," he said, showing her. The light from the candle flame leaped and capered around them. "This is how to take it off. Right here. See?"

She stared at the automatic, gleaming in the candle's unsteady glow. "Hawkshaw, I can't use that—"

He took her hand and pressed the gun into it. "It's got a full clip in it. Sixteen shots. If you have to use it, aim for the middle of the body. Squeeze the trigger, don't jerk it.''

"Hawkshaw, I couldn't—"

"Put out the candle when I put my hand on the knob of the front door. I'll set it so it locks behind me. Let me get out the door and count to twenty before you light it again."

She said nothing. She hugged Charlie against her, and in her right hand she held the gun awkwardly, as if it were some amulet of evil enchantment.

Hawkshaw moved to the front door. Mentally he damned himself for frightening her when there might be no reason for fright. Yet his instincts were going wild now, anxiety buzzing like wasps through his system. He reached for the door's knob.

"Put out the light," he said softly.

He heard the soft exhalation of her breath as she blew out the candle. The house was plunged into darkness again.

He eased open the door and narrowed his eyes. The first glow of a gray dawn edged the eastern sky. The rain had turned to a fine, cool mist.

As he slipped out the door, his heart took a painful vault. The main electrical wire and the phone wire hung limply from the roof, falling over the railing and disappearing into the darkness. Both must have been cut.

He did not pull the door quite closed. He stood, tense and ready, as his eyes swept the shadowy yard. He saw the white van sitting on the gravel drive, too low to the ground and with an odd list to it. To the right, the Thunderbird sat, also too low and at a tilt.

Somebody's slashed the tires, Hawkshaw thought with a sick rush of realization. He moved back toward the door. "Kate," he called softly, "I'm coming back in. It's all right, it's me—"

The clapboards next to his head exploded, showering

him with splinters. At the same split second, a crack like a bolt of thunder shook the air.

Hawkshaw jolted backward, dropping to a crouch as a second shot rent the dawn. The clapboards above him spewed another eruption of slivered wood.

Hawkshaw swore and dived back through the door, cursing his own stupidity. Some bastard was out there with a high-powered rifle, and he'd offered himself up like a sitting duck.

Inside, he sprang to the door's side and yanked it shut. Even as he did so, two more bullets crashed into the door. The first shattered one of its small diamond-shaped windows into a spray of splintered glass; the second slammed into the top set of hinges with a whining scream.

The shock of the impacts spun Hawkshaw backward, but he righted himself. He heard Charlie crying. He felt Kate's shoulder brush his own.

He put his arm around her and pulled her close. "Are you all right?" he demanded.

"Yes, yes, what about you?"

"He didn't hit me," said Hawkshaw, although he felt blood creeping down the side of his face in a slow, warm trickle. Blood dampened his chest, as well. A shard of glass was embedded under his collarbone like a thick needle. He winced and pulled it out.

Kate fumbled to press the automatic into his hand. "Here, take this. You know how to use it."

Hawkshaw took it, slid off the safety. He thought, *This is not a good position we're in.*

Silence closed in around them. It was broken only by Charlie's quiet weeping. A feeble gray light was starting to show itself at the edges of the curtains.

"He's cut the lights and phone," Hawkshaw said. "The tires, too. We're pinned down."

Questions cascaded through his mind: who was the sniper and how had he found them? The gate was locked and he'd heard no car; whoever it was must have climbed the fence.

Where was he shooting from, and how much firepower did he have? He must be up behind the stand of pine trees and jacaranda, and the rifle sounded like it might be a .30-.30, and not a semiautomatic, which was lucky.

The silence closed in again. He pulled Kate nearer.

Then a man's voice came from outside, a strong, angry voice. "I've got you now, you slut," he called. "You're going to pay now. You and your brat and your bastard boyfriend. You'll pay, you unfaithful slut."

Charlie cried harder. Kate clutched Hawkshaw's arm almost convulsively.

"I told you never to go to another man," the voice called. "I *told* you. Now you'll pay. You'll pay."

Hawkshaw tried to brush the blood from his face. From the sound of the voice, the man had moved to the cars now. "Kate," Hawkshaw said, "I'm going to talk to him, try to distract him. Take Charlie and go out the back. Take the kayak and get to the island. Charlie knows the way. He'll get you there."

She clutched at his arm more tightly. "Hawkshaw—I can't."

"You have to. He could shoot the hell out of this place. Set fire to it. Save the boy, Kate." He pressed the gun back into her hand. "Take this. Use it if you have to."

"No. No—you can't face him unarmed."

"I've got my dad's rifle. Go, Kate. Before it gets any lighter."

"But—"

"Go now," he ordered. "Charlie, be absolutely quiet.

You've got to be a real Secret Service man, understand, kid?''

"Yes." Charlie's voice was small and shaky in the darkness.

From outside, the man's voice came again. "Did you hear me, you unfaithful bitch? You'll never touch another man again. I'll burn that house down with you in it.''

"Go," Hawkshaw whispered tersely. He heard her make her way to the kitchen door, quietly open it. When he heard the jingle of the dog's tags, he realized, with horror, that the dog was following her.

"Kate!" he whispered hoarsely. "Don't take the damn dog.''

But it was too late. He heard the jingle on the back deck now. The dog had slipped out with them. Goddamn, he thought. Goddamn.

He held his breath and moved beside the front door with its broken window.

He yelled into the darkness at the sniper. "You've hurt her already," he lied. "You've hit her in the throat. She's going to die if she doesn't get help. If you love her, help her.''

"Shut up, you bastard," the man cried. "It's your fault she's hurt. You can die with her.''

"You've got it wrong," Hawkshaw called back. "She doesn't care about me. Don't let her die. I can't save her. But you can.''

"Step outside," the man shouted. "If you want to save her, step outside and put up your hands. And bring the boy.''

"I can't leave her," Hawkshaw lied. "I've got to keep pressure on the wound.''

"Let the boy do it. You step outside.''

"The boy's too young.''

"Then send him outside, with his hands up."

"No. The boy stays here."

Hawkshaw gritted his teeth. He prayed Kate and Charlie had made it to the kayak, that they could get away before it was light enough for them to be seen.

"I said, send out the boy."

"I said no," Hawkshaw retorted. "But we can talk this over. Wait. Just give me a minute."

He began to edge toward his bedroom. He needed to get to the gun cabinet and grab his father's old .22 and a box of ammo.

But air was rocked by a new fusillade of shots. The living room windows exploded into fragments, and Hawkshaw hit the floor.

The bullets burst over him like a storm. The SOB was strafing the house with shots, his firing crazy and unceasing and wild.

CHAPTER SIXTEEN

KATE'S HEART PLUNGED sickly when she realized Maybelline had followed them out of the house.

She could not seize the dog's leash and force her back inside; she had Charlie in her arms and she still clutched the gun.

She hurried down the stairs and heard Maybelline at her heels, the dog's heavy body thudding on each step. Tears of frustration burned Kate's eyes, and fiercely she blinked them back.

She reached the cement ramp where the kayaks lay. She made Charlie get in, snatched up a paddle and waded as quietly as she could into the water, pulling the little boat into the water.

She heard Hawkshaw shouting from within the house and the gunman shouting back. She could not make out their words because her blood drummed so loudly in her ears.

But she heard the splashing of her own movement in the water, it sounded as noisy as the roaring of a tidal wave to her. And she heard Maybelline's whimper from the shore.

''Mama—Maybelline!'' Charlie whispered in a desperate voice.

Kate, knee-deep in the water, clapped her hand over his mouth. But Maybelline, stubborn as ever, splashed into the water and began to swim noisily toward them.

Oh, God, Kate thought in panic, *how do you get a dog into a kayak?*

She grabbed Maybelline and thrust her onto Charlie's lap. "Hold her mouth shut," she ordered. "And hang on to her."

Charlie was small, and the dog was weighty, but he clutched her tightly and clamped his fingers around her muzzle. Kate slid into the kayak's seat, her heart slamming against her ribs. She let the gun drop to her lap.

She began to paddle as quickly and silently as possible. The sky seemed to be growing lighter by the second, the mangroves black against the paling horizon.

Then, suddenly, a deafening hell of gunfire erupted. A pair of snowy egrets flew up from the mangroves like two ghosts. In horror, Kate glanced over her shoulder to see if Charlie was all right.

He was bent so low he was nearly doubled up, but he kept his tight grip on Maybelline, one hand imprisoning her snout. Kate paddled faster.

Just twenty yards ahead, the river bent out of sight, and fifty yards beyond that was the first mangrove tunnel. Beyond that bend, they would perhaps be safe. Once they reached the maze of mangrove tunnels, nobody could follow them except Hawkshaw.

But the gunfire still shook the air, each crack of the rifle echoing eerily across the water. Kate gritted her teeth and prayed.

Something struck her in the back so hard that she gasped. It was as if a phantom fist had rammed into her rib cage, just below the shoulder. The blow almost knocked the paddle from her hand.

She tightened her grip and put all her strength into reaching the bend in the river. Her back ached dully, but she ignored it.

When they rounded the bend, the shots still roared, splintering apart the backcountry's silence. Kate turned again to look at Charlie. "Are you all right?" she whispered and kept heading for the mangrove corridor.

"Yes," Charlie answered, his voice quivering. "But, Mama—"

"You're not hurt?" she demanded.

"No. But, Mama—"

"Shhh, stay quiet," she ordered.

"But, Mama—"

"Hush," she said, almost ferociously.

Maybelline whimpered and gave a feeble thrash. "Keep hold of that dog," Kate said. "If she falls out, I won't stop for her, I swear it."

Then the kayak nosed into the first long tunnel of roots and branches. Kate felt half-faint with relief. The interior of the tunnel was dark as the deepest pit of a cave.

It was too narrow to paddle, so she pulled the boat along by grasping at the roots and limbs. She did not allow herself to think what might be lurking in those roots and leaves.

When at last they reached another tidal channel, she was startled at the brightness of the sky. It was still gray, and a fine mist hung over the water, but compared to the mangrove tunnel, it seemed blindingly light.

"Charlie," she said, surprised at how steady her voice was, "tell me where to find the next tunnel to get to the island."

"Up ahead," Charlie said. He was crying, but silently. "We'll pass one on the left and one on the right. Take the next right one after it."

The tears in his voice shook her to her soul. "Charlie, are you crying because you're hurt?"

"No. But, Mama—"

Something splashed next to the boat, something big: The water churned and went muddy. *Barracuda,* thought Kate sickly.

Maybelline moaned and struggled to get loose. Kate had a nightmarish image of the dog making the kayak capsize. "Charlie, *hold* her," she said desperately. "For God's sake, don't let her turn us over."

She paddled harder. Again something splashed frighteningly close to them.

HAWKSHAW HAD SCUTTLED into the bedroom. He had no idea where the key to the old gun cabinet was. Hell, he didn't even know if the old .22 would still fire. He yanked the lamp from the night table and smashed the cabinet's glass.

Carefully he reached inside, flicked the lock, then swung the door open. He snatched up the .22 and a box of shells from the cabinet's floor.

The crazed man outside was still firing, but more erratically now, and not as often. Breathing hard, Hawkshaw leaned his back against the wall and loaded the .22.

Then he rose from his crouch and made his way to the bedroom's front window. Broken glass crunched beneath his feet. The old curtain fluttered limply in the humid breeze.

Hawkshaw prayed that Kate and Charlie were safely out of range, that neither had been hurt by the wild firing, that they were in the mangrove corridors, heading toward the island. *Trust her,* he told himself. *Trust her courage, her cool head.*

He lifted the edge of the curtain and peered out. The sky was inexorably brightening.

Another shot tore the dawn air, and Hawkshaw saw the brief flash of its firing. The gunman was behind the van, using it for cover. It would take patience to get a clear shot at him from the house. And it would take luck.

"I've got ammo. I've got plenty," the man shouted. "I can blow that house to shreds. I can blow you all to shreds."

Let him think he's done it, Hawkshaw thought. He licked the sweat from his upper lip. Blood still seeped from his temple down the side of his face. He ignored it.

Without Kate and Charlie here, he could take chances. With them gone, he no longer had to be on the defensive; he could take the offense.

"You—Hawkshaw," called the gunman. "I know your name. How do you like your woman now? Is she worth dying for?"

Hawkshaw didn't answer. Let the SOB think his shots had wounded them all. Let him wonder.

"I can blow your dirty house to bits, I can burn it to the ground," the man cried.

Like hell you can, thought Hawkshaw.

He jammed the box of shells into his hip pocket, dropped to a crouch, and moved across the room to the back window. Silently he heaved up both the glass and screen.

He pulled himself through the opening and landed softly on the deck. He didn't take the stairs. He went to the corner farthest from the shooter and climbed over the railing. Slipping the rifle over his shoulder, he climbed down the scaffolding of the deck.

He had to drop eight feet to the ground, and he did it silently, landing on his feet like a cat. It was nearly light now, and the east was pearly gray, its brightness climbing higher into the sky.

One of the kayaks was gone from the ramp. He looked up the river in the direction Kate was to have gone. There was no sign of human life, only the low, fine mist riding the current's flow.

He saw no trace of the dog. Either the gunfire had driven it to hide in the woods, or somehow Kate had taken it with her.

From the drive, the sniper shouted. "Hawkshaw? Hawkshaw, answer me."

Hawkshaw's blood prickled, but he didn't answer. From the way the sound carried, the man hadn't moved from the cars.

If Hawkshaw swam quietly downstream, holding the rifle out of the water, his movement would be covered by the screen of scrawny Joewood trees that clustered along that section of the bank. He could climb back ashore where the fig thicket began.

And from there, he could make his way through the scrub and get the drop on the gunman from behind. He took the box of shells from his pocket and clamped it between his teeth. Soundlessly he slipped into the rush of the foaming water. He tried not to think of the blood on his body and the sharks cruising under the swift water, hungry and hunting.

From above him, he heard the gunman open fire again. A wild shot split the water next to Hawkshaw's head, temporarily blinding him with the spray of salt.

He swam on.

KATE WAS EXHAUSTED, her heart banging in her chest and pounding in her ears. She cursed her own weakness and kept paddling, although her arms quivered and her fingers tingled with numbness.

She was disoriented, feeling hopelessly lost, but somehow Charlie seemed to know where they were. She entered the darkness of another mangrove tunnel, pulling the boat along by grappling at the hanging roots and branches.

Nothing mattered except to keep going, keep going. Behind them, she could still hear the irregular crack and echo of the rifle, sounding farther away now, like distant fireworks.

Her back hurt, her arms ached, and her hands burned with blisters or cuts—she could not tell, she hardly cared. Her forehead drummed as if it were being beaten, and her vision was blurred, whether by sweat or tears, she could not say.

At least Maybelline had stopped struggling, although she still whimpered and whined from time to time. But for now the dog seemed too frightened to try to spring away or even move. Passive, terrified, she waited for whatever fate into which Kate could deliver them.

Kate had stopped imagining dangers. She no longer thought of barracudas trailing the little boat or of capsizing among the trailing stings of jellyfish. In the mangrove tunnels, she did not think of crabs or snakes falling into the boat.

Such fears took energy, and she needed all her strength to press on. When she pulled the kayak free from the darkness and claustrophobic closeness of the corridor, she blinked at the climbing brightness of the sky, the openness of the gray water before them.

"We're almost there, Mama," Charlie said in a small voice.

She wiped a strand of damp hair from her eyes with the back of her hand. The water seemed to dance and swarm with eerie sparkles. "Where?" Her voice sounded spent and far away from her.

"There," Charlie said in frustration. "Mama, *look*."

It cost too much effort to turn her head to see if he was

pointing, but across the strange twinkling of the water she thought she saw it. The island with the limestone shore.

They had found it. Kate almost sobbed for happiness. But the open water made her nervous, she wanted to reach the shore as quickly as possible, to hide the kayak and disappear into the cover of the scrubby trees.

The paddle had grown suddenly heavier and more unwieldy in her burning hands, but she did not stop. Her breath came in painful gasps, and the strange pain in her back grew sharper, cutting like a blade.

Far above them flew a white bird with an immense wingspan. For a few giddy seconds, Kate almost thought it was an angel leading them to safety. Around them the water swayed and glittered and shot off bursts of dizzying gleam.

Then the kayak ground its nose against the island's limestone slope. Kate stumbled from the boat and fell when the water surged over her knees. She sputtered, rose, and towed the kayak far enough onto the shore that she could help Charlie out.

Maybelline leaped out and sprang through the shallow water to the stony shore. Kate tried to lift out Charlie, but he scrambled out by himself, then helped her drag the kayak completely onto dry land.

He seemed like a very strong little boy to her at that moment, stronger even than she was. "Charlie," she panted, "we've got to hide the kayak and then ourselves."

She gripped his shoulder and discovered she was leaning on him for support. Charlie's face, white and frightened, swam in her vision.

"Mama—" he said, clutching her arm.

"Shhh, hurry," she said. "We'll hide the boat. Then we'll wait for Hawkshaw."

She stumbled toward a thicket of spindly acacia trees, dragging the kayak. Her heart beat as if it would explode. Once the kayak was out of sight, she wanted to go deeper into the island's thickets, to hide as completely as possible.

But she sank to the stony ground. Her legs would carry her no farther.

"Mama!" Charlie cried.

"I'm all right." But she had an irresistible desire to lie down. She half lay, half fell among the weeds.

"I just have to rest a minute," she tried to tell Charlie, but the words wouldn't come.

"Mama," Charlie begged, "please get up. Mama? I'm scared. I think you're shot, Mama."

Feebly Kate put her hand to her back, just beneath the left shoulder blade. She felt something warm and wet. She drew her fingertips back, shaking, and looked at them. They were tinted red with her blood.

"Charlie," she said, with surprising clarity, "don't be afraid. I'll be fine."

Then the world gave a last great swirl around her. It filled with whirling sparkles that faded to darkness.

HAWKSHAW REACHED THE SHORE, the box of bullets still clenched between his teeth, the rifle held over his head. He rose out of the water and lowered the rifle to combat position.

He moved through the trees with sureness and quiet; he was on his own turf, he knew it as intimately as he knew the beat of the blood in his veins.

The vault of the sky was brightening now, and the rude jeer of crows echoed through the air. Hawkshaw slipped the bullets back into his pocket and moved from shadow to shadow, silent as a shadow himself.

The vines and thorns and thistles might have slowed or stopped another man. He moved among them as if they were faithful allies. He held the rifle at ready.

A handgun was his preferred weapon; but he'd handled rifles from childhood and had spent hours training on the Service's rifle range. The old .22 felt ridiculously light in his hands, yet familiar and dependable.

Ahead of him, beyond the screen of trees and shrubs and vines, Hawkshaw heard a scrabbling *snick-snick* noise from the direction of the drive. He recognized the sound; the sniper was reloading.

Hawkshaw kept moving. He watched where he stepped. He did not stir a leaf any more than the breeze did, he stepped on no twig. Mosquitoes lighted on him, drinking his blood. He did not slap at them, he let them drink.

Then, at last, he looked between the branches and saw the van and the Thunderbird and the house beyond them. Standing at the rear of the van, his back to Hawkshaw, was the gunman. Hawkshaw eyed him with almost scientific interest as he raised his rifle.

From the back, the man looked surprisingly ordinary. He was neither tall nor short, fat nor thin. He wore jeans that did not fit well and a short-sleeved shirt of greenish plaid. His hair was hidden by a tan baseball cap, and his exposed arms, the back of his neck were pale.

He turned his head slightly, and Hawkshaw saw that he wore glasses with flesh-colored plastic rims. He had a pointed nose, a receding chin, a thin, almost prim mouth.

The gunman did not see Hawkshaw. He turned his attention back to the house and raised his rifle again. Hawkshaw had the back of the man's neck in his sight now, he could have severed his spine with one shot. But he lowered the barrel, trained the gun instead on the sniper's right arm.

This time the gunman seemed uncertain where he wanted to shoot. Perhaps the silence of the house disconcerted him. Slowly he swept his gun to the left of the house, in the direction Kate had gone. Then he seemed to change his mind and aimed at the house itself. But the barrel still wavered, traveling from one end of the building to the other.

Hawkshaw didn't hesitate. He squeezed the trigger. The old .22 barked to life, shattering the fragile quiet. The gunman screamed and reeled, the rifle leaping from his hands and clattering to the gravel.

Dispassionately Hawkshaw kept the .22 aimed on the sniper in case he had another weapon. But the man fell to his knees, screaming and sobbing and clutching his elbow. Blood dripped between his fingers.

He rolled to his back, still shrieking and weeping, his feet thrashing. His hat had fallen off. His hair was thin and straight and brown. He had a bald spot.

Hawkshaw walked up to the man and stared down at him. The glasses were askew, the face pale and tear-stained. The gunman stared up at him wildly, and his voice was a wail of rage and panic.

"You hurt me!" he cried. "You hurt me!"

"Yeah," said Hawkshaw. "I did."

The man rolled to his side and lay in the gravel, blubbering and grasping his injured arm. Hawkshaw didn't have time for sympathy.

He heard sirens in the distance. Aggie must have heard the shooting and called the state police. *God love you, Aggie. God always love you.*

He knelt beside the man and hauled him up by his

shirtfront. "Where's Corbett? What have you done to him?" he demanded.

"I shot him. I left him in the basement."

"Is he dead?"

"I don't know."

"Tell me everything, you bastard."

By the time Hawkshaw had shaken the facts out of him, the first police car was wheeling into the drive, siren keening. Hawkshaw pushed the gunman away roughly, letting him drop back to the gravel.

A second car came roaring up the drive and pulled up behind the first.

Hawkshaw stood, holding the .22 over his shoulder, his free hand raised. The first officer shouldered his way out of his car, gun drawn. "What the hell's going on? I had to shoot the lock off the gate to get in."

"This guy's a stalker," Hawkshaw said. He told them to call authorities in Columbia. "Immediately. This man shot a detective there. He was left in the basement of an apartment house. At six-thirty-nine Carolina Street.

"And I need somebody to come with me," Hawkshaw said. He nodded toward the dark maze of mangroves laced by the brightly flowing tidal water. "There's a woman and a kid out there."

A stocky state trooper swore. "Out there? Are they all right?"

For the first time, a wave of pure fear chilled Hawkshaw. "I don't know," he said.

CHARLIE HAD NEVER BEEN so frightened. Mama lay crumpled in the grass, her face a scary white.

Beside him, Maybelline whined.

There was a spot of blood on the back of Mama's shirt. It wasn't a big spot—it was no larger than Charlie's clenched fist, and it wasn't getting bigger, but it made him feel sick with panic.

He had seen the red color bloom like a dark, evil flower on the shirt's back, seen Mama's body jolt as if from an invisible blow. He feared then that she'd been shot, but she hadn't stopped paddling.

Now she lay almost as if sleeping except her position was so awkward. Her legs were curled up, one arm flung out, the other arm pinned beneath her.

But she was breathing. Her breath was even, but fast and weak. Fearfully, he touched her forehead. It was wet with sweat, but strangely cool.

Don't die, he begged her. *Daddy died—don't you die, too. Please, God, don't let her die.*

Her eyes fluttered as if she heard his silent prayer. Her fingers groped toward his, found them. "Oh, Charlie," she said faintly, "I passed out. How stupid of me."

Maybelline whined again and wagged her tail.

Charlie tugged at his mother's hand. "Get up, Mama. Maybe that man is still after us."

She gripped his hand tightly, but she didn't try to raise herself. "No. No. He can't follow us here. We're safe here, Charlie. You got us where we need to be."

"But, Mama," he pleaded, "you're *shot.*"

"It's okay," she said. "I'll be fine."

"But you're *bleeding.* Can't you get up?"

"I'm not bleeding much. I'm just—worn out."

She managed to turn her body a little. "Charlie," she said, "just keep holding my hand. And don't cry. Hawk-shaw will find us."

"But, Mama, what if *he* got shot?"

"He'll come, Charlie. You've got to believe it. Just hold my hand. Hang on."

So Charlie believed. And hung on.

CHAPTER SEVENTEEN

DIMLY, AS IN A DREAM, Kate heard Hawkshaw calling.

"Kate! Charlie! Can you hear me? Kate! Charlie!"

She squeezed Charlie's hand. "See, sweetie?"

Charlie rubbed his free hand across his eyes to wipe away the tears. He sniffled.

"Kate! Charlie!"

"Answer him," Kate told the boy. "Get up and wave so he can see you."

Charlie rose unsteadily to his feet. Reluctantly she let go of his hand. He looked impossibly small to have been through so much.

But his shout was loud and strong. "Hawkshaw! We're on the island! Mama's hurt, she's shot—*hurry!*"

He ran to the edge of the water, he jumped up and down, he waved his arms wildly. "Hurry, hurry, hurry!" he cried.

Kate closed her eyes, dizzied with relief. She must have slipped into unconsciousness again. The next thing she knew, Hawkshaw's face hovered above hers, his expression taut with concern.

He touched her cheek. "Kate, you're going to be all right. A 'copter's coming from Key West. We're going to airlift you out of here. Hang on, honey. Just hang on."

She wondered, dazedly, if he was a dream, a hallucination. She managed to lift her hand, to brush her fingertips against his jaw. He caught her hand and held it to his chest.

"The man—" she managed to say "—what happened?"

"The police have him."

"Who—who is he?"

"I've got no idea, Kate. I'm sorry."

A wave of bewilderment swept her. She had been stalked, threatened, driven from her home. Her innocent son and she—and Hawkshaw, too—had been in danger of death. She had been shot. And still she did not know who had done any of it, or why.

AFTER EMERGENCY SURGERY, Kate woke up in the Key West hospital, her back throbbing and her head foggy with pain.

Hawkshaw was there, holding Charlie in his arms. She tried to smile at Charlie. She wasn't sure she brought it off. "Hi, sweetie," she breathed.

"Mama?" he said, his eyes wide. "Are you okay?"

"She's going to be fine," Hawkshaw assured him gruffly. He gave Charlie a pat on his skinny back.

"And you *will* be fine," he told Kate, just as gruffly. "You were lucky. The shot didn't go deep. Stopped just short of your lung. You've got some torn muscles, two nicked ribs."

"And the bullet kept you from bleeding a whole lot," Charlie said, nodding wisely.

"Oh, Charlie," she said, "I'd like to hug you and hug you, but I'm too sore right now."

Charlie looked embarrassed.

"How long do I have to stay here?" Kate asked.

"A couple days," said Hawkshaw.

She saw he had a bandage on his temple, another showing from beneath the neck of his T-shirt. "You're hurt," she said.

"It's nothing."

"It doesn't look like nothing. What happened?"

"I said it's nothing. Listen, Kate. I've got good news for a change. They found Corbett. He'd been shot, left for dead, but he's going to make it. He should make a full recovery."

Kate bit her lip. Tears of relief rose in her eyes, and for once she didn't try to blink them back.

"He'll be all right? You're sure?"

Hawkshaw nodded. "I'm sure. I've talked to Cherry. The shot creased his skull, gave him a concussion. More blood than real damage. He was lucky as hell."

"Mama, you know what?" Charlie asked excitedly. "Hawkshaw *shot* that guy. He swam upstream and he got behind him and he took him by surprise—pow! Just like Sergeant Steelarm."

"It's nothing to admire, kid," Hawkshaw said. "It had to be done."

"He didn't kill him, though," Charlie said, sounding disappointed.

Kate tried to reach for Charlie's hand, but pain stabbed through her back. She let her hand fall back to the sheet.

"The man—who is he? Do they know yet?"

"His name is Johnson," Hawkshaw said. "Ivor Johnson."

She frowned in puzzlement. She did not recognize the name, and yet it resonated a strange chord of memory. "Johnson?"

Hawkshaw nodded. "Brother to the man killed in jail. They were both in on it. You weren't being stalked by one man, Kate. There were two."

She blinked in stunned surprise. "Two? Brothers? But *why?*"

"We don't know. He hasn't been able to say much yet. He's been in surgery, too."

She turned her head away, sickened by the thought of so much futile violence.

"His name doesn't ring a bell? Nothing?" Hawkshaw asked.

"None," she said. She closed her eyes, suddenly too spent to face the mystery.

"You're exhausted," he said. "I'll take Charlie over to Aggie's. We'll stay there till we can get the house back in shape. We'll come back later, when you've rested."

She turned and looked up at him. Neither he nor Charlie had changed their clothes. Charlie was grimy and looked as bedraggled as an urchin. Hawkshaw's T-shirt was torn and bloodied.

Hawkshaw expertly lowered Charlie to her. The boy gave her a small, smacking kiss on the cheek, offered his own cheek in return.

She kissed him and again blinked back tears. "You were wonderful, Charlie. You found the way to the island. You did everything just right."

"Yeah, he did," Hawkshaw said, hoisting the boy to his shoulder again. "Come on, kid. Let's go back and clean up. We look like a couple of bums."

You look like the two most beautiful men in the world to me, Kate thought.

Hawkshaw only nodded goodbye. He said nothing. He did not kiss her or try to touch her. She watched as he carried her son away, the boy's arms once again tight around the man's neck.

KATE DIDN'T LEARN the truth about the stalking until late the next morning. She was sitting up in bed, stiff but mending. Hawkshaw arrived carrying Charlie.

He set the boy on his feet, gave him a handful of quarters and sent him down the hall to the soft-drink machine. Charlie went with clear reluctance. Hawkshaw waited until he was out of sight.

"He doesn't need to hear this," he said.

"You keep carrying him," she said. "And he hangs on to you like he's afraid to let go."

"He needs to hang on for a while. He's had a bad scare. He's not going to get over it fast."

I won't, either, she thought. But she supposed Hawkshaw would. He was trained to get over such things, to take them in stride.

He said, "Johnson talked, Kate. He and his brother had a history of mental problems. When the police in Columbia interviewed Ivor about Kyle, Ivor claimed he was deaf. That he'd been in an accident in college and he lived off the disability. But he was lying. He was deaf, all right, but only in one ear."

"I—don't understand," Kate said.

"He had disability payments, but not for deafness. They were because he had schizophrenic episodes. He claimed the deafness to throw suspicion off himself. How could a deaf man have phone conversations with you and eavesdrop? The police didn't suspect him. But Corbett did."

"But how? If he seemed deaf?"

"Corbett stopped by to try to question him. He noticed a radio in the kitchen. Why would a deaf man have a radio? So he went back for a second time. To double-check."

Hawkshaw fingered the amulet at his neck. "Ivor Johnson was like his brother. An electronic genius of sorts.

He knew how to tap into your phone from the outside, so not even the phone company could trace it."

Kate's stomach knotted with the familiar sick anxiety. She knew such taps could be made. Corbett had been worried about the possibility all along. "His brother was no slouch, either," Hawkshaw said. "He hacked his way into your computer system. Before you had any idea, they knew all about you."

"The damned computer," Kate said miserably. "I should have stopped sending e-mail to Trevor. And everybody else."

"The Johnsons could take turns keeping surveillance on you, phoning you, trailing you. And it was clever, because nobody'd suspect Ivor, and it gave each of them a built-in alibi. Part of the time you were being stalked, Kyle was out of town. Part of the time Ivor was gone. As long as we thought there was only one stalker, they were in the clear."

Kate clenched her fists in her lap. "But why me? I didn't even know them."

"They were walking in the park one day. They saw you sitting on a park bench. Ivor said you looked like you were trying not to cry. And they—wanted you."

Kate's mind plummeted back through time. She remembered sitting on a park bench one morning after taking Charlie to day care. Her marriage was failing, and she'd been certain she would have to divorce Chuck. She'd stared at the ducks on the lagoon and struggled not to weep.

Hawkshaw said, "They saw you. They became obsessed with you. Both of them. Psychologists call it *folie à deux*. 'The madness of two.'"

Madness, she thought numbly. So the answer lay in that one, seemingly simple word. *Madness.*

"I think," said Hawkshaw, "that at first, in a sick way, they wanted to take care of you. Then, suddenly your husband died. They took it as a sign. Ivor came into the bookstore as soon as you went back to work. He tried to chat you up. He said you rejected him."

"Rejected him?" Kate said, appalled. "He tried to— to flirt with me? When Chuck was hardly cold in his grave? I don't even remember it—I was still in a daze. I was in shock for months."

"Kate, these guys weren't rational. They felt rejected again when you wouldn't wear the flowers they left. And they were intensely displeased when Corbett got on their case. When you disappeared, Ivor left town. Sometimes when he'd get upset, he'd take these long, pointless bus trips. But your leaving jarred something loose in Kyle. He decided on his own to torch your place. Then he got stabbed. When Ivor came home and found out, he flipped out just as badly."

"It's insane," Kate said, putting her hands to her eyes.

"Yes," Hawkshaw said. He took her wrists, drew her hands from her face. "It's all right, Kate," he said. "You're safe now."

"But how did he get here?" she asked. "How did he find the house?"

"He bought a one-way ticket from Columbia to Miami. Put his rifle and ammo in his check-in luggage."

"You can do that?"

"Yes, unfortunately. At Miami, he rented a car. Once he reached Cobia, he asked at the all-night filling station where to find the place. He'd come to punish you. He blamed you for Kyle's death and his own unhappiness."

A torrent of revulsion swept over Kate. She wanted to weep, rage, storm. At the same time laughter bubbled in her throat at the sheer absurdity of it. All this had happened because one day two strangers had seen her in the park. Chance and chance alone had made her the object of their obsession.

For a giddy moment she understood hysteria all too well. But her emotions spun so wildly she could not decide whether to laugh or cry or do both at once, so she did nothing. She stared helplessly at Hawkshaw. "I almost caused us all to get killed," she said.

He held her wrists more tightly. "You caused nothing. It was their doing. All of it. But it's over. They'll put Ivor away for life. You're safe again, Kate. And Charlie, too— safe."

"And you saved us," she breathed.

He stared into her eyes. "No. You and Charlie saved yourselves."

"But you kept Johnson talking while we escaped," she said earnestly. "And you're the one who captured him."

He brought his face closer to hers, grasped her shoulders. "I let you get shot."

"Oh, Hawkshaw, you didn't *let* it happen. It was a wild shot—it was freakish." Shyly she reached and put her hands on either side of his face. "You would have taken that bullet yourself—I know you."

"I'm nobody's hero, Kate."

"You're mine. You're Charlie's."

You could kiss me, Hawkshaw, she thought. *It would be so nice. I wish you would. Yes. Do.*

Instead he drew back. He released her shoulders, and she was forced to let her hands drop back to her lap. They felt suddenly empty, and so did she.

He frowned. "You know what this means," he said, shifting his weight and cocking a hip.

She looked at him questioningly.

"It's really over, Kate," he said quietly. "You can go

home. Back to Columbia. Back to your old neighborhood, your job. Charlie won't have to change schools.''

I don't want to go home, she thought, a painfully sharp realization. *It doesn't seem like home anymore.*

He shrugged. ''Or maybe you'll want to go on to Denver anyway,'' he said. ''Put all this behind you. Make a clean start.''

''I—I haven't really thought about it,'' she said. ''So much has happened…''

''Yeah,'' he said. ''It has. And you're welcome to stay on a while to recuperate. If you don't mind coming back to the house. Aggie and the boys are helping me get it back into shape. But maybe you don't want to see it again.''

He gave her a little twist of a smile freighted with sadness. ''Maybe there's too many bad memories there. Maybe you'd just as soon skip it.''

She drew in a shaky breath. ''I don't want to be in your way. We've imposed enough.'' She tried to laugh, but failed. ''I guess 'imposed' is a pretty weak word.''

''No,'' he said. ''You're welcome to stay as long as you need. Only I—'' he hesitated ''—I'll be moving in to Key West late next week.''

''Here? Key West?'' she asked. ''But why?''

She nearly bit her tongue. Hawkshaw didn't have to account for his movements, and he liked his privacy.

He stared past her, at the window full of blue summer sky. ''Sandra's coming,'' he said. ''We're going to talk about getting back together.''

Kate felt as stunned as if she'd taken a second shot in the ribs. ''Oh,'' was all she could say.

Hawkshaw thrust his hands into the pockets of his shorts. ''She heard about this whole thing. It was on the Florida news. Her stepmother lives in Palm Beach. She called Sandra in Hawaii, Sandra called me. One thing led to another.''

''I see,'' said Kate.

''But you're welcome to use the house,'' Hawkshaw said, still not looking at her. ''But if Sandra and I get things smoothed out, I won't be back. I'll be putting it on the market.''

''Oh,'' she said. ''Of course.''

The atmosphere in the room had become charged and awkward. Hawkshaw looked intensely uncomfortable, and Kate struggled against a foolish feeling of bereavement.

Have enough pride at least to save face and lie, she told herself.

''Well,'' she said in a chipper voice, ''I hope things work out. I know you've always hoped to get back with her. I wish you the best of luck. You deserve it.''

''So do you,'' he said. The look he gave her was somber. Neither of them seemed to think of any more to say.

Charlie came into the room, holding two cans of cola. ''I couldn't get the machine to work,'' he complained. ''I had to get a nurse to help me. You want this, Mama?'' He held a can toward her.

Kate forced herself to smile, but shook her head. ''No. Thanks, sweetie.''

''I'll take it,'' Hawkshaw said. But when he took the can, he set it aside, still unopened.

''Help me open this, will you?'' Charlie asked him. ''I can't get the top popped.''

Hawkshaw opened the can for him, handed it back. Charlie sipped, then cast a puzzled glance first at Kate, then Hawkshaw. ''Hawkshaw,'' he said uneasily. ''I think when we ran away from the bad guy, I hurt my foot. Would you carry me?''

"Sure, kid," said Hawkshaw and swept him up. For the rest of the visit he held the boy in his arms. Charlie obviously wanted to be there because it was where he felt safe.

The lump in Kate's throat felt as hard and jagged as a chunk of broken glass.

KATE'S STAY IN THE HOSPITAL dragged out longer than expected. She was physically and emotionally exhausted, and pneumonia set in. It was a mild case, but it kept her weak, and the coughing hurt her incision.

Aggie came to see her every day. On the third day, she came bearing a newspaper and a bouquet of yellow-and-white daisies.

"I'd rather be bringing you these at home," Aggie scolded, setting the flowers on the bedside tray. "It's a fine state of affairs when you come down sick right in the hospital."

Kate gave her an ironic smile. "Nothing else has made sense lately. Why should this?"

"Hmmph," said Aggie. She unfolded the paper, which was the *Miami Herald*. "There's a picture in here of those two sons of guns. You seen it?"

"What two sons of guns?"

"Those two sons of guns that made your life so miserable," Aggie said. "Those jackass Johnson boys. You seen it?"

A shudder chilled Kate. "No."

"Well, feast your eyes," said Aggie. "Though they don't look like much, and that's for sure."

She opened up the paper with an angry rattle and thrust it at Kate. Kate saw two grainy police photos, each showing a man staring emotionlessly at the camera.

Under each picture was the identifying name and age,

Kyle Johnson, 32, and Ivor Johnson, 34. Kate was stunned by how bland and powerless they looked.

They were the sort of men that would seldom be noticed, and if noticed, quickly forgotten. They did not look like sexual predators. They did not look vicious. They did not look mad.

"This article says their doctors told them to live apart," Aggie said. "They weren't good for each other. And for a while they did stay apart. But then the older one moved to Columbia, and the other one followed. Pretty soon they were living together again. But they kept the young one's room. It was closer to your place."

Kate shivered again and pushed the paper away. "I could have seen them a hundred times and never noticed."

"Maybe that's what made them so crazy," Aggie observed, folding up the paper. "That nobody ever took notice of them."

"Maybe it is," Kate said with a sad shake of her head. Later she would try to understand the strange motives and twisted logic of the brothers. But not yet. Her own psychic wounds were too fresh.

She changed the subject. "How's Hawkshaw's house coming along?"

"Better than you'd think," Aggie said. "They got the new windows in, a new door on the front. Most of the bullet holes inside are plastered up. Ozzie and Burt and Gator are over again today."

"You've all been good."

"Hawkshaw and Charlie can sleep there tonight. I told Hawkshaw they could stay with me long as need be, but he says, no. He keeps working to fix things, and the boy works right alongside him."

"They thought I'd be back tonight," Kate said. "Charlie thinks if they get the house fixed up, *I* won't be scared.''

''I think Hawkshaw's right to try to go back,'' Aggie said. ''It's better that the boy face it. No sittin' around feeling sorry for yourself. Just jump in and start putting things right again. That's how folks survive.''

Kate smiled. ''You come from a tough breed, Aggie.''

''You ain't a sissy yourself,'' Aggie said and patted her hand. ''What's the word on Hawkshaw's friend. That Corbett?''

''He's doing well. I thought I'd beat him home, but maybe I won't. Hawkshaw says he's making a remarkable recovery. I can't tell you how thankful I am.''

''Charlie seems well, too,'' Aggie offered. ''He's mighty clingy with Hawkshaw, but I guess that's what he needs now.''

''Yes. I guess.''

''He's going to miss Hawkshaw,'' Aggie said, watching Kate's face.

Kate kept her expression carefully blank. ''I suppose he will.''

''Have you decided if you're going back to Columbia or on to Denver? Hawkshaw said you were kind of wavering.''

Kate shrugged, then winced at the pain. ''Back to Columbia, I suppose. I've been there the last nine years. It's home now. And Charlie knows it. His school's there, his doctor, everything he knows.''

''He doesn't know yet about the fire?''

Kate coughed and winced again. ''No. Not yet.''

''The little guy's got a lot to face.''

''Yes. He does.''

''When will you go back?'' Aggie pressed.

''As soon as possible,'' Kate said. ''Like you said, it's

best to jump right in. We can stay in a hotel while I find a place to live.''

"A hotel,'' Aggie said with disgust. "I don't know why. Stay here, get rested. Rent an apartment by phone. Have it waiting for you when you get there. It's done all the time.''

Kate lifted her jaw to what she hoped was a jaunty angle. "No. Hawkshaw's got plans. He said we could stay at his house, but it wouldn't be right—''

"Then don't stay at *his* house,'' Aggie countered. "Stay at mine. *Mi casa su casa.* I've got room. A hotel, my foot. You come to me. I'll fatten you both up. And I'd love to have a little boy around again.''

Kate was tempted. She liked Aggie, and she didn't relish going back to Columbia, or the prospect of explaining to Charlie that there were still more losses he had to face.

But she shook her head. "No. You're a doll to ask, but it's time for us all to get on with our lives.''

"I know what's going on,'' Aggie said, a combative edge to her voice.

"What?'' Kate asked with feigned innocence.

"It's her,'' Aggie said vehemently. "It's Her Majesty, Lady Sandra. I know. She's called my place for him twice. With orders for him to call back in *private.* And he went off to the Flamingo and did just that. She wants him back again, doesn't she?''

Kate felt a jealous twinge that she knew was foolish and futile. She said nothing.

"Well,'' Aggie demanded. "Doesn't she?''

Kate tried pleading. "Aggie, you know how private he is. I owe him too much to talk about him—''

"I knew it,'' huffed Aggie. "She hears he's in the news, and she wants back in the picture. She snaps her fingers for him, and he's ready to drop everything and come running. He's going to Key West to meet her, isn't he? Cobia Key was never good enough for her. But she's stringing him along again. She never stopped, really. It makes me sick.''

Kate shook her head. "Aggie, Hawkshaw loves her. He always has, he always will.''

"He got his daddy's height, his daddy's looks, and his daddy's dumb streak," Aggie said contemptuously. "I'd like to kick his butt.''

Kate looked away. She didn't want to criticize Hawkshaw, and she didn't want to talk about Sandra.

"He saved our lives," she said.

"It's about time he saved his own," said Aggie.

CHAPTER EIGHTEEN

THAT NIGHT IT RAINED hard again. Charlie sat at the kitchen counter with Hawkshaw, drawing a picture of a belted kingfisher.

The kingfisher was hard to draw. Its crest was wild and spiky, like a punk rocker's hair, and the markings on its wings and tail were complicated.

Suddenly the bird looked stupid to Charlie, like a big-headed clown with a stupid false beak. Tears rose, burning, in his eyes. He swept the tablet off the table in disgust and threw his blue crayon on the floor.

"It's no good," he said, full of self-loathing. "It's dumb." He pounced on the tablet to tear the picture to shreds.

Hawkshaw was quicker. He snatched up the tablet and held it out of Charlie's reach. "It's not dumb," he said. "It's a good picture. Kingfishers look weird, so pictures of them have to look weird."

"I hate it," Charlie said with passion. Then he put his elbows on the counter and his fists to his eyes. He cried.

Beside him, he heard Hawkshaw swear softly. "I'm sorry, kid," Hawkshaw said. "I shouldn't have brought you back here. I should have left you at Aggie's. Come on, I'll take you back."

Charlie felt Hawkshaw's hand on his shoulder, and he cried harder. "I don't want to go to Aggie's," he said angrily. "I want to stay here with you."

"I'll stay at Aggie's, too. We'll come back another night. Come on. I'll carry you."

"No," Charlie said, wrenching away. "You don't have to carry me anymore. I'm not a baby."

Hawkshaw didn't touch him again, but he knelt by his side. Charlie, ashamed of his tears, refused to look at him.

"Look," Hawkshaw said softly, "a lot of things happened to us in this house. It's got bad memories, all right? They make a guy feel funny. I know. I feel it, too."

"I'm *not* scared of this house," Charlie insisted, although he was. He was both frightened and fascinated, and he wanted to leave it, yet he didn't want to leave it.

This afternoon he had helped Hawkshaw patch bullet holes in the kitchen counter. They had found a bullet the police hadn't taken, and Hawkshaw said Charlie could keep it, that it would be like a medal, a war souvenir.

Hawkshaw had drilled a hole through the bullet casing and strung a thong through it. He'd fastened it around Charlie's neck. "There," he said. "That's to remind you always that you're a good guy, and you were stronger than the bad guy. It's your medicine, your mojo."

Charlie had frowned in puzzlement. He liked wearing the bullet; it made him feel like a great adventurer. But he didn't understand. "What do you mean, medicine? Mojo?"

"It's like your personal magic," Hawkshaw had said. "It'll protect you. See this?" He showed Charlie the small carved stone he wore around his own neck.

Charlie had looked at it and nodded. Before, the stone had always just looked like a shiny, irregular pebble. But he saw it was shaped like an animal.

"What is it?" Charlie had asked. He fingered the bullet around his own neck as if it were indeed magic.

"A medicine man in New Guinea gave this to me,"

Hawkshaw had said. "He said it would always protect me, keep me safe. And see? It has. It's my mojo." He tapped the bullet on Charlie's chest. "And this is yours."

"Wow," Charlie had said in awe. With the bullet he'd felt protected, almost invulnerable.

But that had been in the sunshiny daytime. Now it was dark and rainy again, and the house creaked and groaned as if haunted.

Hawkshaw touched Charlie's arm. "Charlie, there's no shame in remembering. It's too soon to come back. I was wrong to try it. Let's go to Aggie's."

"No," Charlie protested, pulling away again. "I'm not afraid of this house. I'm *not*."

Yet Charlie was afraid, and deeply, but he didn't understand why. He faced away so that Hawkshaw couldn't see his tears, but he couldn't stop crying.

He wasn't afraid of the bad man; the bad man was in jail and he would probably stay in jail forever. He could not get out, Hawkshaw promised. Hawkshaw said there would be guards and guards and guards around him, for years to come.

And Charlie wasn't afraid of the bad man's brother. He'd been told about that other man and knew he was dead and could never hurt anyone again, ever. Hawkshaw had made that clear.

Charlie wasn't exactly afraid of the house, and he wasn't afraid of the backcountry—the backcountry had saved him and Mama after all, but—but—

And Charlie cried harder, so hard it tore at his chest and made his body shake. "Charlie," Hawkshaw said, "come on. Let's go to Aggie's."

Hawkshaw gripped Charlie's shoulders, but Charlie stiffened and struck at the man's hands. "No, no, no," he cried, "I'm *not* afraid of the house! I'm afraid for my mama! I let her get shot—she could have died."

"Charlie, Charlie," Hawkshaw said, his voice ragged, "it wasn't your fault, kid. Never think that for a minute."

"I should have helped her," Charlie stormed. "There's all sorts of things I should have done."

"Jeez, Charlie, don't do this to yourself," Hawkshaw ordered, spinning him around to face him. "Now, listen to me, kid. And listen good."

And Charlie listened. Hawkshaw told him that he'd been the bravest kid Hawkshaw had ever seen, that he'd done all sorts of things right, that he'd helped *save* his mother.

"It's human nature to blame yourself if somebody you love gets hurt," Hawkshaw said. "But what happened to your mother, it's not your fault. So you can't blame yourself. Understand me? Understand?"

Hawkshaw talked and Charlie listened until he'd almost stopped crying. Hawkshaw gave him a handkerchief, not a tissue, but a real man's handkerchief to wipe his eyes and blow his nose.

"I want to stay here," Charlie said stubbornly. "I mean it. I'll *show* this house I'm not scared."

"We'll talk about it," Hawkshaw said. "In the meantime, you may need a little extra mojo, that's all. Here. You can wear mine, too, for tonight."

He took the thong with the little stone from his neck and put it around Charlie's. "There," he told Charlie. "You're carrying about as much mojo as a man can."

"Awesome," murmured Charlie. "But I really do want to stay."

Then the phone rang. Hawkshaw frowned and went to answer it. Charlie watched, clutching the two mojos in one hand, the wet handkerchief in the other.

"Sandra," Hawkshaw said. "Well, no, honey, it's actually not a good time. I've got a kind of c-r-i-s-i-s on my hands right now. Can I call you back?"

Charlie frowned. He didn't like Hawkshaw talking to Sandra; he hated her and was jealous of her. He stalked to the couch and flopped down on it, clutching a pillow to his chest.

"Sandra, it's a kid," said Hawkshaw. "Yes, it's her kid. No, I'm not pulling the same old stuff on you again. I'd rather talk about it later. Sandra?"

"I *hate* Sandra," Charlie whispered to Maybelline, who snored on the floor beside the couch. "I hope she falls off his boat and a whale swallows her."

Maybelline took no note of this hideous fantasy. She snored on.

"She can't take care of him herself," said Hawkshaw. "She's still in the hospital. And he's having a—kind of bad night. I know you're not having such a great night. I know that. I know it. Sandra? Will you listen?"

Hawkshaw kept talking and talking to the lady named Sandra. Charlie was spent by his own emotions. He tried to block out the sound of the conversation by putting his hands over his ears. He closed his eyes so he wouldn't even have to see the room while Hawkshaw talked to her. He sniffled a bit. He burrowed his head into the pillow.

And before he knew it, he had fallen into exhausted, dreamless sleep.

WHEN HAWKSHAW AT LAST set down the phone, his shoulders ached with a strange tiredness. He gazed at the patched bullet holes in the counter. He put out a forefinger and touched one. The patching compound still felt damp and fragile.

He glanced at the silly cat clock that ticked on the wall.

It had come through the gunfire unscathed, and Hawkshaw was peculiarly grateful it had survived. He stared at it a long moment.

He had talked to Sandra for almost twenty minutes. He turned toward the couch and saw Charlie sleeping in the lamplight. The boy lay on the cushions as limply as a rag doll, his feet tangled in the ancient afghan, one arm dangling over the floor.

Charlie's lips were parted, his breathing regular. The tear streaks, dried now, still glistened on his face. But he seemed at peace.

Hawkshaw did not have the heart nor the stomach to wake him. Let the kid sleep, let him get through the first night facing the demons in the house. Let him prove to himself he could.

Hawkshaw would not chance wakening him by carrying him into the back bedroom. He would let him sleep on the old couch, with all the lights on.

Hawkshaw left him only long enough to bring a blanket and pillow from his own room. Then he bedded down for the night on the other side of the coffee table. If Charlie woke, he wouldn't be alone.

Maybelline rose, grunted, huffed, and sighed. She hobbled to Hawkshaw's side. She turned around, grunted, huffed, and sighed again. Then she lay down beside him, her warm flank against his thigh.

He wrinkled his nose. Maybelline was not the best-smelling dog in the world. And the floor was ungodly hard. But he didn't mind because he didn't suppose he'd sleep anyway.

He got up again, took up the little night case that contained the letters and postcards and took it back to his blanket. He lay down again, leaning on his elbow. He opened the case.

He took out a bundle of letters. They were from his mother. His heart beating hollowly, his stomach tight, he began to read them. And to think. Of what he'd said to Charlie. And to Sandra. But he'd never dared say to himself. Until now.

THE HOSPITAL RELEASED KATE three days later. Charlie and Hawkshaw conferred seriously and decided the old blue Thunderbird would serve as the most splendid and festive means to convey her back.

Kate smiled when she saw the car, but she truly dreaded returning to the house. In heart and mind, she rebelled against staying there.

"Don't make any plans for a while," was all Hawkshaw, tight-lipped as usual, had said. He had hardly visited her the past two days. He'd bring Charlie, or both Charlie and Aggie, then drift off down the hall.

He was beginning to separate himself from them, Kate could tell. But she wondered if Charlie would ever understand. Or if she would ever become reconciled to what had taken place in her own heart.

Hawkshaw was nearly silent on the ride back to the house. He had, thought Kate, reverted to his old aloof self.

But Charlie, of course, chattered incessantly.

"And I stayed in the house three whole nights," he said. "Even though it's still got *bullet holes* in it."

"You're incredibly brave," Kate told him, because he seemed so proud of himself. But she had to fight down the shudder that skittered through her nerve ends.

"I did it," Charlie said, nodding excitedly. "I really did. Three whole nights now. I got my mojo working. I faced the demons."

Mojo, she thought, bemused. *Facing demons.* That line

of patter sounded as if it must be Hawkshaw's. She wondered if, once she entered the house again, she could outface her own demons.

Charlie seemed to read her thoughts. "I'll help you so you aren't scared," he said. "You don't have to worry. Those bad guys are gone for good. There's only us good guys left."

It cost her a twinge of pain, but she turned in the seat and touched Charlie's chin affectionately. "You're the very best of good guys," she said. "And I'm proud of you."

Charlie beamed. "Know what?" he said confidentially, "There's something else that'll help you be all right. I made you a mojo, too."

"Charlie, that's enough," Hawkshaw said sternly. Kate glanced at him. Unsmiling, he kept his eyes on the highway.

She turned back to Charlie, felt another pinch of pain, but hid it. "Can you tell me what a mojo is, at least?"

"Can I, Hawkshaw?" he asked, bouncing up and down on the seat.

"I will," said Hawkshaw. "It's a term a New Orleans guy in the Service always used. It means like a charm or a talisman. Maybe it's magic, or maybe it's just something special to you."

"Hmm," Kate said, cocking her head. "You two have been dabbling in magic?"

"You'll see," crowed Charlie and bounced harder.

Hawkshaw said nothing.

"Look, look!" yelled Charlie, pointing up. "It's a frigate bird, Mama! See? They call it the magnificent frigate bird."

Kate looked up, narrowing her eyes against the blazing

sky. Silhouetted against the blue was a single bird, great and dark and breathtakingly graceful.

She smiled. "You certainly learned your birds, Charlie."

"Yeah," said Hawkshaw. "He certainly did."

Her smile grew stiff, but she kept it in place as she turned to him. She forced her voice to stay cheerful. "That's one more thing we have to thank you for, teaching him so much."

"A guy should never stop learning," said Hawkshaw.

THE HOUSE DIDN'T LOOK nearly as bad as Kate had feared. The broken glass had been replaced, and there was a new front door. Burt and Ozzie were hard at work, priming the patched holes in the siding.

"They're going to paint the house," Charlie said excitedly. "It's going to be good as new."

"Easier to sell," she said brightly to Hawkshaw. She knew he wouldn't want to keep the house if he and Sandra were reuniting.

He only shrugged.

Burt and Ozzie greeted her with a mixture of concern and jollity.

"You all right?" Burt asked. "Them sawbones fix what ailed you?"

"You *look* all right," Ozzie said, taking her hand between his, which were huge and rough with callouses. "But pale. Rest is all you need. We won't be round making noise. We're quitting for today, let you have your privacy. You just take it easy."

"Aggie sent over enough food for an army," said Burt. "You don't have to worry about food."

"She sent over her Key lime pie," grinned Ozzie. "I

always said nothing has the healing powers of Ag's Key lime pie.''

She smiled up at the big, sunburned men, touched by their kindness. ''You're good neighbors.''

''I am,'' Ozzie said and dug an elbow in his brother's ribs. ''He's only just middlin'.''

''Oh, shut up and let's go,'' Burt grumped. ''Don't keep her out standing in the sun. Charlie, take your Mama inside where it's cool.''

Charlie grabbed her hand and led her up the stairs. ''Ozzie let me put putty in some bullet holes,'' Charlie told her. ''It's cool, like modeling clay. Big guys use it. To fix things.''

Hawkshaw paused to exchange a few brief words with the men, then quickly caught up to Kate and Charlie. He unlocked the door and swung it open for them to enter.

She swallowed, fearing that the sight of the living room would awake a swarm of terrifying memories.

But when she stepped inside, she was struck by how the sunshine poured its brightness through the new windows. The interior walls were already patched and painted a clean, gleaming ivory.

Everything was as neat and polished as she'd worked to make it before—surely Aggie had assisted in this miracle.

But it was the kitchen counter that claimed and held her attention. It was festive with garlands of crepe paper and bunches of balloons and bouquets of wildflowers. A white banner hung over it. WElComE HomE!! said letters written in different colors of glitter, red, blue, green, and purple.

Aggie's pie sat proudly in the middle, heaped high with swirls of meringue. Next to it were two packages wrapped in gaily colored paper and festooned with curling ribbon.

"Oh," Kate gasped in surprise. Charlie's hand tightened around hers. Maybelline danced her welcome dance around their feet.

"I made the banner," Charlie said, pointing. "Hawkshaw helped me."

She stared at the laboriously-made letters sparkling out their crooked rainbow of greeting. How hard he must have toiled over it.

"Oh, Charlie," she breathed, "it's beautiful."

In the drive she heard the men's truck pulling away. "We should have asked them in, to join the party," she said, a hitch in her throat. "And Aggie and Gator, too."

"We did ask," Hawkshaw said. "They said keep it small. They didn't want to overwhelm you."

"I picked the flowers, too," Charlie said with pleasure. "Over at Aggie's. And Hawkshaw and I got the balloons last night at the grocery store, on the way home from the hospital. They got *helium* in them."

The balloons, the colors of jewels, gleamed and bobbed on their ribbons.

"Aggie made cookies, too," Charlie informed her. He led her to the counter to point out the iced sugar cookies studded with colored candy bits. "We can have pie or cookies. Or we can have both."

Kate gazed down at him, helpless not to smile. He would be going absolutely sky-high on sugar, but for once she wasn't going to worry about it—much. "Let's have the cookies and save the pie for later," she told him.

"Okay," said Charlie and pounced on the cookie with the thickest frosting. He bit into it, then looked up at Hawkshaw. "Can I show her now?"

Hawkshaw nodded.

Charlie took another bite and grabbed up the first package, thin and rectangular. "Come sit on the couch and open it," he said, his mouth full of cookie.

Kate cast Hawkshaw a questioning look. Again he nodded. He and Charlie had apparently thought this out in some detail. She let Charlie lead her to the couch and sat beside him. Hawkshaw sat on the boy's other side, his face inscrutable.

"Okay, open it now," Charlie instructed. He bounced with excitement.

Kate unfastened the ribbons and undid the crackling paper. She found herself staring, baffled, at an old Sergeant Steelarm comic book with a torn and faded cover.

She thought, *I have no idea what it means, but I guess I should say, "Thank you."*

She struggled to look properly delighted. She opened her mouth to thank Charlie, but before the words came out, he took the comic from her. "Tell her, Hawkshaw," he said.

"Charlie never looked at this comic before this morning," Hawkshaw said.

"I can read it, Mama—" Charlie said "—almost."

He opened it and put his finger under the first story's title. "'The B-b-battle For Great Sands,'" he said, his face showing the strain of his concentration.

He pointed to the caption over the first panel. "'It is night in the j-jungles of B-b-b—'" he looked to Hawkshaw for help.

"Sound it out," said Hawkshaw. "You can do it."

"'Bur-ma,'" Charlie said with a determined frown. "'It is night in the jungles of Burma. Sergeant Steelarm leads his men through the darkness and heat. Suddenly—'"

Charlie pointed at several yellow starbursts with lettering in them. He looked happily up at Kate. "This is the sound of guns. 'Bam! Pow! Budda-budda-budda!'

"Then Sergeant Steelarm says, 'Night attack! Hit the dirt!' Then there's more guns, 'Bang! Ka-blam! Bratta-bratta-bratta!'"

Kate looked at him with amazement. He was reading—not with ease or speed or total accuracy. But he was *reading*.

Slowly, stumbling from time to time, Charlie forged his way through the story. It clearly took effort, and often he had to stop and ask for Hawkshaw's help. But after six pages, he reached the story's finale.

"And Sergeant Steelarm says, 'One more win for the free world. It may seem like only a small win, but it counts, boys. It counts.'

"And the comic book says, 'The fight for fre-fre-freedom is never small. It is the most—m-magnificent—fight of all. The end.'"

Kate fought back tears. "Oh, Charlie," she said. "That was *wonderful*."

"Yeah," Charlie said with a pleased grin. "I guess it was, wasn't it?"

She put her arm around him, hugged him hard. "But how did you do it?"

Charlie shrugged. "I don't know. It just started to happen, sort of."

Hawkshaw said, "He learned words in the bird book. He could recognize the same ones in the comics. So—he worked at it."

She hugged Charlie's shoulders harder, and her chin trembled. *You did this,* she thought, studying Hawkshaw's carefully controlled face. *You did this for him. You with your laid-back ways and endless patience.*

Her emotion swelled until she could not bear to look

at him. She leaned and kissed Charlie's cheek. "I'm so proud of you. So proud."

Charlie flinched from the kiss and disentangled himself from her arm. "Wait," he said. "There's more. There's the mojo I made for you."

He sprang from the couch and raced back to the counter, snatching up the second package. He ran back and thrust it into Kate's hands, then flopped down beside her.

"Charlie," she murmured, "I just don't know what to say—"

"Open it, open it," Charlie urged, his eyes eager upon her face, watching for her reaction.

Kate began to undo the ribbon, trying to disguise the tremor in her hands. The package was almost the same shape and size as the first, only thinner. Another comic book? she wondered, unwrapping the paper.

"Oh, Charlie," she breathed.

She held a homemade book made of tablet paper. It was held together by a spine of green tape and staples. On the cover was one of Charlie's drawings of a great blue heron. In his awkward lettering, he had written CHaRLiE's BooK oF BiRDs By CHaRLiE.

"You like reading and books," Charlie said. "So I made you a book to read."

Kate opened it to the first page, which showed another heron drawing. "LittLE BLuE HERon," he had printed crookedly beneath it.

She could not stop her eyes from misting. The book had only twelve pages, but they seemed the twelve most beautiful pages she'd ever beheld. An illuminated man-uscript on vellum, ornamented in gold leaf, covered in gemmed leather, could not have seemed more marvellous.

"The birds're all standing in the water," Charlie explained, "because I can't draw feet so good."

She stared in wonder at each picture and its label: little blue heron, great blue heron, tricolored heron, green-backed heron, black-crowned night heron. The egrets—the great, the snowy, the reddish. The brown pelican and the white. The belted kingfisher and the magnificent frigate bird.

"Do you like it?" Charlie asked anxiously.

"I will never love a book more than this," Kate said. She did not bother to try to hide her tears or to wipe them away. "This is my favorite book in the whole world."

"I'll write you a better one someday," Charlie promised. "Maybe I'll write lots. I'm going to be a bird scientist when I grow up."

"You'll be a wonderful bird scientist."

"It's pretty hard to write a book," Charlie admitted.

"I'm sure it is," she agreed.

"The pictures aren't so bad," he said. "But the words are murder."

She bit her lip. Hawkshaw handed her a handkerchief, clean and folded. "Here," he said without emotion. "You're soggy. You're going to drip on your book."

She took it and wiped her eyes and with no pretense of dignity blew her nose.

"My kingfisher's kind of goofy-looking," Charlie said critically.

"That's not your fault, it's the kingfisher's," Hawkshaw said.

The dog stood at the door, looking mournful. She whined. "Maybelline wants out," Hawkshaw told Charlie. "Why don't you take her outside?"

"You really like it, Mama?" Charlie asked, a note of pleading in his voice.

"I love it. I love you," Kate said. He suffered her to kiss him on the cheek again, then he leaped up and rocketed out the front door. But he had to stand and hold the door open until Maybelline sauntered through in her own sweet time. It slammed shut behind them.

Hawkshaw and Kate sat in silence. The space between them, now that Charlie was gone, seemed infinite. She wanted to tell him thank-you, but how could one begin to say thank-you for a gift so immense?

"I—I want to tell you—" she began. But her throat constricted, and she had to pause.

"I think I better go keep an eye on them," Hawkshaw said uncomfortably. "He's not too used to being out by himself yet."

He rose and left her alone with her bouquets and balloons and Key lime pie and the comic book and the bird book that was the most beautiful book in the world.

CHAPTER NINETEEN

AT NINE O'CLOCK, Charlie went to bed. Kate had been waiting nervously for this event, half in dread, half in anticipation. All evening long she had been silently rehearsing what she must say to Hawkshaw.

Since picking her up at the hospital, he'd hardly spoken to her. He did not seem to want her to speak to him. .He probably feared an emotional scene and wanted no part of it.

What little communication occurred between them seemed always to route itself through Charlie. Now, Charlie lay asleep in the repainted back bedroom. With chagrin he'd asked Kate to keep all the lights on, he didn't yet want to sleep in the dark. She left them on.

As she made her way to the living room, her nerves twitched with self-consciousness. "Hawkshaw," she intended to say, "I have some things I want to say. I know you'd rather I didn't, but please hear me out."

She tried to prepare a facade of perfect calm. But Hawkshaw was not in the living room, although the lights were still on. Neither was he on the back deck or the front deck.

At last she saw him come from out of the shadows of the side yard and stand on the dock. He looked across the water toward the mangrove islands. They were black as ink against the luminously starry sky.

Barefoot, he wore the familiar battered shorts and nothing else. He looked as much a part of the backcountry as if he were its solitary Adam, created out of its very clay.

She took three deep breaths and padded down the stairs, barefoot herself. She walked up behind him. He never glanced in her direction, and she doubted he could have heard her approach, yet he knew she was there, she was sure of it. He had a sixth sense about such things.

"Hello, Kate," he said, his back still to her.

"Hello," she said.

"Charlie asleep?"

"Yes."

"He's had a few nightmares. Bad ones."

"Yes. I'll have his doctor talk to him when we get home."

Hawkshaw nodded.

From somewhere a night heron cried. A fish splashed.

"You should get some rest," Hawkshaw said. "Not overdo it."

Kate took another deep breath. Instead of calming her, it made her a bit dizzy. But she forged ahead.

"Hawkshaw," she told him, "I have some things I want to say. I know you'd rather I didn't, but please hear me out."

He sighed. "No. There are things I should say to you first."

"No," she said with a stubborn shake of her head. "Please. First, thank you for taking us in when we were nothing but strangers to you. For that alone, you deserve our everlasting gratitude."

"Don't thank me," he said. "Thank Corbett. He set it up."

She squared her shoulders until they felt rigid. "I do thank Corbett, but I thank you, too. Secondly I want to thank you for saving us from Johnson. It sounds so—

inadequate. A person says thank-you so often that it seems meaningless in a case like this. But I don't know what else to say.''

"You don't have to say anything," he muttered. He raised his eyes and studied the stars. Tonight they were like a rich spill of diamonds across blue velvet.

"Third," she said, "I don't know how to thank you for helping Charlie the way you have. Terrible things happened to him down here. But so did wonderful ones. You saved him from all that was terrible. You gave him everything that was wonderful. And for that, again, thank you is inadequate.''

"He's a good kid," Hawkshaw said.

"He's a kid who's learning to read. And to me, that's a miracle.''

He shrugged. "I was glad to help. It—passed the time.''

Kate didn't know which desire was stronger—to hug him or to shove him into the water. He took compliments worse than any man she'd ever met.

She stuck to her script. "I called the airline from the hospital. Charlie and I are going back to Columbia day after tomorrow. We'll go back to our own world. And give you back yours.''

He turned to her, and his face seemed to be made of silver and shadow. "Day after tomorrow is too soon," he said. "The doctor doesn't want you traveling yet.''

"I can take it," she said. "I feel fine.''

"You've got no place to go," he pointed out. "And Charlie doesn't know about your condo.''

"I've made a week's reservations at a motel," she said. "We'll find a furnished place to rent. We've imposed enough.''

"It's a lot of changes to put Charlie through," he said.

"You should take your time. You're welcome to stay here."

She leveled her chin. "I know that. But the worst is over. We need to go back and get our lives in order. And it's not right we stay here. It's not fair."

She saw his shadowy brows draw into a frown. "Right?" he echoed. *"Fair?"*

She folded her arms as if to emphasize how self-sufficient she was. "Hawkshaw, your wife is coming back," she said matter-of-factly. "I know it's what you want, and I—sincerely—want you to be happy."

Pretty sincerely, she thought, miserable with her own pettiness.

"You want me to be happy," he said.

"Yes," she insisted. "And frankly, if I were reconciling with my ex-husband, I wouldn't be happy if he were living with another woman. Does she know we're here?"

He put his hands on his hips. "Yeah," he said, a wryness in his voice. "She knows."

"Well," Kate said, struggling to keep her tone crisply businesslike, "I'm sure she's a lovely person. But she couldn't like the arrangement."

She couldn't clearly see his eyes, but he seemed to look her up and down. "No," he said. "She doesn't much like it."

"See?" Kate said. "I don't blame her. I wouldn't like it either in her place. And there's more to it than that."

"There is?" He took a step toward her.

She fought the instinct to retreat. She held her ground. "Yes," she said. "You and I slept together. I know it meant nothing to you. I know that she was always on your mind. But it would be better for us all if I moved on before she gets here."

"She's not coming here," Hawkshaw said. The night breeze stirred his hair.

Kate's heart seemed to stumble and fall down hard. "What?" she said.

"She's not coming here," he repeated. "I told her not to come."

Kate tried hard to keep her mind from skidding into an illogical spin. "Well...you're going to her then. Either way, it's better I leave. I mean, my staying at your house would be..." she searched for a word and could only find one that was infirm and prim "...unseemly."

"I'm not going to her, either," he said. "It's over between us. I don't want her."

He reached out his hand and took up a strand of her hair, running it like silk between his fingers. "I want you, Kate," he said softly. "I don't deserve you. But I want you. If you'll have me."

Her breath lodged in her throat. She stared up at his face, indistinct and ringed by stars.

He put his hands on her upper arms.

"I—don't understand," she whispered. "You love *her.*"

"Once, for a long time, I thought I did," he said. "It was a mistake, all the way. Everybody told me. I wouldn't believe it then. Now I do."

She broke away from him, wheeled and walked to the end of the dock. Her chest hurt, and she still could not get her breath. Her thoughts had gone so helter-skelter she could not sort them out.

She looked out at the moving water, breaking the night's brightness into fragments. "You don't just stop loving one person and start loving another one," she said.

She felt him move behind her, close enough so that she could sense the heat of his body. "I didn't want to stop loving her," he said. "Do you know why? It would prove I'd been wrong about her and me. I couldn't admit that—it was a blow to my damn pride. But I never knew her, really. I knew what she could seem to be. I knew what I wanted her to be."

"And suddenly the scales have fallen from your eyes?" Kate asked. She could not keep the flippancy from her voice. She wanted it for protection.

"No," he said. "Not suddenly. If I loved only her, why did I start wanting you? At first, I thought it was sex, that was all. But it wasn't that simple."

The skin between Kate's shoulder blades prickled. "You acted as if it were."

"I pretended it was."

"You pretended well."

"I almost fooled myself," he said. "Kate, look at me, don't turn your back. You asked me to hear you out. I ask the same of you."

His hand clamped gently on her elbow, and she allowed him to turn her to face him. Her midsection fluttered with fearful hope.

He said, "I never once thought about Sandra that morning after Cherry called. I could think only of you. And Charlie. The whole time, only the two of you. Then when I finally got to the island and saw you lying there, hurt…my God. I was scared you were dying. Part of me wanted to die, too. Some things ended for me in those seconds. And different things began. It just took a while to understand."

He was close enough that she could see the glittering water reflected in his eyes. She breathed, "But when she called you, you wanted her back."

He shook his head. "I'm not proud of that, Kate. Old

ideas die hard. It was like a reflex. And yet it was a reflex that I knew had gone wrong long ago.''

He took a breath, moved his hand to her face. ''The first night we were back here, she called. You were still in the hospital. She had a fit because Charlie was there and I needed to pay attention to him, not her. For the first time I had to admit that she could be charming, but her selfishness was absolutely colossal.''

He paused, took her face between both his hands. ''That night I got the nerve to read the letters my mother had written to us. And I thought, 'They're alike, Sandra and my mother.' My God, I can't tell you how much alike. Why didn't I see it when it was happening? Why didn't I understand what I'd done? What darkness in me made me choose her?''

He shook his head, bent closer. ''Then I made myself read the letters my father tried to write me. He knew. He saw. He tried to tell me. Once he wrote 'There's a kind of woman who doesn't want you. But she doesn't ever want you to be free, either. She doesn't understand love. She only understands power.' That was Sandra. She understood only power. But you, Kate, you understand love.''

Her pulses leapt crazily. ''You mean…you and me?''

''I mean you and me—and Charlie. Would you stay, Kate? Stay here? We'll build it back up, start the guide service again, make a home. Would you? Could you want such a thing?''

She nodded, unable to speak. She wanted it more than she could say.

He bent, brushed his lips against hers, then drew back only slightly and pressed his forehead against hers. ''For days, I've been trying to figure out how to say this to you, wondering if I knew how to say it at all. Or if you'd listen if I had the nerve to say it.''

A fine tremor ran through her as she raised her hands to her shoulders. "That's the most that I've ever heard you say," she said with a swallow.

"It may be the most you ever hear me say," he answered. "I'm not a loquacious guy."

"Actions speak louder than words," she said and raised her lips to his.

His mouth took hers with a tender greed that shook her. The night heron cried, and the tidal rivers ran on, tugged by the pull of the sea.

IT WAS HELD OUTSIDE, beside the river, and it was a beautiful wedding, everybody said so.

Corbett, who came down clear from Columbia, was best man, and his wife, Cherry, had a wonderful time crying into her handkerchief. Their leggy, giggly teenage daughters were delighted by it all. It was "outstanding," said one. "The absolute ultimate," said the other.

Aggie said everything was beautiful as could be, although she did have doubts about the cake. She had baked it herself, and it was somewhat lopsided, even Charlie admitted that. Burt and Ozzie harrumphed that, yes, they supposed the wedding was beautiful if you went in for that sort of thing.

Gator, who always talked more, said Mama looked pretty as a speckled pup. She wore a short dress of something floaty and pale-green, and her hair shone red-gold in the sunshine, like new minted gold. She had a thing like a crown on her hair, with a pale-green veil.

Mama's friend Carol wore the same color green, because she was the Maid of Something. Carol had come clear from Denver, and she was another one who said the wedding was the most beautiful she'd ever seen. She caught the bouquet when Mama threw it. Charlie thought Gator might like Carol. He hung around her, bringing her cups of punch and telling her stories about the backcountry that made her eyes get big.

Hawkshaw actually wore a suit. And a tie. And shoes. So did Charlie because he was important to the wedding. He carried the ring in his pocket and handed it to Hawkshaw when the time came. Charlie liked that moment a lot and thought it and the cake and ice cream were the best part. He could have done without all the kissing, though.

The reception went on and on, with people laughing and joking and drinking champagne and eating Aggie's good cake. Maybelline waddled among the guests, a green chiffon ribbon and a sprig of baby's breath fastened to her collar. The Corbett girls giggled and thought she was "too cute" and "hugely cool."

Charlie had liked the wedding, and he loved the idea of living in the backcountry and being able to call Hawkshaw "Daddy." But the reception itself soon bored him and made him restless beyond bearing. He escaped, with a paper plate full of cake, a glass of lemonade, and his pockets stuffed full of mints.

He made his way to his secret spot in the trees beside the river. He had an old lawn chair there, and a table made out of a plastic milk crate, and he had stashed his favorite comic books in a safe place.

He'd already taken off his jacket and the horrible, choking tie. Now he kicked off his shoes and peeled off his socks and stripped down to his undershirt. At last a guy could breathe.

He stretched out on the old lawn chair, his head propped on an ancient crocheted pillow Aggie had made years ago and said he could have. Back in the yard, the reception kept on going full steam, as if it was never going to end. Charlie could hear the adults and their everlasting talk, talk, talk.

He paid them no mind. He lazed in the chair and sipped his lemonade. He ate his cake. He nibbled his mints.

In the trees sat a pair of blackbirds, singing. Redwinged blackbirds, to be precise. A grackle hopped from branch to branch, making small, harsh cries. It was a boat-tailed grackle, black and shiny-chested, a male.

Charlie recognized the birds by name, and it gave him a nice, private satisfaction. But he still wanted more from the afternoon.

He opened his comic and lost himself in another, more exciting world. Charlie read about treasure and adventure in Burma. He read about heroism and not being afraid.

In the trees, the birds sang on.

Looking For More Romance?

Visit Romance.net

Look us up on-line at: http://www.romance.net

Check in daily for these and other exciting features:

Hot off the press

View all current titles, and purchase them on-line.

What do the stars have in store for you?

Horoscope

Hot deals

Exclusive offers available only at Romance.net

Plus, don't miss our interactive quizzes, contests and bonus gifts.

PWEB

Strong, seductive and eligible!

THE AUSTRALIANS

Stories of romance Australian-style, guaranteed to
fulfill that sense of adventure!

This June 1999, look for

Simply Irresistible
by Miranda Lee

Ross Everton was the sexiest single guy the Outback had to
offer! Vivien Roberts thought she was a streetwise Sydney
girl. Neither would forget their one night together—Vivien
was expecting Ross's baby. But irresistible sexual attraction
was one thing...being married quite another!

*The Wonder from Down Under: where spirited women win
the hearts of Australia's most independent men!*

Available June 1999
at your favorite retail outlet.

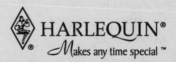

HARLEQUIN®
Makes any time special ™

HARLEQUIN · CELEBRATES

FIVE DECADES OF ROMANCE

In June 1999 Harlequin Presents® gives you
Wedded Bliss—a great new 2-in-1 book
from popular authors

Penny Jordan & Carole Mortimer
2 stories for the price of 1!

Join us as we celebrate Harlequin's 50th anniversary!

Look for these other
Harlequin Presents® titles
in June 1999 wherever
books are sold:

HER GUILTY SECRET
(#2032) by Anne Mather

THE PRICE OF A BRIDE
(#2033) by Michelle Reid

ACCIDENTAL BABY
(#2034) by Kim Lawrence

THE GROOM'S REVENGE
(#2035) by Kate Walker

**SLEEPING WITH THE
BOSS** (#2036) by
Cathy Williams